CW00646570

To my family.

Past,

Present

&

Future.

Lavender Bathwater

and

The Secret

of

Pear Tree Cottage

By Evelyn Throup

Copyright ©2022 : Robert Alexander Merrett.

Cover photograph : Francis Gerard Wilson.

Multi award winner @franwilsonphotography

First published 2022

All rights reserved

Without limiting the rights under copyright

Reserved above, no part of this publication may be reproduced, stored in or introduced into a retrieval system, or transmitted, in any form or by any means (electronic, mechanical, photocopying, recording or otherwise) without the prior written permission of both the copyright owner and the publisher of the book.

First edition

Disclaimer.

Although the author and publisher have made every effort to ensure that the information in this book was correct at press time, the author and publisher do not assume and hereby disclaim any liability to any party for any loss, damage, or disruption caused by errors or omissions, whether such errors or omissions result from negligence, accident, or any other cause.

Chapters

Chapter One

Pear Tree Cottage (1974)

No matter whether it was in the quiet stillness of a winter night or on lazy sunny summer days, Pear Tree Cottage had a whispering breath that spoke to Lavender in such a way that she knew it was more than just grandma's house. Each rounded stone of the whitewashed walls lay in observation. Black oak beams held the low ceilings aloft and probably started their life when Vikings inhabited the land. Every knot and nail in these beams held a memory, and anyone looking at them could still see the shipwright's curve in the shape of the ancient vessel, from which they had previously belonged, and that sailed the seven seas. The hearth by the fireplace had been worn smooth over the centuries by the feet of Lavender's ancestors, no doubt as they had stoked the fire and stood, in a grateful pose, with their backs against it luxuriating in the warmth of the flickering heat.

The wavy, strawberry blond hair of Lavender Bathwater was just over three feet long and had never been cut, save for a neatening two-inch trim at the ends by her mum when she was little and since then annually by her grandma. Tomorrow would be Lavender's tenth birthday, and it appeared as though all would follow the usual routine. After tea and a game of "Beggar-my-neighbour" with grandma, Lavender went upstairs for a hot bath full of bubbles. A multitude of soaps of all shapes and sizes, colours and smells adorned the bathroom. Sampling them with delight, Lavender wondered if that was the inspiration for her name. After her bath, and wrapped in her warm pink fluffy dressing gown, Lavender returned to the kitchen where grandma had pulled out one of great-grandad Augustus' creations, a solid oak stool with his trademark symbol carved on the edge of the seat. No one was certain if the sign meant anything, but Lavender imagined it must do, otherwise, why would it be there at all.

"Come on, sit thisen down, lass," called grandma, gesturing to the stool at the same time as Lavender crossed the kitchen wrapped snuggly in her dressing gown.

Lavender climbed up on to the stool and as she sat perched and waiting, brushed her hair. She could see her reflection in the kitchen window opposite and noticed that snow was starting to fall in that extra light floaty manner that looks like it isn't going to land but just keeps swirling gently in the air for hours. As she gazed at her face in the glass, she felt peaceful and safe, as though she were caught in a snow dome.

Her gaze was broken abruptly by a rattle of the cutlery drawer as grandma took out a pair of her special scissors and began to cut the damp ends of Lavender's hair.

Grandma liked to collect a lock of hair each year and keep it in an envelope. This year was no different except that Lavender had a stronger than usual attachment to her hair and wasn't sure why. When grandma finished, she tied up a lock of the hair, with a piece of string, then left it on the Welsh dresser to dry next to the row of blue willow china plates, that stood proudly waiting for grandmas next home-cooked meal. Unlike many of the items of furniture in the cottage, the old worn dresser was several centuries older than great-grandad Augustus. Although he did not make it, he had apparently "tinkered with it" to create a secret hiding place accessed through a concealed panel between its two main doors. On each annual haircut day, grandma would repeat the same tale about collecting family hair and the secret compartment Augustus had made to house the family locks, as she prepared the hair for safekeeping.

"It's settlin', lass," said grandma as she peered out of one of the little squares in the kitchen window, whose lower corners were now softened into curves by the resting snow.

"We're in for a cold few days and nights so best get the fire banked up tonight."

On nights like these, grandma had a familiar ritual that had the benefit of encouraging a cosy and solid night's sleep. It started with filling two stone water bottles with hot water and putting them in the centre of each bed in the front bedroom. Next would be a hot cup of cocoa, which had to be drunk from a red mug as that made it taste so much better. Then Lavender sat glowing in front of the fire while grandma told stories of her forebears. As she listened intently, the bath that had been soaked in had the accumulating effect of turning Lavender into her own version of a hot water bottle.

In the front room of Pear Tree Cottage, the fireplace was set in a large, grey stone arch that went most of the way up to the ceiling. It was raised to sit in the middle, a couple of feet up from the flagstone hearth that fronted its width, preventing the danger of setting fire to the carpet from any burning wood that might have a wish to spit itself out of the flames. Delius, grandma's tabby cat, sat in his usual spot on the plinth at the side of the fireplace with his bottom so close to hanging over the edge that his fur was highly likely to singe if an extra dry piece of wood became consumed in flames. Delius was somewhat of a mystery, having appeared on the front doorstep of Pear Tree Cottage one dark autumn evening some five years ago and then refusing to leave. No one knew how old he was or where he came from, but everyone was sure that Delius needed to be just where he was.

The coal hole just outside the kitchen door had been stocked up ready for winter, yet the unseasonably warm weather meant that even now at mid-January, there was still three-quarters left. Earlier in the day, Lavender had replenished the wood basket and grandma had filled the coal scuttle which now both sat on the hearth in anticipation of the swirling snow and cold winds, and a bitter frost in the morning to follow. Every stone of the fire surround and hearth now had a homely warmth to it that radiated into the room and the rest of the cottage. When the fire had settled in like this, it felt even more as if the whole cottage was alive.

Outside, on the opposite side of the street, was the working men's club where twice a week the last remaining local mill had its brass band practice. Tonight, the deep vibrations and tuneful harmonies of their latest competition music were emanating from the club hall, sending both grandma and Lavender into a stirring moment of musical gratitude.

"That's 'Nimrod', Lavender. Makes the hairs on the back of my neck stand on end, it does," grandma announced.

She was busily sewing new toggles on her granddaughter's hand-me-down duffle coat and settled in her high-backed chair near the fire.

With her hot cup of cocoa, Lavender sat on the hearth and listened more carefully to "Nimrod". She was rummaging through an old and very worn Cadbury's chocolate tin, which now contained an assortment of buttons of every conceivable size, shape and colour. On the hearth, Delius lay curled up tight against Lavender's leg, purring in sheer pleasure as if he were a buzzing hive of bees. Because the buttons looked so pretty, Lavender decided to make a rainbow out of them on the hearth. She was carefully sifting through the contents in search of a gold one, to complete her mini work of art, when she pulled out something a little unusual. There had been quite a few items other than buttons in the tin, like bits of card, safety pins, screws and several washers, but this was more like a very worn tarnished coin. It had a symbol that looked like two circles, one inside the other, and two wavy lines going horizontally through the middle. On the other side was a simple outline of a man's head with his eyes closed.

"What's this, Grandma?" said Lavender with sudden interest.

"I'm not sure, lass, give it here and let me have a closer look," grandma requested.

She put down the coat, now complete with new toggles and held her hand out. Lavender placed the object into her grandma's palm.

"Oh, that old thing, there's nowt special about that. I would hazard a guess it belonged to my aunt Fanny. I inherited a tin of buttons from her years ago and they all went in together."

She paused as if to dig down into dusty memories and then continued, with a little mystery in her voice.

"My mother reckoned it's an amulet, but then she allus did have funny ideas."

"What's an amulet, Grandma?" Lavender asked curiously.

"Well, it's a mystical object or coin from ancient times that's said to convey a special power to the person who possesses it. An amulet might also be magic or sacred, blessed by the church or royalty. It's obviously been in that old tin ever since me mother kept buttons in it. Don't you be getting any magical ideas about it though, it's not something you should mess around with so pop it back in the tin," grandma replied, passing it back to Lavender.

Lavender took the amulet and pretended to place it back in the tin, but instead kept it concealed in her hand.

As a teenager, grandma had frequently called in to see her aunt Fanny on the way home after a day's work at the mill and the two had become close, especially while Fanny was going through the tragic events of 1928. Grandma began to reminisce stories about great-aunt Fanny's escapades as Lavender listened and continued to hold the amulet tightly in her hand.

"Right lass, it's time to be mekin' tracks," said grandma, as her particular ancestral instalment came to a close.

The amulet tingled in Lavender's hands as if she had rescued something quite rare and precious, and so she guarded it secretly as she swallowed the last cold dregs of cocoa. Feeling tired now, she happily made her way up the narrow stairs that led directly to the front bedroom. This was grandma and grandad's room. It was furnished with two single beds and in the colder months when grandad was away, Lavender shared it with grandma, seeing as though it was not nearly as cold as the back bedroom. Despite this, the windows were often frosted over in the mornings, and you could still see your warm breath misting the air. Delius followed Lavender upstairs to the bedroom, and as she moved the hot stone water bottle to the end of the bed, he curled up in the centre where it had been. She climbed into the bed, still holding the amulet tightly in her hand, and waited for grandma to come upstairs, but as she lay there, her eyes became extraordinarily heavy. Within seconds Lavender drifted off to sleep with the sound of Delius purring, and her grandma downstairs shovelling ash on top of the fire to bank it up for the night and keep the frost at bay.

Chapter Two

Delius

Tap, tap, tatatatap. Tap, tap tatatatap. Lavender had reached a point where her stomach felt as though it was in her mouth. Her body had frozen stiff, and the fine hairs on the back of her neck were raised in fear. Lavender was in the rear of The Turk's Head Inn, one of the more popular drinking establishments in Brigden, of which Fanny Gill was landlady.

Being a landlady was an occupation that suited Fanny who was somewhat unusual and striking in appearance. She was very tall and imposing with a large bosom, a loud, deep voice and a massive head of curly red hair; that said to any observer, you really shouldn't mess with me. Her husband, great-uncle Tom Gill, by contrast, seemed nearly half her size and was a quietly reserved man. Tom had not returned home from a walk on the moors he had embarked on twelve months previously. On the evening of his disappearance, he was found dead on the canal towpath. His clothes were muddy and sodden, and the boots he was wearing were two sizes larger and not his own. When Fanny was given back his clothes, she found a secret pocket in his coat. In it was a small leather pouch containing two gold coins or 'amulets' and a tattered piece of paper, worn and brown with age. In his wallet, he also had a map and a letter from his sister.

After the last drunken patron had reluctantly staggered out of The Turk's Head and Fanny had bolted the heavy dark green double doors, she reached into her apron pocket and took out the letter Tom had been carrying that fatal day.

"See for thisen, lass," she said, handing it over.

It read:

My Dearest Thomas,

Here is the map our great-grandfather Tobias drew of the area. He lived on a farm near the canal and according to family legend, at the age of about ten, he found two amulets on the moor side above the farm that soon after brought upon him vivid dreams and insight. Some of these dreams frightened him and made him delirious. Eventually, it is believed, the amulets were reburied to preserve his sanity.

Tobias's insights were carefully noted, but then disastrously burnt in the farm fire that also saw him lose his life. All that remains are the family tales that tell of the

Venetius Stone marking an ancient sacred place, long since lost.

The stone bore an inscription by the prehistoric inhabitants of the land. It is said to comprise two uprights about seven feet high with a curved crossbeam stone of a similar length. There was an inscription on the cross stone and others on the pillars depicting the seven amulets. To people who hold them individually, the amulets impart the gifts of essential elements, allowing things to be done that ordinarily cannot be done, but more importantly, when they are placed together in a special case, the ancient protective force of "Stoikheion" is formed, bringing equal balance between peace and plenty. Make of all this what you will, but guard your knowledge close, many a tragic tale has followed those that pursue it.

Your ever-loving sister
Katie

Fanny had been quite bewildered and confused since that fateful morning. What had Tom been doing with the amulets? Did they and the other curious articles in his possession have something to do with his untimely death? Laying out the map on the table for Lavender to see, the area's many distinct features were clear and familiar to her, even though it was from a long time ago. It pointed out the canal, rivers and dales of the area, the woodland around Brigden and the Goddodin moors, the ancient cities of Ripon and York, some castles and some less familiar landmarks.

On the map, Brigden looked much smaller to Lavender and just outside a sprawling wooded area, roughly where a prehistoric stone circle was marked. "Maiden Castle" was written on a large oval shape on the moor side above the town with a smaller circle nearby marked burial ground, not far from Obadiah – the famous giant rock that overlooked the valley. Curiously, there was an X written there in different ink and circled.

"All this flummoxes me, lass, and I still can't seem to let these out of my sight, but one thing is for certain, it's summat someone's badly after," said Fanny.

After a few minutes pondering the map, she picked both pieces of paper up and folded them to fit into a small white envelope.

"I think you should put them somewhere safe," said Lavender.

"Aye lass, I'll put it in 'ere," she said, holding up a small flat gold case with intricate patterns on it and circular symbols engraved on the back.

The symbols were much like the pattern on the amulet she had found. Lavender remarked how unusual it was.

"Aye it is that. Tom was very possessive of his case. He came by it only a month or so before he died, on one of his historical investigation trips in York. Strange thing and I never liked it. It has a lock of hair in it that looks like it's a thousand years old. Gives me the frights it does, things started to get very strange after he came across it. Happen it's possessed or summat. Tomorrow when I'm at church, I'll hide it there and put an end to the matter."

She opened the case and placed the envelope inside with the lock of hair before putting it in her apron pocket, then pulled out her hands, spreading her left hand in front of Lavender's eyes. They both looked down at the shining gold amulets in her open palm.

"See here, lass, the symbols on here are like some of those on the case," Fanny continued.

Lavender instantly recognised one of the symbols she had seen on the amulet from the button tin, with two circles and two wavy lines running through them.

"What will you do with them?" Lavender asked curiously.

"I'm not sure, lass, that's been a matter I have struggled to decide on for a year now. The thing is, ever since I've had them, I've been having the most vivid dreams and the strangest feelings, it's hard to let them go," she replied, before putting the amulets back in her apron pocket. "Anyroad, while you're here you might as well help me reckon up the money from the night's takings," Fanny continued.

Fanny and Lavender walked through to the back room behind the bar. They sat down at a table and started counting and stacking pennies, ha'pennies and farthings into piles to make it easier to work out the night's takings. In the quiet of the back room, the echos of the last patrons' footsteps and voices faded into the night air. In the calmness, Lavender considered asking Fanny about the tattered piece of paper, great-uncle Thomas had with him, but her pondering was interrupted by the distinct and increasing noise of clogs, rapping the cobbles. The sounds hastily echoed along the back alley and then stopped abruptly nearby.

"What's going on outside?" Lavender asked curiously.

"I'm not sure, lass, maybe it's young 'uns up to no good. I've had to deal with all sorts on my own since Thomas passed away so mysteriously," Fanny replied in a deliberately raised and intimidating voice.

There was a long silence in which they both sat motionless, listening. Lavender held her breath and began to feel her heart thumping louder on the walls of her chest. Eventually, outside the back-room window, the silence was broken by the ominous, muted chatter of two young men whispering and then suddenly, the lights went out. Almost immediately after, they both heard a tap, tap, tatatatap on the moonlit window that faced onto the long alley, and on which was cast the vague shadows of, without doubt, some unsavoury characters. Petrified, the lump that Lavender had in her throat now felt like it was almost choking her.

Tap, tatatatap, tap, tap. It was at this point that Lavender realised she had started to leave a dream. She noticed the sensation of the warm amulet in her clenched hand, there was some light on the other side of her eyelids, and she could feel the sweet relief of an escape from danger and the security of her warm, comfortable bed.

Tap, tap …

But what is that noise? Lavender thought to herself, *I can still hear it, and it's most definitely real.*

She opened her eyes and peered into the diffused silver moonlight which entered through a gap in the thin floral curtains. On the bedside table next to her she had a small dark blue box that her grandma had given her to keep the most precious thing in; her mother's pendant with the most beautiful array of blues, silver and gold in it. As Lavender opened her hand slowly, a gentle yellow light shone from her palm, and she locked her gaze down on the amulet. The tarnish had gone, and the amulet was now a gleaming radiant gold and shone as if it had its own power lighting up the dark corners of the room. She slowly and quietly leant over and placed the amulet into the box and closed the lid, snuffing out the light.

Grandma's bed was the nearest to the window. She was in a deep sleep and oblivious to the tapping noise. Lavender could hear the silence in-between the tapping. It was that peaceful dead quiet you only get when the air is full of floating snowflakes and settled deep on the ground. Eventually, curiosity overcame Lavender's wariness, and she decided to take a look at what was causing the noise. She crept out of bed, taking extra care not to wake grandma and walked across the bedroom towards the window. With each step Lavender took, the cottage let out a gentle squeak and then a creak as if in relieved gratitude for easing stiffened bones with an ohh and an ahh. This, in turn, disturbed grandma, to the point where she moved onto her back and started to snore, adding syncopation to the rhythm of the squeaking, creaking and tapping.

As Lavender approached the frosted glass, she could see the moonlight was putting on a unique show, like crystals of diamond glitter in the hard frost that had formed intricate patterns on the bedroom window. Beyond was a dark face-like shape silhouetted in the moonlight that appeared to be moving and then another tap. Tentatively, she reached out her index finger to place it on the glass, and then she noticed the strangest thing. The frost's beautiful pattern was the same symbol that she had seen in her dream and on the amulet. It was identical. Lavender closed her eyes tight in disbelief and then pinched her arm hard to check if she was awake.

Then another tap came, and she abruptly opened her eyes, feeling like she was waking from another dream. Again, she put her finger up to the glass towards the dark shape, this time putting it on the frosted glass to make a small peephole in the ice. Now the room was deathly quiet, the creaking had stopped, and Lavender stood like a statue. Grandma's snoring had also ceased, to the point that Lavender was a little unsure whether grandma was still breathing. Even the small brown leather-cased travel clock that sat open on grandma's bedside table had stopped ticking. It was precisely 3.00 am

With great trepidation, Lavender slowly put an eye up to the peephole in the frost. Just as her eyelashes met the glass, a large yellow eye blinked back at her from outside. Lavender let out such a high-pitched scream and jumped so high that grandma sat bolt upright in bed with her eyes wide open and shouted, "where hast tha been?", simultaneously, there was a loud hiss from the window, and a scramble of claws against bark as Delius flew down the pear tree and across the snow-covered front garden.

At the front of the cottage, the pear tree stood so close to the walls that it was if the building was formed around it. Grandma had said that pear trees were a way to keep evil spirits out of buildings and so we would always be safe inside. Maybe that was true, but for Delius, the tree provided him with a perfect ladder to the bedroom window, that during warmer days and nights, was his very own open front door. Lavender rubbed over the circular symbol she recognised, that was so striking in the frost, to widen her viewing hole and saw that Delius must have been moving on a branch but now sat like one of those gothic lions outside the town hall. A statue on top of the stone gate post staring up at Lavender.

Grandma had laid straight back down and was again snoring as if nothing at all had happened. As Lavender stood there, she could see the hole in the frost closing up before her eyes and with it a new pattern, this time with just the circles and no wavy lines, and around it what looked like some of the features from the map found in great-uncle Tom's pocket. She rubbed her eyes to check her vision, and sure enough, it was just as she had seen in her dream, the woods, the moor, dales and the river, even the oval and circular-shaped objects on the moors.

With the most gentle footsteps she was able to make; Lavender worked her way back across the bedroom. But instead of returning to her bed, she felt an almost hypnotic pull onwards, out to the landing and down the stairs. Halfway down the staircase was a small window just two feet square that sat in the cottage walls, which were so thick they could easily have been in a castle. She felt a need to look out of the window to check on this side of the cottage. It required leaning right into the recess and again to rub at the frost on the glass. The ice was not as harsh on the single window on this side of the house. At first the moonlight outside drew her eyes to the sparkling, glinting snow, then to Delius who had worked his way around the cottage, as if to either knowingly follow Lavender, or to guide her to some yet unknown place. Whatever the reason, Lavender looked at Delius sitting on the edge of the medieval stone wall, that was now no more than an ornament in the centre of the lawn. As she did so, he winked slowly and just stood there as if not wanting to be the first to move.

Lavender trusted that something outside was waiting to be discovered, and that despite the cold night and the occasional gently floating snowflake that tickled and teased the bare trees in the garden and Delius's nose, he might be her guide. From the small cloak cupboard, she pulled out a large pair of green woollen socks and one of the hand-knitted cable knit jumpers that grandma had made Lavender back in the autumn, and quickly put them on over her pyjamas. Next, she squished her feet into the yellow Wellington boots that were now just a little too tight and put on her duffel coat, hat, scarf and gloves, then ever so quietly lifted the sneck of the back door. It was time to venture out into the night.

Chapter Three

Fred Keighley

The snow had drifted at the back of the cottage and was near the top of Lavender's boots as she stepped from the kitchen door into the backyard. Delius was waiting. He opened his mouth as if to meow, but no sound came out, just a small puff of misty breath in the night air. There was nothing strange about the lack of noise. Delius was mute and other than an occasional hiss or purr, was utterly silent. If he wanted to get some attention, he would typically leap up on the piano and start to paddle his paws up and down the keys to make himself known.

Lavender made her mouth into a wide O shape, took a deep breath, and slowly blew out into the cold night air. She pretended to have been puffing on one of grandad's funny shaped pipes that sat like ornaments in a hole on the fireside wall.

The sky was clearing now, and the moon shone brightly on the snow which allowed her to see well enough, despite the time of night. With soft crunching footsteps in the snow, Lavender wound her way around the cottage and out of the front gate. She paused for a moment to look up at the bedroom window then turned down Bridge Street following Delius. The curious thing was, Delius, didn't walk while Lavender was watching him. He would sit and observe, and as soon as Lavender looked away or even blinked, he had moved further along the street. Lavender looked back again at the cottage to make sure there were no lights on, and when she turned around, the cat had disappeared. She scanned the street for Delius whose dark tabby coat had stood out as plain as day against the snow, but he was nowhere to be seen. She looked toward the streetlamp in front of the working men's club on the opposite side of the road, where the Wades Mill brass band had rehearsed earlier, but that now sat dark and silent. Then she looked right towards the turning to Bradley Street. Delius was sat on the butcher's shop windowsill which was painted in a distinctive red. The sign written proudly above the window in gold letters proclaimed:

F. Keighley. Butchers.

As well as being a shop, this was the home of Fred Keighley and his son, also called Fred, one of Lavender's closest friends. Fred was a tall slim boy with blond hair, blue eyes and a disarming smile that worked charmingly around girls and ladies. Fred and Lavender had known one another ever since they could remember. Along with Alice Sutton, who was the spitting image of Lavender, the three children had spent many happy days playing in the fields, woods and sometimes in the beck, or anywhere else they could explore for that matter.

Delius often followed grandma to the butchers on a Tuesday and was quite familiar with the meat there. But even more than that, he preferred Friday supper time and a routine trip a little further down the road to the fish and chip shop where there was sure to be a titbit of haddock to reward the journey.

Lavender expected Delius to have moved as she approached the shop window, mainly as she was so close and had looked away several times. Still, he just sat there with a nonchalant look on his face and his stripy tail wrapped tightly around his legs.

"What is it?" whispered Lavender into the cat's ears. "Are we here? Is this what you've brought me out for? A half an ounce of Fred Keighley's best beef mince?" Delius didn't answer but looked up knowingly.

I wonder if I should try and wake Fred up, thought Lavender as she looked up at the bedroom window.

Delius sneezed as if to agree this was the right course of action. She crouched down and scooped snow into her gloves, cupping it into a ball and then threw it up at the dark window. Duff … it was the perfect sound, not too loud and sharp to the ear but soft and deep. She waited. Delius waited. Again, she made another snowball and repeated her action. There was another duff on the window.

Lavender knew Fred was a sound sleeper as they had been camping together many times. The last time was the previous summer's choir trip, when a rather ravenous pig had woken everyone except Fred. The pig had escaped from the farmyard, wandered into the camping field and was snuffling at the food supplies and snorting at the canvas. Fred slept through the whole thing, much to his disappointment in missing out on such a hilarious event.

Lavender bent down once more and scooped up an extra-large pile of snow and squashed it a little harder this time to make a solid snowball. She stood up and threw the projectile as hard as she could, realising after it was too late that Fred Keighley had opened the window and was peering outside with bleary eyes. The snowball landed smack on his forehead, and he let out a barely muffled ouch, his head disappearing back inside followed by a distinct thud.

At first, Lavender couldn't help but giggle as she stood waiting to see what Fred would do. But for what felt like far too long, nothing happened.

What if I've knocked him unconscious? she thought.

Lavender was on the point of whispering loudly up to the open window when a paper aeroplane glided out and spiralled down through the clear night air to arrive precisely in her grasp. Fred's head cautiously popped out of the window. He gestured for her to open the paper, then pointed up the street before quietly pulling the window closed. Lavender opened up the aeroplane.

"Meet me in the back snicket, the front door will wake my dad," it said.

A back door led out into a yard; otherwise, Lavender realised using the shop door would have tinkled the brass bell. This naturally alerted the entry or exit of a customer and would likely have woken up Fred's mum and dad. Lavender went ahead and turned down the narrow dark snicket between the row of buildings that led to the yard at the back of the butchers. She suddenly realised she was on her own and Delius had vanished completely. Still, by the time she reached the other end of the passageway Fred was crunching his way through the snow towards her.

"Are you alright?" said Lavender, concerned about the thud she had heard from Fred's bedroom.

"Aye, but I'm more bothered about why you're 'ere. I was in the middle of a right good dream when you woke me up with your snowball."

"That's just it," Lavender replied, "It's a dream that's brought me here."

Lavender explained the amulet she had found in the button tin and then the dream she'd had of great-aunt Fanny, the note, map, the case and the gold amulets, then waking up at the tapping on the window at the back of The Turk's Head Inn. Fred's jaw dropped as Lavender explained the details of her dream.

"What is it, Fred?" she said, looking at Fred's perplexed expression. Fred's mouth was still open and for a second Lavender thought he'd frozen to the spot in the cold night air.

Eventually, he spoke; "That's really weird. I was just dreaming about being at the back of The Turk's Head. A couple of lads were chasing me, so I ran down the ginnel and jumped down a coal hole to hide. They were just a few feet away from me, and I heard them whispering to each other.

Then one of them started tapping on the window of the inn. That's when I woke up."

Quite aghast, Lavender was now stood as Fred had been moments before.

"You don't reckon we were somehow in the same dream, do you?" said Fred. "And that this map and the amulets of your great-aunt Fanny's really exist. Do you think they might lead us to an important discovery?" he continued.

Lavender nodded in confirmation. "I think you might be right, Fred, and I have an idea. Will you meet me before church service tomorrow?"

"Why, Lav, what do you have in mind?" Fred questioned.

"Just trust me, I have a plan," Lavender replied secretively.

Fred agreed and then, being a good soul, walked Lavender back to Pear Tree Cottage.

"By the way," said Fred with a cheeky smile, "happy birthday."

"Thanks," said Lavender, smiling back as she turned around the side of the cottage and disappeared from view.

Delius was waiting at the back door when Lavender returned. He looked at her with an approving smile in his eyes as she lifted the sneck on the door. Delius slinked into the warm kitchen, then through to the front room fireplace that still radiated heat like the comforting hug of a dear friend. Lavender took off her gloves that were now a bit soggy. Her fingers tingled back to life as they warmed up, and her nose started to run. She removed her hat, scarf, boots and socks, then hung her coat back up in the cloak cupboard and ever so gently made her way back up the narrow stairs. Lavender felt safe, hearing grandma in the bedroom snoring deeply. She knew she had not been missed. Entering the room she climbed into bed, taking a last look at the clock, silent on grandma's bedside table. As she did so, she noticed it started to tick once more. It was still 3.00 am.

Chapter Four

St Paul's

The bright winter sunlight cast shadows of the pear tree
branches through the bedroom curtains and onto Lavender's
face. Her eyes squinted open, and she noticed that grandma had
already gotten out of bed. Delius was sitting on the dressing
table opposite, staring intently at her as if waiting for some
early morning conversation. Lavender stared back, trying not to
blink and wondering who would give in first, until the stairs
creaked one after the other. Grandma came into the bedroom
with a breakfast tray complete with boiled egg, buttery toast
soldiers, a pot of tea and homemade jam from last summer's
raspberries.

"Happy birthday, lass. I'm treating you this morning;
you can have breakfast in bed as it's your special day."

Lavender sat up and plumped up the pillows behind her
as grandma put the tray on her lap. The egg was already
cracked open, and within minutes the soldiers had mopped up
the runny egg yolk, the white had been consumed, and the shell
had been placed upside down as if it were still a complete egg
waiting to be eaten. Once Lavender had polished off the toast

and sat with her cup of tea, grandma went to the wardrobe and pulled out a brown paper bag with a small bundle of envelopes and some presents inside. No matter what was inside though, the one thing Lavender really wanted for this, and every birthday, was something she knew she wouldn't be able to have: her mum and dad.

At four years old, one perfect afternoon in early May, with the sun shining brightly in a nearly cloudless sky, and the pink blossom, like candyfloss, dabbed elegantly on the cherry trees in the park, Lavender said goodbye to her mum and dad. As they hugged and squeezed her tight, little did they know it would be for the last time. Destined for a long-delayed honeymoon in the Yorkshire Dales, they had ventured off in their Trafalgar blue 1963 Morris Minor with wooden-framed rear doors, registration number 40BWW. They had planned to stop in York on the way for lunch and were last seen at "Ye Olde Moon Inne." What happened after that has remained a mystery. Curiously, the next morning their Morris Minor, still packed with their suitcases, was parked outside Pear Tree Cottage. Lavenders parents had disappeared without a trace.

Delius joined Lavender as she made her way through the cards and presents. He seemed interested to investigate them and the discarded wrapping paper. There was a selection of gifts; books, a new dress, some chocolates and the pink and white roller skates that she had been hoping for. Then Lavender got to the last present, which felt like yet another book. She noticed the distinctive smell of musty old paper and leather immediately that she began to pull off the wrapping paper. The book she held in her hands was kept closed by a length of thin brown twine tied in a bow, and embossed on the red leather were the words "My Scrapbook - by Katie Peach".

"You took such an interest in the story of Aunt Fanny, I thought you might like this family heirloom. My mother started this as she used to like collecting all sorts of bits and pieces and writing favourite poems and family sayings in it. Anyway, keep a good hold on this, lass. When I reached twenty-one it was handed down to me and I added to it. When your mother was twenty-one, I gave it to her, but now…" she took in a wavering breath and sighed, pausing for a moment. "Now it's coming to you, much too early I know, but I want you to have it as you might as well start adding to it rather than it sitting in a box."

Lavender pulled the twine bow and released the cover to turn over the first page. The book sprang open with a multitude of newspaper clippings, cigarette cards and pieces of paper that had been inserted between the pages.

The first page confirmed the contents with a most vague description.

"A collection of things and what not. By Katie Peach."

Lavender flicked through the bulging pages until a point in which the book fell naturally open, about halfway through at a particularly tatty and aged piece of paper, accompanied by some of Katie's writing on the opposite page. She read:

"This strange rhyme was in my brother Thomas's possession when he died and still to this day, it has not rightly been fathomed.

"This is the place thou comes from,
And the old moon shone long ago,
Thereupon fair Maiden's castle,
Peace did reign without a foe.

Together, seven made all content,
'Til invaders divided their gain.
Disguised with shining stones they came,
Our perfect vale obtained.

On horse's wings, they rode to us,
By the hundreds, red and gold.
Alas, they took our peace and plenty,
But they could not take our souls.

But though many moons will surely pass,
The seven, together, still are true.
Content can still be found in them,
When they are restored to thee.

Take heed my offspring to this rhyme,
Thy future blessings rest in time.
Though I shall not chance to see,
Ye still may find thy blessings be."

She continued to read: "Last night I lay in bed and reread it
before I fell asleep, then I woke abruptly from a dream at three
o'clock. I dreamed I was walking by a river in the summer sun
with a wise old man, some sort of respected elder, I think. He
wore simple clothes made of roughly woven wool, including a
tunic. We stopped and stood to watch, where, on the other side
of the river, there was a beautiful black horse with tears in its
eyes. On its back it had a Queen's body, and it was escorted by

at least twenty Roman soldiers. Then it unfurled magical wings and flew off into the sky. There have been stories of the Brigantes in our family ever since I can remember, and many have been forgotten over the years, but whoever wrote this scrap of tattered paper is a mystery. I decided to keep it safe in this record, in the hope that someday the person it was intended for may read it. The only thing I do know is that Maiden Castle is a Brigantian fort and burial ground, and this rhyme appears to describe the time when the Romans arrived in the area."

Lavender was quite perplexed and became rather pale as she read the words in her head, and in growing curiosity closed the book and turned to grandma.

"What does this mean?" she asked.

"Well, lass," she replied, "it was typical of my mother putting two and two together and coming up with five. She had a knack of dreaming the future and the past, being in connection with people and between things. Knowing things that by ordinary means could not be known. Anyway, it's a gift a rare few of the women in this family have had and writing this extraordinary insight down is summat your great-grandmother decided to do."

There was a long pause while grandma seemed to drift off to some faraway place in her mind and then, changing the subject, she continued, "Na'then, you'll have plenty of time to read but for now times getting on, you've had quite a sleep in this morning so best get thisen up and dressed if we are going to attend church service on time."

Lavender had the sudden recollection of the previous night and her arrangement with Fred and leapt out of bed with a dramatic sense of urgency.

"Steady on, lass, what's got into you?"

"Don't want to be late, grandma, I have things to do."

"Well, you'd better get your skates on then!" Grandma laughed at her own joke, but Lavender was on a mission and had already got to the bathroom and was soon running the hot water, ready for a wash.

It was a bitterly cold morning outside, though there had been no more snow and the sky was clear and bright. Inside, the cottage had retained some warmth. The fire was still "in", smouldering and shifting as it relaxed under white ash. With a poker used to prod and disturb the embers, and with some fresh wood, it wasn't long before it came back to life. Grandma knelt by the fire and pulled aside the black metal door below the flames and started to shovel the ash into a bucket.

"It will be just right when we get back from church."
She stood up and took the bucket of ash to the back door, then
continued, "I'll just get the beef in the oven, and then we can
get off."

Lavender wasn't surprised that they would have roast
beef for Sunday lunch despite the fact there was just the two of
them. Grandma had a habit of always cooking for an army,
regardless of how many mouths needed feeding, so there was
never a short supply of food.

Stepping out of the front door into the snow-covered
garden, the evidence of last night's activities was plain enough
to see. A series of footprints went around the cottage, out of the
front garden, down Bridge Street and back again. Lavender
also noticed the cats paw prints, but only up to the front gate.

"Whatever's been going on here?" exclaimed grandma,
pointing at the array of footprints in the otherwise pure and
smooth snow. "There must have been some children messing
about last night," she continued.

"You're probably right, grandma," replied Lavender,
feeling a little relieved that last night's adventure had not been
questioned.

They headed across the road, which was quieter than usual and made their way to St Paul's Church, a short five-minute walk into the town.

"I wonder when Grandad will get home. Do you think he will see me on my birthday, grandma?"

"You never know, lass, you never know," grandma replied without commitment.

Grandad had his own haulage business which consisted of one green lorry that seemed enormous to Lavender. He was often away on long trips to far-flung places like London or Glasgow, so there were times when he wasn't around much. When grandad was home, he was pretty quiet. It seemed to Lavender that he spent a great deal of time either reading or sleeping in the small study that was just off the side of the front room, or that he was out walking on the moors above the small town. He had this particular kind of presence that Lavender missed when he was not home. But when he returned home, she could sense immediately that he was there. It was if inside him was the calm depths of the oceans, silently knowing, not necessarily doing but just being.

As the steps to St Paul's came into view, Lavender saw Fred Keighley stood waiting by the entrance. His head was down, he was shuffling his feet in the snow, and he had both hands planted snuggly in his trouser pockets for warmth. She ran ahead to see him.

"Mind you don't slip and break your neck," grandma shouted after her.

Fred looked up to see Lavender heading up the church steps towards him.

"Happy birthday … again!" he greeted her.

"Thanks, Fred. Now you do still remember what happened last night, don't you?"

"Aye, how could I forget?" he replied.

"Well, we'll have to be quick while we are alone to talk. Great-aunt Fanny played the church organ all those years ago, and I remembered her saying that she would hide the note and map in church. If we get in early, we can search for it. I think it might be hidden somewhere near the organ."

Lavender and Fred both sang in the church choir, making it reasonably easy to look around the chancel and the organ area before the service. Being in good time, they were the first to enter the vestry where the choir put on their robes. It was only a small room of wooden panels with a tiny arch window and cupboards running along the inner wall. The cupboard doors were made from the same wooden panelling as the rest of the vestry, making them invisible to any new visitors. After getting changed into their choir robes, Lavender and Fred set about searching the room, then the nooks and crannies of the choir stalls and the organ. Within minutes though other choristers started to arrive and they had to abandon their search.

"We'll just have to try again after the service," said Fred, a little disappointed.

"I'm not sure we will get the chance, Fred. The Mothers' Union ladies are always chatting for ages afterwards with their coffees and custard creams."

The vestry was getting jam-packed with the whole choir now crammed into the small room. Fortunately, it would soon be time to make the choirs procession down the western aisle out to the back of the church and then forward down the nave to the choir stalls. Generally, by now Miss Peddler the organist would be playing some sort of nonsensical but pleasing music. Instead, beyond the vestry door, all that could be heard was the congregation gathering, accompanied by their echoing footsteps and muffled voices.

Just then, the choir mistress Mrs Moles came in and announced that Miss Peddler was unwell and that her elderly mother, Mable, would be stepping in to play the organ.

Unfortunately, everyone knew that this could be rather disastrous as Mable was nearly deaf and consequently would usually start playing either too early or too late. Even if she did start on time, it was often at the wrong speed, so singing along to the hymns was like chasing a speeding car on a pushbike. Mrs Moles tapped Fred Keighley on the shoulder and requested that he go and sit with Mable with the intention of prompting her when to start playing and help her with her speed. Fred was quite relieved as he always seemed to get stuck in front of Malcolm Majors. Majors was a rather large and jolly bass singer with a huge belly who had a habit of hitting the choir boys on the head with his hymn book to encourage better singing. Fred looked at Lavender with a knowing smile and then went out of the vestry's back door and round to the organ to sit next to Mable. Within a few seconds, the church organ's familiar sound and vibration started, and the choir made their way out into the church.

The service proceeded as usual, but even with Fred prompting Mable when to start playing each hymn, he struggled to prevent her from speeding up as she went along. Each time Mable began to play too fast, Fred would tap his hand at a slower speed on the top of the wooden frame in which the lower keyboard sat. This happened during every hymn but seemed to be getting worse through the service. By the time it got to the last hymn, which happened to be "Jerusalem," Mable started off like the clappers. As the choir began singing, "And did those feet in ancient times …" Fred was tapping the organ with a particularly hard and apparent gesture. The action of hitting the instrument in such a fashion suddenly dislodged something under the frame which fell with a clatter onto the floor. Mable seemed oblivious to this, continuing at an ever-increasing pace to what seemed like the Grand National's finish line and the awaiting coffee and custard creams. Fred looked down at the floor with great astonishment to see a bright piece of gold that could be precisely what he and Lavender were searching for. In his excitement, he quickly stomped his highly polished leather shoe on top of the metal, feeling it bend a little with his weight.

Oh Lord, he thought, as he waited with a fear he had broken it, but also with great excitement for the chance to pick it up.

As the vicar recited the last prayer and Mable closed her eyes in deeper reverence, Fred bent down. He picked up the object, seeing immediately that it had a series of intricate circles engraved on the front, damaged a little now by the dent he had made with his Sunday-best shoes. He quickly put it in one of the deep pockets of his red cassock and closed his eyes. The feeling of excitement was making his heart beat out of his chest.

Wow, he thought, *I can't believe I've found it. Wait till I get out and show Lavender.*

After the choir returned to the vestry, there was usually a quick exit and not much hanging about. But even before the vestry door was closed, Malcom Majors already had his deerstalker hat on as if he was Sherlock Holmes, eager to solve some mystery.

With the rapid departure of choristers, Fred was able to whisper his news to Lavender, and they made a plan to catch up after dinner. Lavender could hardly contain herself.

How exciting, I wonder what we will find and where the map will lead us? she thought, her mind drifting off into untold adventures.

Lavender and Fred left the vestry and joined grandma and Fred's mum and dad at the back of the church where they were engrossed in conversation.

"Well, that was a belter," laughed Fred's dad, "I thought I was at Brands Hatch with Niki Lauda in the driving seat by the end of the service."

Grandma interrupted with an announcement, "You'd be most welcome to come for Sunday dinner, seeing as though it's Lavender's birthday."

"We'd love to, but we have to go and see mother," said Fred. "But you can go if you want son if that's alright with you, Annie?"

"Aye, of course it is, Fred. These two are thick as thieves, wouldn't want to split them up," grandma replied.

Chapter Five

Grandad

When they opened the front door of Pear Tree Cottage, grandma and Lavender were greeted with the most beautiful smell of roasting meat, mingling with the smoky heat of a slowly burning log. Delius didn't move from his usual perch by the fire, except for a slight opening of his eyes in that smiling way that cats do when they are in a state of bliss.

"Ee, whatever next!" exclaimed grandma as she stepped inside.

There in his rocking chair sat grandad, still with boots and flat cap on, but fast asleep and obviously back from a long trip in his lorry. Grandad woke with a startled twitch, his eyes popping open and staring blankly ahead.

"I thought you weren't back 'till late tonight, Arthur?" grandma said as she took off her boots.

There was what seemed like an incredibly long pause before grandad gave an exceptionally long yawn.

"Ahhhhhhhrghhhhhhhh … Aye well … I thought seen as it's a special day, I'd decide to work through and sleep when I got home."

He stood up and took off his cap.

"Come 'ere, birthday girl, and give us a hug then."

He held out his arms and Lavender skipped over with her arms outstretched. As she reached grandad, he plonked his cap on her little head, "Ee by gum, you've grown up since I last saw you!" he continued.

Lavender squeezed him tight, feeling so safe in his arms and with the familiar smell of oil, cherry tobacco and the wool of his jumper.

"I'll have to get on with dinner now, and you need to go and get a wash and clean up, Arthur," grandma instructed.

For the first time since he discovered the gold case, Fred and Lavender were left alone. As they stood there still warming up from their walk back from church, Fred reached into his pocket and pulled out their discovery.

"Go on then, you open it," Fred said, handing the case to Lavender.

She hesitated for a moment and then took it from him. Being bent a little out of shape, the lid was not budging, but eventually, with some effort, she prised it open with a click. Sure enough, inside was the small white envelope that great-aunt Fanny Gill had put there that night in the back of The Turk's Head all those years ago, but the lock of hair she had seen was gone. Lavender sucked in a sharp breath as she saw it and then paused, looking at Fred with wide-open eyes.

"You can breathe out if you want to," he said, trying to break her statuesque pose.

As if to follow his instructions, she blew out a long breath, handed the case back to Fred and carefully opened the envelope to remove the folded piece of paper inside.

She read out loud:

"You dreamed a dream to find me,
That power has been given to you,
From the first piece of gold, you touched.
There's so much more you can do.

Touch a second, and see our union,
A connection unbreakable true
And follow the path it will take you.
To your intention, your destiny true

Now you must search for the lonely traveller,
With a ruby that glows for you,
To guide you far beyond here.

And make you a traveller too.

Signed,

Mary Bathwater"

Lavender stared at the note, then at Fred, then back at the note. Confused, she turned it over as if she expected the anticipated text to appear on the other side, but instead, it was blank. Why was there a letter from Lavender's mum? Confused at the difference to her dream, she pulled open the envelope again to check for the map. It wasn't there. Yet still, the case with the envelope was hidden in the church, just as she had believed in her heart it would be.

"What on earth do you think this means, Fred?"

"I haven't a clue, but one thing is for sure; your mother got to it before us," he replied with disappointment. "Pass it 'ere and let me 'ave a look," he continued.

She held out the note to Fred, but it lifted straight out of her fingers before he could take hold. In a whirl the paper was sucked into the flames of the fire, then with a flash it turned to smoke vanishing up the chimney.

Delius, who had remained at peace until this point, leapt from the plinth and across the room to the piano. He jumped up and parked his bottom on the high keys at the end with plinking sound. Lavender and Fred stood in shock by the fire.

"What's Delius trying to tell us?" shouted grandma from the kitchen.

Being a cat unable to make any kind of meow left Delius resorting to numerous other methods of communication. Jumping up on the piano keys was his favourite.

"Err, not sure," replied Lavender, somewhat lost for words.

"If you two are not doing anything, you can come and set the table ready for dinner," grandma continued.

As the children went into the kitchen grandad came back into the front room and took the place of Delius at the piano. He never actually played any tunes but instead had a weekly ritual of exercise that involved playing a crescendoing series of scales. It was a sound that Lavender had come to relish on Sunday mornings, a sound that seemed to be designed to speak to every crack, crevice, stone and timber, every concealed space within the thick-set cottage walls. The rippling, rising and falling notes vibrated into each pore of the cottage in their own language. Not understood, but nonetheless felt.

The Yorkshire pudding was cooked in a big tray, nicely crisp on the bottom and around the edges yet still soft in the middle. Depending on how you liked it, there was just the right kind for everyone and usually plenty left over for pudding. Leftovers were Fred's favourite part when visiting Lavender's for Sunday dinner as they always had Yorkshire pudding with golden syrup drizzled over to finish. Today was no exception.

After the main course had been demolished, and grandad had loosened his belt to let out a little room in his expanding waist, grandma got up from her chair announcing, "There's some Yorksha's left. Would anyone like some for pudding?" grandma winked at Fred.

"Yes please, Mrs Tilly," said Fred without the slightest hesitation.

There was a combined replete sigh from everyone at the table, as the last crumbs were scraped from the plates, and the dinner concluded.

Grandad gently rubbed and patted his somewhat rounded belly, exclaiming, "Ee, there's not a pot washed, nor a po emptied and a house full of strangers!" to which everyone laughed.

However, no one was quite sure exactly what it meant except that the food was very satisfying. It wasn't long before the kitchen had been cleared; Lavender and Fred went to build snowmen out in the garden, while grandma and grandad sat quietly together by the fire.

"What shall we do now?" said Lavender, sticking twigs for arms in the side of the snowman as Fred wrapped his scarf around the neck.

"We could have a snowball fight?" Fred replied.

"I meant what shall we do about this mysterious note, Fred?"

"Oh … Nowt we can do I reckon, unless you get to see your great-aunt again," Fred replied.

"Well, I've been thinking about the dream and what the note said. I think my dream is because of the amulet I found yesterday," said Lavender.

"Wow, you found an amulet? I read a story about them only a few weeks ago, don't they give people special powers or cure illnesses or summat?" asked Fred.

"Well after what has just happened, maybe they do. I found it in my grandma's button tin. I think I will ask her to tell me more about great-aunt Fanny in case there are any clues to this mystery."

"You're not going to tell her about the dream and the note, are you?" This was more of a statement than a question from Fred but had the effect of planting the thought in her mind.

"I might tell her about the dream," Lavender replied. There was a long silence.

"I wonder what happened to the other amulet that your great-uncle Tom had in his coat pocket? The amulet from the button tin is one of them, so the other might be nearby," Fred said in a pondering manner shuffling his hands around in his own coat pockets as if to search hopefully for a miraculous discovery.

"That does it!" said Lavender in a sudden outburst of enthusiasm, "I will ask grandma tonight. She must know something."

They returned to the cottage, hung up their coats and laid their gloves out on the hearth to dry, the bobbles of snow caught in the wool slowly turning to tears on the warm stone.

"Now then you two. Would you like a nice cup of cocoa to warm you up before Fred goes home?" grandma offered as they stood on the flagstone hearth.

"Yes please!" they replied in unison.

As grandma made the cocoa in the kitchen and grandad and Delius were sleeping soundly in the rocking chair, Fred took the gold case out of his pocket once more. He handed it to Lavender.

"You should have it seeing as though it belongs to your family," he said with a tinge of disappointment in his voice.

Lavender took the case and to avoid any questioning, pushed it underneath the piano to hide.

"I wish we had a way of finding that map," Lavender whispered to Fred as she returned to the hearth.

Just as she spoke, grandad made a deep snorting sound. He awoke with his eyes wide open, as if with a sudden realisation and at the same time abruptly raised his right hand in the air pointing up with his index finger. Delius jumped down from his lap as grandad sat there almost as if in a trance. His finger held in the air until Delius jumped up on the piano and started walking down the keys.

"Hear all, see all, say nowt, that's my advice," he said as he lowered his finger.

"What's going on in there?" grandma shouted out from the kitchen, knowing very well that something was of interest if the cat needed to raise his proxy voice.

No one replied. They all just sat there in silence as if heeding grandad's advice. Suddenly, the lights went out, leaving the room lit only by the fading winter daylight and the glow of the fire. Grandma's face entered from the kitchen in the illuminated glow of a birthday cake and ten candles.

"Happy birthday, Lavender," grandma sang as she walked in and put the cake down on the small dark table; another of great-grandad Augustus's creations.

""Go on then, lass, make a wish!" grandad prompted.

Lavender took a deep breath, closed her eyes, and after a slight hesitation, blew all the candles out.

"Now don't tell us your wish or it won't come true," grandma advised.

Chapter Six

Aunt Margaret

Later that evening, after Fred Keighley returned home, grandma and Lavender sat at the card table engrossed in a game of "Canasta". At the same time, grandad stoked his pipe and pondered his week ahead. He was considering whether the snow would abate enough to make his next trip less perilous than the last when the lonely, distant sound of a motorcycle broke the quiet of the evening. As the sound meandered its way between the drystone walls of the winding country lanes, it gradually became louder and in the mind's eye could be imagined quite clearly on the route it was travelling, finally coming into town and turning into Bridge Street outside. It came to a stop in front of Pear Tree Cottage where the engine idled for a while and then turned off with a rapidly reducing puttputtputttt. Shortly after, there was a familiar squeak and clunk from the front gate, followed by a confident knock at the door, not with a hand, but with a hard object.

"Surely it can't be who I think it is at this time of night?" said grandma in surprise, and somewhat annoyed at the inconvenient distraction at a critical moment in the game.

Grandad took a couple of sucks of his pipe and blew a not insignificant plume of smoke from the corner of his mouth.

"I'll go and see shall I, Annie?" he replied, taking the question as a subtle hint. He put his pipe on the plinth by the fire and walked over to open the door.

"Aye up, Marg, you must be nithered. What's brought you over on such a cold night?" he asked.

Margaret entered the room and immediately started peeling off her woollen coat and removing her white "brain-bucket" style half helmet and snow-covered boots.

"Well," said Margaret, somewhat flushed in the face and a tad out of breath, "between you, me and the gatepost, Arthur, there's summat that wer callin' me over and so I just had to come and see you."

"Who me, are you sure?" said grandad.

"Aye you, ya daft 'appeth," Margaret replied intransigently.

Margaret, affectionately referred to as Aunt Marg, was distantly related to the family though the exact relationship was unknown. She seemed about the same age as Lavender's grandparents and was somewhat of a mystery to most that knew her. Marg was widowed at a young age and lived alone in the end stone terrace house of four that was sat relatively isolated overlooking the town, with the Goddodin moors at the back. Her figure could be best described as round, that is no matter which way you looked at her; she was the same width. She always carried a black walking cane with a rounded handle inlaid with mother-of-pearl, there was even a special holder on her motorcycle for it. She had long silver hair tied up in a bun which was fine most of the time but happened to look quite ridiculous with a motorcycle helmet on. Apart from her small, dark and piercing eyes, the other dominant feature of Margaret's face was her jowls. They were disproportionate, unusually fleshy and seemed to have a life of their own moving independently from the rest of her.

"Don't mind me," continued Margaret, as she took up residence in one of the winged high seat chairs opposite the fire and rested her right hand on the cane.

"We won't, Marg," said grandma. "We're just in the middle of a game, so if you don't mind, we'll finish off this round and then I'll put the kettle on."

Grandma debated putting a "Canasta" down on the deck but decided against it as it was early on in the round, and there were plenty more points to be made. Instead, she kept her cards concealed and threw a seven of hearts down.

"You shouldn't have done that, Annie!" Margaret commented, as if she had been analysing every move through the entire game.

Annie looked over and responded with a frustrated scowl. Without hesitation, Lavender picked the seven of hearts up and with a barely contained grin, placed all her cards down on the table, including a red "Canasta" and pronounced "Chip!"

"Well, I'll be!" said grandma with surprise.

They totted up their scores with Lavender now moving clearly into the lead.

"Seeing as though you won that round, you can make the tea lass, and as for you, Marg, whatever is to do?" she continued.

Margaret was at this point, staring blankly into the fire in somewhat of a trance. The room fell silent except for the breathing of the flames that licked the back of the chimney. Margaret didn't respond but remained sitting and motionless. Her usually piercing eyes were now quite wide and glazed over with the warm firelight reflecting in them. Arthur looked across the room to Annie and winked at her. They had both witnessed Margaret having one of her "turns" before, and it appeared this was another such occasion. The first time Annie and Arthur had seen this happen was when Mary was a child and they had been visiting Margaret's house on the moors. Without warning Margaret had announced a cryptic foretelling of their daughter's travel, that only years later was realised. But her "episodes" were not uncommon. The last time it had happened was only recently while Margaret had been out in Robert's Park with her grandchildren feeding the ducks, she had become transfixed looking at the ripples on the lake and was woken from her locked gaze by her granddaughter wading into the water, trying to feed the ducks, then slipping backwards with a splash.

While Lavender was preparing a pot of tea in the kitchen, Margaret's gaze finally shifted from the flickering flames and on to the stone hearth. She let out a long eerie groan and shook her head, jowls wobbling.

"Tha shall 'af to watch thisen on tha travels, Arthur … ohh aye … I see a man's discarded coat on the hearth, and the fire's gone out," she declared ominously.

Arthur looked at Annie and rolled his eyes as if to say, "Marg's finally lost her marbles".

"Whatever are you saying, Marg?" said Annie with concern.

"I'm saying, mark my words, if I see the fire's snuffed out then there's danger coming, and it's near te't fire which means it's someone close. Aye it's as plain as day to me," Margaret replied with a seriousness that sent a shiver down the spine and could only be met with an equal amount of fear from anyone listening.

After a few moments of silence, grandma got up and walked to the kitchen to check on Lavender.

"It's getting late, lass, and you've school tomorrow. I think it's time for bed. Come and say goodnight to your grandad and Aunt Marg and I'll come up and see you in a bit."

Lavender looked over at grandma with a deliberately sad expression. As she looked into her pale green eyes, Lavender knew this wasn't about going to bed because it was getting late, or that there was school tomorrow. Grandma was just trying to shield her from why Marg was here.

"Promise you will come up and see me before I go to sleep," Lavender said.

"Of course, lass, now off you go," grandma replied, giving a gentle touch on Lavender's arm for reassurance.

Lavender ran back into the front room and gave grandad a big hug.

"Goodnight, sleep tight, lass," he said as Lavender skipped off and made her way up the narrow stairs.

"And goodnight to you too, Aunty Marg," Lavender called out with a final farewell as she got to the landing.

As grandad was home, Lavender went to her bedroom at the back of Pear Tree Cottage. The back bedroom dropped a couple of steps from the landing and was the only room where anyone over an average height didn't have to stoop to avoid banging their head on the door frame. The prospect of head injury was peculiar to all the other doorways, especially the staircase in the cottage which bore the sign "Duck or Grouse" as a jovial warning to anyone taller than 5 feet 6 inches. By contrast, the back bedroom seemed quite cavernous in size and even housed a large double bed in which Lavender had now tucked herself and was gradually warming up. While she was lying waiting in the semi-dark, the bedroom door creaked open slightly, creating a wedge of light from the landing. The low, long shadow of Delius slinked silently into the room and vanished as he jumped up onto the pillow next to her. Lavender sat up a little and leant over to the bedside table and switched on the lamp. With a casual curiosity, she picked up the leather-bound book that had been given to her that morning, and which lay next to the blue pendant box on the table. It naturally fell open to the page she had read before, so she turned the subsequent page. It was blank. Turning the next page revealed a rubbing of the amulet she had found in the button tin, then a second, very similar, but with a different circular symbol. Underneath Katie had written the following words.

"Are these the amulets of Great-grandad Tobias Gill?

I took these rubbings from the gold coins that Tom had with him when he died. Is it possible that they were the same ones our Great-Grandfather Tobias reburied? I do not know but what a strange coincidence if they are not. The family tales tell that after discovering the mysterious amulets on the moor side above his farm, Tobias contracted scarlet fever and became gravely ill. His wife was so worried that she called for the family and lit candles to prepare for his imminent death. Miraculously, Tobias recovered from his raging fever, hallucinations and unconsciousness to recount that he had been placed under the Venetius Stone to be cured. In his unconscious state, he had been told that the stone was a sacred place at the centre of Brigantia where healing ceremonies were performed. Following his recovery, Tobias began experiencing vivid dreams. He named his discovery on the moors the

'Amulet of Dreams' and the 'Amulet of Union' because of their distinct effects."

Lavender paused to consider the story. It made sense now that she had dreamed such a vivid dream too and that perhaps the "Amulet of Dreams" was now working its strange magic on her. But what about the "Amulet of Union?" Where was it and what effect could that have on a person. There was so much to think about, but her eyes were growing heavy now. She closed the book, still intrigued by what she had just read. Her mind wandered into the events of the last 24 hours. She went over the curious dream that was as real as anything that happened after she woke in the night. What did it mean and was there anything she could do to find out? As she lay quietly and deep in thought with the gentle sound of wind and snow swirling against the small window outside, she started to feel as if she was not alone. That she was being watched over, guided and protected, as if she was part of something much more significant than just herself.

As this feeling grew, Lavender became aware of an absolute stillness that had wrapped itself around her in a powerful embrace, as though time had stopped. The muffled voices from downstairs were now silent. The wind had paused itself, and Lavender imagined that each flake of snow outside was currently suspended, motionless in the air. For what lasted like an infinite moment, everything was entirely at peace.

The iron knocker bounced against the front door as it closed behind Aunt Margaret, breaking Lavender's trance. Then in reverse of its arrival, the engine of her motorcycle could be heard starting up with a putttputtttputtt. It meandered idly back up Bridge Street and away to the moors above town. It wasn't long before the stairs cracked with their familiar night-time voice and grandma's head peeped through the broadening wedge of light in the bedroom doorway.

"You're still awake then I see, lass," grandma spoke softly as she entered the room and came to sit on the bed, "and I see you've been looking through the family book."

"Grandma," said Lavender tentatively, "You know how you were telling me about Great-aunt Fanny last night before bed?"

"Aye, I do, lass," grandma replied.

"Well, do you know what happened to Great-Uncle Tom?" Lavender continued.

Taken aback, grandma responded quickly to Lavender's question, "Whatever has made you ask that, lass? You know it's been a mystery to us all, and summat your mother was obsessed about. How did you know about Uncle Tom anyway? Have you read something in this 'ere book?"

Grandma asked so many questions that Lavender wished she had not said anything, yet at the same time, she knew that without doubt, this was a serious matter.

"I had a dream last night, grandma, and part of it was that Great-Aunt Fanny had a mysterious letter and map which Great-Uncle Tom had with him when he died."

"Nay, lass," grandma replied, dismissing Lavender's memory, "You must have heard about it somewhere in the past, and then dreamed of it after last night's story. Your mother thought as much too, but no map or letter was ever found. Eventually, everyone in the family apart from your mother came to the conclusion it was just another one of Fanny's bizarre stories."

"Do you think Mum knew something that no one else did then, grandma?" questioned Lavender.

"I think she believed a lot that the rest of us didn't, and so it's difficult to talk about."

Grandma explained that Lavender's mother had become a little obsessed with the mystery of Great-uncle Tom. She had spent many hours visiting distant relatives and searching through old newspapers and microforms in public libraries to learn more. Grandma recounted how her daughter thought she had discovered that Tom was the member of a long since disbanded society, a group attempting to find the mystical secrets of the Brigantes. She also suspected he had aquired a precious Brigantian artefact, that had been lost for over two thousand years. Tom believed he was directly descended from them. Not being taken seriously got your mother a little fed up and eventually she stopped talking about the whole thing. But look, lass," grandma continued reassuringly, "it's all in the past now and not at all something you need to concern yourself with. Now, you get thisen off to sleep and let's hope this snow eases up; otherwise, the school might not be open tomorrow."

"Night, night, grandma," Lavender said, yawning.

"God bless, my little one," grandma replied as she turned off the bedside lamp and turned to leave. She stepped back into the landing, and as the wedge of light narrowed back to darkness with the closing of the bedroom door, she whispered, "I'll see you in the morning."

Grandma's gentle words had the effect of placing Lavender back into that place of perfect peace she had been just a minutes before. Within a few short moments, Lavender was fast asleep.

Chapter Seven

The Old Barn

Halfway up the long garden that stretched behind Pear Tree
Cottage was a large, old stone barn. It now acted as a workshop
and garage and had been three generations since it was used for
its original purpose. There was a low wooden door into the
barn from the garden and a large black double door leading out
onto the side street with "Don't Park!" painted on roughly in
white. This allowed plenty of access for grandad's lorries, the
first of which was the old ex-WW2 army lorry that he had
started out in business with after the war. The second was his
regular lorry that he now used. The barn was a perfect place to
keep them safe and protected from winter weather and service
them. In addition to the lorries, there was what seemed like lots
of other junk stacked against walls, in the old hayloft and what
looked like a car underneath a large tarpaulin in the far dark
corner of the barn.

As Lavender sat at the kitchen table stirring golden
syrup into her porridge, she listened to her grandparents
discussing the likelihood of grandad being able to start the lorry
on such an icy morning and then to get it safely out of the barn

and on to the main road. Grandad was already dressed in his work overalls with his flat cap on, though grandma was still wearing her nightie and dressing gown. It had become particularly icy through the night, and there had been further snowfalls, making the prospect of both starting the lorry and getting it out on to the main road rather slim. In anticipation of this, grandad had drained the radiator in his lorry the night before, and grandma had put an enamelled bucket of water in the Yorkshire range oven overnight to warm, to refill the radiator.

"Ahh!" grandad exclaimed, after he gulped the last dregs of tea from his mug and stood up from the table, he followed this with clacking sounds as his tongue moved from the top of his mouth with great satisfaction. "Right. I'd better get on as I need to be up in Glasgow around lunchtime."

"I heard on the wireless that the road over't top is blocked Arthur. You'll never make it."

Grandma had already mentioned this only five minutes before. Still, grandad seemed oblivious as he put on his overcoat and adjusted his cap.

As he opened the back door, he turned to grandma with one of his typical replies, "Is that so, Annie?"

He said it in such a way that it was neither a question nor a statement, leaving anyone entirely stuck as to how to respond. Despite being just a short distance from the cottage, Lavender had only seen inside the barn twice before and was intrigued to see more, so sensing an opportunity to explore, she jumped up from her chair.

"Can I come and help?" She asked enthusiastically.

"Go on then lass. You might as well make yourself useful. News is out that the school is closed today anyway," grandma replied.

"Once you've cleared the snow let me know, I'll come up with the bucket of water, Arthur," she continued.

The dark early morning still cloaked the sky as grandad and Lavender crunched their way through the icy, snow-covered garden to the barn. Everything was absolutely still, as if frozen in time, just like the snowman Lavender and Fred had built the day before and that now watched them. Grandad lifted the solid iron latch with a clack, and the barn door slowly creaked open with an eerie welcome.

There was a distinctive smell in the barn that infused the nostrils, a combination of oil, rusty metal and wood. There was also the ambient heat from a paraffin heater that sat under the engine of the lorry to keep the edge off the perishing cold.

Grandad made his way through the darkness across to the other side of the barn. He pulled back the bolts on the double doors and swung them inside.

"We'll never get out of here, Grandad," exclaimed Lavender with a sense of doom, "We'll be stuck here until the snow melts in the spring."

The snow outside looked insurmountable, whipped into a drift higher even than Lavender herself. The snow certainly was pretty bad, and even grandad had doubts about getting out, though he didn't express them. Instead, he grabbed one of the shovels near the door and handed it to Lavender, then picked one up himself. He spat into each of his dry hands and clapped loudly, rubbing them furiously together while blowing into them.

"Come on, lass, let's not give up before we've started. I'll shift the drift from the door, and you climb over and make a start out in the lane."

Lavender copied her grandad and warmed her hands up in the same way, then lifted her leg up high and took a giant stride into the deep snow and into the lane. Within half an hour, the passage was clear out of the barn and down the narrow side street.

"Go and let yer grandma know we're ready for the bucket now, lass," grandad instructed as they both made their way back inside the barn.

The sun was breaking the horizon, turning the clouds into shades of red, pink, and burnt orange as Lavender and her grandma got back to the barn with the bucket of hot water. Inside, grandad was stood on a pair of stepladders taking off the radiator cap. Grandma lifted the bucket up to him. "Perfect timing," he said, reaching down.

He took the water and carefully poured it into the radiator, replaced the cap, then closed the bonnet.

"Can I get in?" said Lavender as grandad walked around to the driver's door.

He looked over at grandma and winked.

"You can go as far as the bottom of the street, lass – if it gets that far!" grandma replied.

With no hesitation, Lavender pulled herself up into the lorry cabin, that to her felt like she was climbing into a giant, but friendly, iron beast. She looked at grandad as he again spat in his hands and clapped them loudly together before starting the lorry. There was a deep, slow, almost reluctant whirring from the pits of the engine, then suddenly a thundering roar echoed around the barn, as the lorry came to life and a plume of bluey-brown smoke filled the air. Grandma beat a hasty retreat from the barn and into the garden, waving her arms around as if she were swatting a cloud of flies in a summer cow meadow.

"Think on Arthur and heed what Marg said last night!" she shouted back.

Grandad shifted the lorry into gear, and with a jolt, it sprang forward into the alley. The lane was winding at the back of the barn and very narrow in parts, with cobblestones and high walls on either side that made the transit down it even more perilous. Still, Lavender hung on to her seat as they bounced and slid towards the main road at the bottom, excited to be going for a ride, even though it was brief. About ten yards from the bottom of the alley, grandad started to brake. The wheels locked and slid silently over the frozen cobbles and the driver's side narrowly missed the high wall by a hair's breadth before coming to a halt on the main road.

"Wow, Grandad. That was FUN!" Lavender yelled in excitement.

"Aye well, best not tell yer grandma what fun it was. Off you go now, lass, and I'll see you tomorrow when I get home," grandad winked at her as he said it and Lavender climbed down from the lorry cab and slammed the door shut.

"Bye, Grandad," she shouted after him as he turned into the Main Street. "Don't get stuck in Scotland!"

Lavender made her way back up the alley and into the barn. She pushed the doors back to close them and looked around, realising just how massive the barn was with less in it.

The air hung with a mixture of the cold morning frosty nip and the slowly dispersing fumes from the lorry. Although the air was toxic, the fine particles had a magical quality. They sparkled in the harsh early morning light streaming through the loft windows high in the barn. This was the first time Lavender had been alone in the barn and had a good look. There's so much stuff in here, she thought, as she moved around the old lorry to get a better view wondering what she might find.

In the distance, grandma's voice could be heard shouting from the kitchen:

"In you come, Lavender, you'll catch your death out there and don't forget to close the barn doors."

But Lavender was becoming transfixed as grandma was calling. She looked at Delius who had taken up residence on the tarpaulin in the corner of the barn and who seemed to be calling her over to investigate with his large knowing eyes.

Lavender slowly made her way across the flagged floor towards the large shape in the corner. Judging by the amount of dust and muck, it was likely to have been sat there for years. As she got closer, she could see that it must be a car of some sort. In curiosity, Lavender lifted the corner of the tarpaulin to reveal a tyre and wheel with a dirty chrome hub cap with an "M" in a circle in the middle. She lifted it further and saw the bluey-grey paintwork of a car that, though she hadn't seen it before, seemed vaguely familiar.

"Lavender!" grandma called out again, reminding her of the request to come in from the cold.

Lavender dropped the tarpaulin and turned quickly on the heal of her Wellington boot as if doing a pirouette, but rather than resembling the balance of a graceful ballerina, her legs threw up into the air. She landed abruptly, with no cushioning to her head and an audible crack. Delius flew into the air and scampered out of the doorway as her eyes flickered and closed. The white winter light that streamed into the barn through the high loft windows began to fade to grey and extinguished as if it were a snuffed-out candle. After a few moments laying in perfect stillness on the cold hard stone flags, Lavender became aware of a growing dizziness that spun uncontrollably in her head. If I could open my eyes, this spinning might stop, she thought. Still, Lavender's eyes felt exceptionally tired as she tried to open them, the effort to do so was as if she were pushing up a heavy weight, but eventually, she managed to see a little. Her attention was drawn back to the tarpaulin and the wheel revealed underneath. With each passing second, her eyelids regained more of their strength and the barn brightened to the point where part of the chrome hub cap on the car began to gleam in a star-like fashion.

Lavender pulled herself up and made her way over to the tarpaulin. On top of the tarpaulin were some old coats and a carpet bag. She grabbed the items, sending a plume of dust into the air, and moved them to the side of the object so that she could completely pull back the cover. She bent down to the corner nearest to her and pulled the tarpaulin up and over to reveal a dark blue car with wooden-framed doors on the back and red leather seats in the interior. On the front was a chrome emblem that said "Morris" and on the back door in chrome letters "Minor 1000." She pulled on the handle to the driver's side door that grudgingly broke open. As its stiffness broke, the door gave a deep, grated, metallic whine. Lavender sat down inside, closing the whining door behind her with a final clunk.

The first thing she noticed was a distinctive smell, a blend of rust and leather. There was also something else she couldn't put her finger on, but nevertheless, a scent that felt somehow homely and safe. She closed her eyes again and took a long deep breath through her nostrils, examining the cool car air, searching for its identity. Then, beyond her eyelids, she became aware of a shining red light and a faint tinkling sound somewhere in front of her.

She opened her eyes. Almost in her face was the steering wheel's centre, which had a red glass-like circle, with a white "M" in the centre. The morning sun streaming through the loft window had caught it so that it was now sparkling and glistening with ruby-like stars in the car. The beauty of the light transfixed Lavender.

It seemed to be accompanied by the sound of fairy-sized tubular bells that she imagined were being brushed with a cotton bud. A softly spoken female voice behind her broke Lavender's hypnotic gaze.

"Don't look around, darling, and do not fear, I am with you still if you choose to believe."

Despite the shock in realising she was not alone, Lavender felt calmed by the voice from the back seat and eager to see who it was. Still, she kept her eyes down while she listened.

The voice continued "The 'Amulet of Dreams' was the start, and now that you're here, the next step is to believe more than you fear. Now the glovebox will open, put in your hand, there's an amulet you'll find there, it belongs to this land. A word of warning though, you'll need to conceal, eyes are watching and waiting to steal."

Lavender raised her eyes from the floor and looked across at the glovebox in the dashboard. Reaching across to the small door, it dropped down of its own accord, allowing her to place her hand inside. The glovebox was full of a wad of papers, so she grabbed hold of them and pulled them out onto the passenger seat. The collection of documents fanned out loosely across the shiny-red leather and a photograph within jumped out to catch Lavender's eyes. It was a photograph she had never seen before of herself when she was about four years old with her mum and dad in front of Pear Tree Cottage. Lavender gasped when she saw it and automatically looked up into the rearview mirror. As she did so, her eyes met the familiar hazel eyes of her mum looking back at her. She was caught in a trance for a split second. A single tear rolled from each of her mother's eyes and a cascade of memories played in her mind.

She turned around quickly, calling out to her, "Mum!" But as she did so, her mother had gone.

Chapter Eight

Confused!

When grandma had found Lavender in the barn, she was unconscious and cold, with a soft pearl tear resting in the corner of each of her eyes. No matter how loudly she spoke, or how tightly she nipped her skin, Lavender failed to wake, there wasn't even the slightest flinch. Consequently, grandma ran down the garden, past the house's side, across Bridge Street and down Cavendish Lane to the doctors. She burst through the door of the large Victorian house as if she were leading the charge of the Light Brigade, puffing and panting and gasping for breath.

"Doctor Wheatley," she said in more of a wheezing breath than a voice, "Doctor Wheatley ... I need him quickly ... please ... come quickly, it's our Lavender, she's out cold."

Mrs Arkley, the elderly receptionist who had worked at the surgery for nigh on fifty years, leapt into action from behind her desk, like a rusty coiled spring. She opened the internal door of Doctor Wheatley's office and informed him of the emergency. Fortunately, it was still early, and Doctor

Wheatley hadn't yet taken his overcoat off following his arrival just a few minutes before.

"Come on then, Mrs Tilly, take me to your Lavender," he said calmly grabbing his black bag in one hand and his cap in the other.

In no time at all they had reached Lavender, finding her still laid out on the flagged floor.

By now though, her eyes were starting to open, and she was letting out a weak moaning noise and then a few words that didn't make sense, "oaaaahhhh, uhhhh, the smell … has gone."

Doctor Wheatley carefully examined her and then instructed grandma to call an ambulance. A hospital would need to check her over to be safe.

Once grandma had made her phone call and returned to the barn, they both acted as crutches to guide Lavender back to the cottage. They lay her down on the couch near the fire until they waited for the ambulance to arrive. Lavender half-raised her eyelids and muttered something incoherently about her mother, before closing her eyes once more. This continued several times as she continued to repeatedly traverse the doorstep between sleep and wakefulness. It wasn't long before the ambulance arrived. Lavender was carried into the back of it and taken to Scordale Hospital for observation.

"I expect she will be back before you know it Mrs Tilly, but, in the meantime, if you need me let me know."

Then as she was carried into the back of the ambulance he turned to Lavender; "I'll see you later little one," Doctor Wheatley said reassuringly, before closing the ambulance's rear doors and nodding to the driver.

Sure enough, Doctor Wheatley was correct. Lavender and grandma were back home in front of the fire, with Delius for quiet company, just after lunchtime. They had been advised to keep warm and away from bright lights and avoid too much noise, making the fire's flickering glow and the pale winter sunlight just about right for recovery. The gentle breathing of the fire and the purring of Delius, nuzzled in the nook of her neck, was like comfort for Lavender and in the first hour or so that passed since returning home she continued to drift, along with her thoughts, in and out of sleep.

The silence was broken abruptly when grandad telephoned, having pulled over his lorry at a lonely red telephone box that stood like a beacon in the snow near Carlisle. He called to let grandma know he was safely over the Pennines and well on his way to Glasgow.

"Ee, Arthur," she started, "All through the night I'd been worrying that summat was going to happen to you today, but all along it must have been Lavender that Marg was referring to in her rambling premonition."

"Why, Annie, whatever's 'appened?" he replied with concern.

Grandma began to explain, then just as the pips sounded, indicating the need for extra money, it was quickly agreed he would call again when he got to Glasgow for an update.

Later in the afternoon, Lavender started to waken more fully. By teatime, her tummy was rumbling, and she was feeling ready to do something rather than just lay there. Her thoughts were becoming more transparent, yet she was having difficulty making sense of what had happened, what was real and what was not.

Did I get in the car or not? Was Mum there or was I dreaming? Was the dream real?

The thoughts circled around and around in her mind, without answers, until they were interrupted by the distinct pattern of knocks on the front door. Tap, Ta, Ta, Tap, Tap … Tap, Tap. Both Lavender and grandma recognised the knock instantly as the arrival of Fred Keighley.

"Are you ready for a visitor, lass?" grandma asked, as she stood up and headed towards the front door.

"Yes, grandma, and I'm ready for something to eat too!"

She opened the front door and sure enough, Fred was stood there with his usual charming smile.

"Hello, Mrs Tilly, I've been helping me dad in't shop all day...Is Lavender in?" he said hopefully.

"Aye, lad, she is, but she's had a bit of a nasty fall so you'd best not stay too long, 'appen half an hour." Grandma stood aside to let Fred in and then continued. "I'm just going to pop into the kitchen and put the kettle on and make some sandwiches for tea, so I'll leave you two to catch up on events."

Lavender sat up a bit too quickly in a burst of excitement and instantly felt light-headed and woozy that was clear enough for Fred to see. He took his coat off and sat down beside her on the settee to steady her in case she passed out.

"What's been happening then, Lav?" he asked with concern.

"That's the thing, Fred, I'm not too sure what happened. I was in the barn after my grandad left this morning and found my mum and dad's old car, covered up in the corner, gathering dust. At least I think it's their car. But on the other hand, I'm not sure. Then I fell over on the stone floor and passed out. Now I have this horrible taste stuck in the back of my throat, like strong onions and whisky. The next thing I remember is getting in the back of an ambulance," Lavender sounded confused.

"What is it you're not sure about, Lav?" Fred asked.

"I'm not sure if I saw the car or not. I think I got in it, and I think I saw my mum in the back seat, but then I might have been dreaming it after I fell over. I just don't know what to believe."

It was now clear to Fred that Lavender doubted herself and this was getting her quite upset.

"Now listen, Lav, you've been through quite a rough day today so no wonder you're having difficulty making sense of this. How about we meet up in a couple of days when you've rested and try to work things out. It will all be clearer for you then, and we can go up to the barn, have a look at the car, and maybe you can ask your grandma about it too."

Fred was taking control, but a bit too much for Lavender. She felt uneasy discussing the car with her grandma, especially after her talk the previous night and her eagerness to move on from the whole topic.

"I'd rather not mention it to grandma at the moment. I think it might be my mum and dad's old car so it could be a bit of a touchy subject, but it would be good to go and have a look together when I'm feeling better," Lavender agreed.

"Well, if you're feeling up to it, how about Thursday after school? That's if we're back at school by then," he said, peering out of the window at the snow that had just started to fall again.

"Sounds good to me, and I think we're going to the pictures on Thursday evening as Alice has some free tickets for 'Charlotte's Web'."

Alice Sutton's grandad was the local cinema manager at the Cavendish Picture House. It was a place, Lavender, Fred and Alice went to regularly as they would get complimentary tickets. Lavender called to grandma in the kitchen to check on the arrangements.

"Grandma! Are we still going to the pictures on Thursday after tea?"

"If you're up to it, we are. Why do you ask, is Fred wanting to come?" grandma replied.

"If that's OK, yes I'd love to come too, Mrs Tilly," Fred answered for himself.

Grandma came into the front room with a tray of tea, sandwiches, Battenberg cake and Yorkshire Parkin and put them down on the little trolley that was mainly there for the purpose. Fred leant across without hesitation and picked up a sandwich, taking a bite without a pause for breath.

"I suppose you'd like to come straight after school and have tea then, Fred," grandma asked with a wry smile.

He looked at her, eyes wide open and nodded eagerly, still chewing on a mouthful of cheese and pickle sandwich. Lavender looked across at Fred and winked. A wink that conveyed a message they both understood.

Chapter Nine

Back to School

The following two days had been relatively uneventful. In fact, Lavender's thoughts of the curious events had drifted to the vague area at the back of her mind where she began to doubt that they actually occurred. By the time she left for school on Thursday morning, it was as if they were simply a series of vivid dreams.

After Fred left on Monday evening, grandad phoned again from Glasgow to get an update on Lavender. The snow finally stopped falling, in fact by Thursday morning, the weather warmed up to the point where all but the snowdrifts against the walls on the moors and hilltops had melted, and the rivers were overflowing in the dale bottoms. School reopened on Thursday too, which meant that Lavender had time to recover from her fall without any time away. Her days were spent staying warm by the fire and doing an assortment of the activities done when one was kind of ill, but not too sick to lay in bed, making spiced biscuits, doing jigsaws and playing card games. So, it came as quite a jolt when on that clear, bright Thursday morning, a rather strange event occurred on the way to school. An event that returned Lavender's memory straight back to her mum's eyes in the back of the car and the words she had said.

Albert Road primary school always appeared a homely building to Lavender. It was one of those traditional Victorian schools with a double cross-gable roof at either end that had had a girls' entrance under one gable, and a boys' entrance under the other. There was a small playground at the front of the school and a larger one at the rear. The infants used the entrance originally assigned to the girls and the juniors used the boys. Robert's Park was opposite the school on the other side of a steep cobbled street, and this was used as an extra playground at lunchtimes on warmer days. Robert's Park had always been a place where Lavender, Alice and Fred would meet before school. They would go on the swings or play catch and other games, and even though today was cold, it was no exception.

Lavender followed her regular routine, which was to walk down to Fred Keighley's butcher's shop and meet Fred. Delius went with Lavender as far as the shop and then sat on the red windowsill watching until the pair had gone around the corner and out of sight. Alice lived close to the school, which meant she would meet the other two on the park swings or roundabout if the swings were occupied.

On this particular morning, Lavender and Fred arrived first. They were sat on the slowly rotating roundabout waiting for Alice and deciding on who would be the first to hide in a game of hide and seek.

"I know" said Fred, "let's count it out and see who gets to hide first."

He began counting, "Alla malla mink monk, tink tonk tuzzi, vouzzi vouzzi agadi, va va, vac!"

"OK, I'm on first then," Fred said, jumping down from the roundabout and heading to the trees and shrubs at the side embankment.

"Hey, you two, what about me?" Alice shouted as she entered the park gates and walked across to her two friends.

"You need to count me in too," she continued.

"Alright then," said Fred as Alice approached the roundabout.

"I'll count then. Eenie meenie macca racca, air arr dominacca, ticca pacca lollipopper, umm, pum, push!! … You're on, Lavender, you get to hide first."

Fred and Alice sat on the roundabout and closed their eyes.

"Count to 100 and no cheating," said Lavender as she spun the roundabout around and ran off towards the edge of the park.

Having spent many long summer days exploring the nooks and crannies of Robert's Park, all three of the children knew it well. One side had quite a slope and had a variety of landscapes. The main area was flat for games where the roundabout and swings were. The side that Lavender headed for had a path weaving through a variety of shrubs that went along and up a steeper embankment. There were also many mature trees and some enormous boulders that she knew would make a great place to hide. By the time she had got up to a group of the taller, thicker oak trees, her two friends had reached fifty-three of their count and were speeding up rapidly. Lavender stopped briefly and with panting breath looked up at two of the largest trees that were growing close to one another. Behind them was the sheer face of a boulder that was as big as her grandad's lorry. One of the trees had a hollow at ground level that Lavender had not seen before and that looked as if it was just large enough for her small frame to hide in. A squirrel darted across the bare soil beneath the tree as she surveyed it, then effortlessly spiralled the trunk until it was hidden somewhere aloft. Mirroring the exact path of the squirrel, a shiver ran up Lavender's legs, curled her spine and disappeared in her neck. Her body relaxed and then, as if an invisible rope was tied around her waist, the dark tree hollow drew her towards it.

Approaching the hollow, she turned sideways, stepped her right leg into the tree and lowered her head. Next, she pulled her arms and shoulders down and then turned again into the tree as she lifted her other leg in. Inside the hollow it was warm, and looking back through the hole towards the daylight, Lavender felt quite snug and safe, as if she was receiving a secure hug from her father. She could hear Fred and Alice's raised voices counting … 94,95,96 and in anticipation of the imminent search, turned herself around to face the back of the tree to hide.

"100, coming ready or not!" the two friends shouted in unison.

Fred zoomed off down the southern side of the park, and Alice took the northern steeper side where Lavender was hiding. It wasn't long before Lavender could not only hear but feel the footsteps approaching her concealment and the snapping of twigs on the ground growing closer. She became aware that her perceptions had changed entirely, that although stood in a dark enclosed space, she was able to experience the world beyond it more entirely than if she were outside, or indeed than she had ever experienced it before. Stood inside the tree with her back to the sound, in her mind's eye Lavender could see exactly where the noises were coming from, she felt them through the gentle vibration of the ground as if her feet were the tree roots that twisted, curled and tentacled their way into every available crack and crevice of the earth. The tree hollow was thin at the back and had a small slit just in front of her face that she could see through towards the boulders and tree behind. Looking through the crack, it seemed to Lavender that she was the eyes of the tree itself. She could see a robin redbreast high in the tree opposite's small branches, scanning the whole park with its tiny eyes. She immediately became one with it, feeling the bird's perfect little heart beating. The fluffing of feathers as it shook to plump up its insulation against the cold morning air and feeling a shiver as it did so. She could see from here as the bird saw: the whole park, the school across the road and the children, starting to arrive with their parents, the town beyond, even Delius, sat on the pear tree outside grandma's cottage. Lavender's attention to every detail both great and small left her feeling a complete unity to everything as if she were everything. There was also sense that Fred was already getting fed up with his lack of success. Alice was getting closer and more sure of herself, moving as quietly as she could through the large trees towards the face of the boulders at the back of the park. Through a narrow break between the rocks, Alice eventually reached the access to Rombus's cave.

Local stories had it that Rombus was a giant man who lived several thousand years ago. He and his wife had terrible arguments which ended one day when she chased Rombus out into the valley and threw stones at him. Eventually, he took it no more and fled to the moors where he picked up huge boulders and hurled them down into the valley in anger and frustration. It was these huge boulders that formed the cave that became his shelter.

Alice trod as quietly as she could on her approach the cave, convinced that Lavender had made it her hiding place. Now that she had moved behind the tree, Lavender could see Alice with her own eyes through the small gap in the bark. Unnervingly, she could also see something else in her mind's eye, someone already inside the cave. He was a tall, thin man with a gaunt, almost grey face and dark eyes. His hair was long and straggly, and he wore a thick dark grey trench coat, and she could sense clearly that his intentions were far from good. The closer Alice got to the cave, the greater the sense of dread

Lavender felt. What would happen if Alice went inside the cave? Maybe she wouldn't go in. Perhaps she will turn around and search the trees and shrubs instead, thought Lavender. Alice was only a couple of feet from the gap between the boulders now. Lavender started to feel quite sick in the stomach, she felt a breath of misty air against her neck as if it was the man's waiting breath in the cave.

Lavender could take it no longer, letting out in a high-pitched shriek, "Alice, don't go in there!"

Alice turned instantly in the soft ground and, losing her balance, landed with an undignified flop on her bottom. In her moment of disorientation, a tall, thin, cloaked figure emerged from the boulders, almost like an apparition, floating and flapping like a coat on a washing line fluttering in the breeze. Then he disappeared into the trees and undergrowth as quickly as he had appeared.

Fred heard all the commotion and ran up to the other side of the park as if he was a sprinter in the 100 metres on sports day. By the time he got to her, Lavender had prised herself out of the tree hollow and was standing over Alice's dishevelled figure.

"What was all that about?" said Alice, looking up in a somewhat confused fashion, hair dishevelled and hands and legs streaked with mud.

"Didn't you see that weird man come out of the cave when you fell over?" Lavender replied.

"No, I didn't. Are you sure you're not seeing things?" Alice responded with some annoyance.

"Yeah, I'm sure ..." then she hesitated, "at least I think I'm sure. Did you see anything, Fred?" Lavender asked for conformation.

Fred had not been in a perfect position to view the cave area. Still, he had noticed that something strange had happened after Lavender shouted her warning. The air had very suddenly and abnormally changed. It went from being quite breathless to an icy breeze that had swept down the park. It then quickly deadened again, creating a rustling of the few remaining leaves that were frostily welded to their parent trees, and causing the birds to flock from their lofty positions and away into the blue.

Fred explained what he had noticed and then went on, "Anyroad, there was summat, I'm sure of it. Things have been strange around here since we had our dreams at the weekend and ..."

"And that's not all," Lavender interrupted, "when I had my accident on Monday, something even weirder happened."

Alice looked even more perplexed and asked for the full story after getting a hand up from her two friends. Lavender went right back to the beginning, concluding by explaining both how she felt and what she was aware of while hiding in the tree hollow.

"Well, I'm not sure what to believe, and honestly, I think you two have probably lost the plot," said Alice sceptically, "but I do know we're going to be late for class register if we don't get a move on!"

"Come to my house for tea after school, and I'll prove it to you," Lavender replied as the three friends started out across the park towards school.

Chapter Ten

Morris Minor 40BWW

By 4.15 pm, the sun was starting to set as Lavender, Alice, and Fred entered the old barn from Pear Tree Cottage's garden. They had arranged with their parents to walk to Fred Keighley's butcher's shop and collect eight of his famous Cumberland sausages for tea on the way to Lavender's house. Before going to the cottage, they now had the opportunity to investigate the barn without being missed. This required a high degree of stealth. The three of them silently navigated the front gate. They invisibly ducked below the study's low windows and then the kitchen where they stopped to see grandma. She was busy baking something delicious at the kitchen bench. As the three of them peered from above the windowsill to check on what the delightful food might be, grandma spontaneously burst into song, making them all duck down and freeze like rabbits in a spotlight.

"Lloyd George knew my Fa-a-a-the-er, Father knew Lloyd George," she sang with a repeat of the same line ad infinitum to the tune of "Onward Christian Soldiers".

Within seconds, a gloriously mismatched rhythm and untuneful sound accompanied her as Delius must have scarpered off to the piano to join in.

It was hard to contain their hysteria as they crouched below the kitchen window listening to grandma. Once they got beyond the cottage, and into the garden, they all felt a huge relief to be safe enough to burst into laughter. Their composure had been regained by the time they had reached the barn and, as they pulled open the door, a more serious approach had been taken. Inside, there was barely enough daylight left to see the car in the building's darkest corner and still covered in tarpaulin. The carpetbag and coats still sat undisturbed with dust on top. Lavender went directly across to grandad's wooden workbench that was one of the few places in the barn not covered in a tool-hoarder's paraphernalia. Above the bench on a rack of shelves were an assortment of rusty tins and jam jars. They had every conceivable nut, bolt, nail and screw you could imagine as well as a variety of tools hung on a pegboard. She unclipped a large, rather heavy torch from the board, switched it on and turned around like a searchlight scanning a prison camp for furtive escapees. She stopped as the powerful beam of light pointed towards her waiting friends and cast their long shadows across the covered car.

"Come on then, you two, let's see what all the fuss is about," said Alice, heading towards the dusty grey shape in the corner.

Lavender removed the carpetbag and coats with a déjà vu image running through her mind. Had she remembered correctly? She gulped in fear at the thought of nothing interesting being there, and of appearing a freak. Fred put his school satchel, now also containing the sausages, on the flagged floor and pulled up the tarpaulin cover to reveal the car. It was exactly as Lavender had seen.

"It's just an old car, nothing special about this," Alice commented, completely underwhelmed by the sight of it.

"Go on, Alice, you get in first then," Fred encouraged.

Getting into the car by the passenger door was impossible as it had been parked within six inches of the barn wall. Alice opened the driver's door, which just as before let out a reluctant, stiff and grating metal whine, then climbed into the driver's seat.

"Budge over then," Lavender instructed, whilst giving her a gentle nudge on the shoulder.

Alice moved into the passenger seat, and Lavender joined her inside the car.

They sat there for what seemed like an incredibly long time, waiting for something to happen.

"Oh, this is stupid, let's go," said Alice feeling both ridiculous and bored.

"Check the glovebox, Alice. There'll be an old photo inside of Lavender and her parents if she's right," Fred instructed.

Lavender pointed the torch at the glovebox, and Alice opened the door and pulled out a wad of papers and put them on her lap. As she did so, Lavender noticed the torch beam had caught something shiny, a momentary glint of light at the back of the glovebox.

"Wait a minute … I think there's something else in there," said Lavender in excitement.

Alice tutted with a barely concealed indifference as she reached to the back of the box and pulled out what resembled a coin.

"Oh wow!" exclaimed Alice sarcastically, and then continued, "some grotty old coin!"

Lavender looked stunned and in a state of disbelief as she stared at the tarnished gold disc.

"Can I see it?" Lavender requested rather politely, but Alice appeared not to hear, suddenly she was entranced by the object in her hand.

She closed her eyes and clenched her hand into a fist, as if to possess the gold or for the gold to possess her.

"Alice, pass it here please," Lavender asked more forcibly, but still, Alice sat there, fist clenched and eyes closed.

"Alice … give me the gold NOW!" Lavender shouted in both frustration and annoyance at Alice. Was she playing games or was she genuinely in some sort of possessed state?

"Here, let me," said Fred, gesturing Lavender to swap places.

Lavender climbed out of the car, and Fred jumped in next to Alice. For a few seconds, he just sat there in silence observing her, trying to figure out if she was faking her catatonic state. If she was putting on a show, she was a great actress. With some concern he noticed her clenched hand was starting to shake, and her knuckles were turning white. He leant over and put his mouth close to her ear.

"Alice … Alice, it's me, Fred," he whispered gently.

With the briefest twitch, he thought he saw her eye movements.

"Alice, everything is alright. We are going to have our tea now at Lavender's cottage, and then we are going to the pictures," he continued with his soft, calm voice.

Alice's eyes twitched again and then blinked and opened. She turned her head to face Fred and Lavender and spoke to them without a single change to her expression.

"Now I understand."

After speaking, Alice remained rigid with a vague distant look in her eyes. As Fred continued to whisper to her, eventually her muscles loosened, and she started to respond to his voice. Her hand fell open on top of the wad of papers and in her palm sat a familiar sight, an amulet the same size and colour as the amulet that Lavender now had in her box. Lavender gasped as she saw it.

"It looks like the amulet I found in the button tin."

Tentatively, Fred took the coin from Alice's hand, then held it out for Lavender to see. She pointed the torch to examine it closely and as she did so noticed it was the same in every detail except the symbol on the front was a little different. It had the two circles, but instead of the wavy lines, it looked like the sun with eight rays of light emitting in lines from the outer circle.

Lavender immediately recognised what looked like the other amulet great-aunt Fanny had and like the one she had found in the button tin.

"Are you alright, Alice?" said Lavender, a little concerned.

"I'm OK, just feeling a little dizzy and different," Alice replied.

"In what way do you feel different?" asked Fred.

Alice paused a moment and then replied, "I feel like there's so much more to the world, like it's got layers and layers that we cannot see or hear or touch, but that I can feel exist."

Alice drifted off into some other distant place while she was talking and, while they listened, her two friends drifted off with her.

The torch flickered a little, dimmed and then went out, plunging them into that semi-darkness that arrives after the gloaming. It returned the children's attention from the faraway place they had all somehow visited together. Fred broke the silence as he climbed out of the car and picked up his satchel off the floor, then, looking down at the amulet in his hand, he put it in his trouser pocket.

"This is getting weird," said Fred. "Not only are you seeing events and objects beyond the here and now, but I think these amulets are far from just some superstitious mumbo-jumbo. I think they are affecting those who have them in their possession."

"Mrs Tilly will be sending out a search party if we don't hurry up and go in for tea. Here, Alice, pass me that wad of papers and we can have a look through them later, maybe there's something that will help us work out what the meaning of all this is."

He pulled out the sausages from his satchel, wrapped in butcher paper, replacing them with the glovebox documents.

"Well come on then," he continued, "I don't know about you, but my stomach is rumbling like your grandad's lorry."

"Well about time an' all, I was just about to send out a search party. Now, Fred Keighley, where's them lovely sausages of your father's?" said grandma as the three friends entered the warmth of the kitchen.

Fred dutifully handed over the hefty package with a smile.

"Can I smell some gingerbread men, Mrs Tilly?" Fred asked, with an over-exaggerated sniff and his nose pointed high in the air.

"There might be young man if you pop out to the coal hole and fill that scuttle up for me before you take your boots off."

The empty copper container was waiting by the back door to be replenished, rather than in its normal place by the fire. Fred eagerly picked it up and headed out.

"Now, you two, might make yourself useful and set the table while I get these sausages in. It's toad-in-the-hole, mash potato and onion gravy tonight so I hope you're all hungry," grandma continued.

After tea was complete and the washing up done, grandma decided she would have some peace and quiet in the study.

"Last complete performance starts at seven, so we'd best be leaving at six-thirty," grandma informed them as she left the front room and plonked herself down in the little room with a book.

Fred picked up his satchel and took out the papers from the car. There was quite a bundle to shuffle through, and most striking to them all was the photograph of Lavender and her parents that seemed to jump out from the rest. Lavender picked it out and looked carefully at it. There was no doubt she hadn't seen it before, other than her recollection of the event on

Monday morning. They split the rest of the papers up between them and carefully worked their way through each item; an Automobile Association membership, a few old tax discs from the 1960s and other car documents. He paused and turned back a few papers, pulling out a folded serviette with some roughly drawn sketches and handwriting which said: Possibly lost standing stones hiding in plain sight.

"Wow, look here, Lav, this looks interesting!" Fred exclaimed holding up the serviette.

"Let me see," she answered as she took it from him. "It sure is, Fred. That's my father's handwriting, and this sketch looks like the fireplace in Pear Tree Cottage, and this looks like …"

Alice interjected, eager to see the sketch and clearly with some excitement, "Can I have a look at the serviette, I have a feeling we may need it."

Lavender passed the serviette to Alice, who opened it up and flattened it out on the floor to gain a broader look.

Printed in the top corner of the serviette in fine old English lettering was "Ye Olde Moon Inne, York."

"Look here," said Alice, pointing to an animal on the moors drawn carefully on the paper. "It looks like Obadiah and the lost sheep on the moors!"

Obadiah was a massive rock with a striking resemblance to a giant wolf crouched to the ground, with its nose and ears clearly distinguishable. The shadows in the rock crevices made him appear black and white. Obadiah sat on a Jurassic rock escarpment that interrupted the landscape between the moors and the surrounding valley. Legend had it that the huge wolf was struck by a bolt of lightning as it chased a flock of sheep across the moors, turning the creature into a rock. The sheep had long since gone.

"You're right, Alice. If that's Obadiah, then those are the moors above town," Lavender exclaimed in growing eagerness.

The few handwritten words were somewhat cryptic and left the three amateur detectives slightly baffled.

"I'm not sure what this means, but I think your mum and dad were on to something here," Fred added.

Lavender picked the serviette up, folded it and put it with the small photograph and whispered, "I'm going to keep them safe in the case."

She went over to the piano and reached her hand underneath to pull out the old gold case belonging to great-uncle Tom Gill.

"Wait!" said Fred in an urgently raised whisper, "I'm a bit worried about that old case."

"What on Earth do you mean, Fred?" Lavender replied.

"Just that strange things seem to happen with it. Before you put anything else in it, try putting this old tax disc in and see what happens."

Fred passed Lavender a small circular light blue tax disc marked Aug 65 from the wad of papers and placed it inside the empty case, then closed it with a secure click.

"Right, now open it up," Fred continued.

Lavender pulled the lid back off. She took out the tax disc and held it up as if to examine some secret watermark.

"No, looks OK to me. Here," she said, passing it back to Fred.

Exactly as before, as soon as it touched Fred's fingers, it flew off into the fire, and in a flutter of flames, it drew straight up the chimney. Alice cried out in astonishment as they all stood looking at the fire.

"What just happened? Where's it gone?" she continued.

Fred was less excited. In fact, his response was quite contrary, relatively calm, and assured in the knowledge that his hunch was correct.

"I think I'd better keep these safe and hide them upstairs," said Lavender cautiously.

"Is there anything else here that we need to keep as well?" she continued, sifting through the other papers.

Mostly there was little of interest, except for a few items that did spark their curiosity: A small envelope with "Katie Peach 7th September 1884" written on the front. A street map of York and an envelope addressed to Mary Bathwater. Lavender felt that somewhere in the recesses of her brain the envelope marked with her great-grandmother's name was both familiar and important, though she couldn't put her finger on why.

The map had two places of significance circled and handwritten notes in the margin. One was around "Ye Olde Moon Inne" and the other on a famous street that Lavender remembered visiting once before called The Cringles that noted "Meet at inn, 12.30 pm, snug." Lavender opened the envelope and pulled out a letter. It read:

"Dear Mrs Bathwater,

I am writing regarding your letter of the 14th April where you expressed an interest in my Grandfather Manasseh Snowzell's work to uncover the history of Brigantia. I would be most interested in discussing this further and suggest a meeting in person to share our knowledge. From your description, I believe you may also have one of the missing Brigantian Amulets, and I am most eager to see it in person.

Please contact me by telephone on York 55323 to arrange a suitable time and place to meet.

Yours sincerely
Isaac Scrubb
14th April 1968"

It didn't take a great deal of deducing for the three friends to join together some tantalising pieces of this evolving puzzle. With hushed tones and engrossed, excited chatter, they recounted the information they had. Lavender summarised it to check they all agreed.

"It looks like we have two of the amulets that my Great-uncle Tom had in his possession when he died and that I saw in my dream. It seems like the dream occurred because I held the first Amulet of Dreams. The second amulet from the car is a little mysterious. Still, It could be the Amulet of Union, if the description in my book of Brigantia is correct. We also think that my parents may have met with this Isaac Scrubb fella in York before they went missing. Possibly to discuss the amulet. In all, there are supposed to be seven amulets that each impart a different power to the person who possesses them. Another thing about the amulets is that if they are all brought together, peace will reign across the land. From what I can gather, my mother and father were investigating my family history and the history of the Brigantes. The question is: who is the traveller mentioned in the riddle on my mum's note and the one that we must search for?"

"Wait!" Fred interrupted, "I think I know where the traveller is, or rather, what it is."

"What on earth do you mean, Fred?" Alice and Lavender both exclaimed in unison.

"I mean, I think we've already found it! It's not a person but an object. I think it might be the car in the barn. A Traveller is the name of that type of Morris Minor!"

They already had what they needed; it was the amulet that Alice found in the glovebox. There was a deadly silence as the three friends sat in deep thought and contemplated what this meant which had the effect of jolting grandma from the engrossment she had in her book. She looked up at the clock and, realising the lateness of the hour, jumped promptly from her seat.

"Come on then, you three, if we're going to get you to the pictures in time for the first feature, we need to be makin' tracks."

Chapter Eleven

The Cavendish Picture House.

The cinema sign was mounted high on the Cavendish Picture House and could be seen from quite a distance across the town. Its neon blue and red enticed patrons from afar into the cinema's warmth and plush comfort, especially on a cold, foggy evening like tonight when the electric colours dissolved into the atmosphere like a dye in water. "The Cavendish," as it was known was preserved with love by Alice's grandfather, Willy Sutton, for whom it was the great focus of his life.

Brigden had four cinemas and tragically, like many others up and down the country, many had been neglected or changed beyond their former glory. But, with its original character, the Cavendish was the favourite of most who lived in the area.

In the town of Brigden, Willy was what might best be described as a character. To his wife's constant frustration, Willy loved the cinema more than anything else in his life. He devoted much of his energy and attention towards it. Many would say he was indeed married to the cinema as well. Willy had inherited the cinema from his father and had grown up in it, spending his early years, even as a small child, carrying films, polishing the brasses and winding the film in the projection room. Since he was seven years old, he kept a list of every film that had played at the Cavendish and how many people had visited. More importantly, he had a canny knack of knowing what films people would like. Willy was a genuine character; in that, he was entirely himself at all times. He would not pretend or shy away from speaking his mind or to laugh out loud if the occasion demanded it. This often seemed an eccentric trait, but it was entertaining and endearing to Lavender and her friends. He was generous and kind, particularly with children and those dealt a poor hand in life, or who were downtrodden somehow. For these, he would carry out small and deliberate acts of kindness or attention to show them they mattered.

What also made the Cavendish so special was its unique character, built on the designs of a provincial architect and crafted by local tradesmen. It was one of the few buildings to be opened during the Great War. Building commenced in May 1914 on this new-fangled, magical moving picture house. A few months later and it would not have been constructed at all. This provided a sense of progress and hope and a brief escape from the gruelling pain of those keeping the home fires burning. It was not overtly grand like so many of the picture palaces, but what it lacked in size, it made up for in homely character. The small entrance foyer had marble steps and a mosaic floor, ornate English oak-framed glass doors. Polished brass fittings ordained the same oak-panelled doors. They had a small fireplace providing warmth to the eager patrons as they collected their tickets from the booking office. Everyone knew the little family of staff who worked there, just like the many other shops and businesses in Brigden.

Mrs Chamberlain was the efficient cashier who managed to sell all 731 customers their tickets and get them into the building at light speed. The projectionist, Mr Moores, who was pedantic about getting the films just so, could usually be spotted peering through the projection room porthole, like a searchlight operator waiting for the advancing air-raid. The confectionary and ice cream were sold by Miss Hughes, an elderly spinster who was always at the ready, with her apron on and pencil in hand. She seemed to flit about with nervous energy and high anxiety as she proudly managed her display of sweets and chocolates behind the concessions counter.

The more spacious foyer leading to the stalls seats or the balcony, via a flight of stairs, was modest in size and an intimate space. In its fashionable heyday, before the matinees and evening performances, light lunches and afternoon teas could be consumed here. In all the years of its existence, it was the only area of the cinema that had changed. Even then, it was just to accommodate Miss Hughes's concessions counter.

The other notable member of the cinema "family" was Miss Jackson. Rarely was she seen outside of the auditorium where she checked the tickets and did her knitting during the performances. In fact, it seemed as if it was her second home. The only time she moved was to make a cup of tea for the rest of the staff after the film had started, before returning to her usher's seat. Apart from Miss Hughes who appeared to be at least 80 years old and began working at the cinema in 1919 as a waitress and Alice's grandfather, the rest of the staff were in their middle age. All had worked at the Cavendish for over twenty years. The children felt like they were part of the cinema family too, as they were well known to them all in many ways.

Mrs Tilly walked the children across the main road, through the winding streets and over the canal bridge to Cavendish Lane where the cinema stood like a welcoming beacon in the otherwise grey evening air. Underneath the brightly lit archway of the entrance, Willy, Alice's grandfather, stood smartly in his evening dress suit. He had his hands together behind his back and was greeting the evening patrons.

"I'll meet them in the foyer at the end of the show, Mr Sutton." Mrs Tilly advised Willy from the pavement.

She would typically have used his first name, but as he was "on duty" so to speak, she referred to him more formally. Willy opened one of the ornate doors and gestured them inside.

"Good evening, Mrs Tilly, but no need to fetch them. I can drop them off on the way home if you don't mind," he replied and then passing them three tickets he continued, "You children go and see Miss Hughes for a drink each and a box of Fruit Pastilles and then find yourself a seat in the balcony, I've saved you three seats up there tonight."

"Wow, we can go upstairs, Mr Sutton?" Fred checked with excitement at this rare privilege.

"If you're quick, you can. Go on, skedaddle!"

Miss Hughes handed them each their allotted drinks and boxes of sweets in typically spritely fashion, after which they leapt up the staircase three steps at a time before screeching to a halt in front of Mrs Jackson. The latter sat in the doorway with her knitting in hand, looking intently over the rim of her glasses at a gentleman on the back row.

Fred reached the door first and launched into conversation quickly, "Hello, Miss Jackson, we've got tickets for the balcony," he said proudly, whilst thrusting the said tickets towards the distracted usher.

Her eyes never dropped from their fixation, nor did her hands move to take the tickets, instead she just continued to knit.

"Miss Jackson!" he repeated in a raised tone attempting to break her stare. Miss Jackson put her knitting down in her lap and held her hand out to receive the tickets.

"I'm just keeping an eye on that shifty-looking bloke," she whispered, nodding her head towards a man on the back row.

The children walked straight along the rear aisle behind the back row of seats until they had walked past the man in question. He certainly did come across as rather odd, not just because he was sitting at the back on his own but also because he was wearing a thick great coat in what was quite a warm place. Lavender let out a silent gasp as she approached him. She noticed that the man had an uncanny resemblance to the person she had seen in Robert's Park that morning with a thin face and long unkempt hair.

Once the three had taken up residence on the front row, Lavender whispered to her two friends, "I'm not joking now and don't look behind you, but that weird man at the back is the same man I saw hiding in Rombus's cave this morning."

Alice and Fred's curiosity proved too much to bear, and they almost immediately turned their heads to see for themselves.

"He's gone!" said Fred in shock.

"Oh yes, that's weird. I'm glad though, he did look odd, and it was giving me the jitters thinking he would be behind us in the dark," Alice continued.

Just then the glistening brass chandeliers hanging from the ornate plasterwork of the barrelled ceiling began to dim, and the velvet curtains opened to the familiar sound of the Pearl and Dean adverts.

After a couple of short films, the curtains closed and the chandeliers relit for the intermission. Being an inquisitive boy, Fred took the opportunity to turn again and look behind at the back row of seats, which by now had nearly filled with patrons. However, there was still an empty seat where the odd-looking man had been. He could see Mr Moores in the projection room looking through his porthole at the line of people waiting to buy refreshments from Miss Jackson's ice cream tray. Mr

Moores waved at Fred to come up and see him. Fred had been up to the projection room once before, where he had developed a fascination for seeing the big reels of films, each with their own series of condensed images that flicked and hummed and whirred their way past the brilliant light of the projectors and then through the lens. It was, he thought, magical to see them appear on the colossal screen some one hundred feet away.

"I'm just going to go and see Mr Moores," Fred blurted out, as he launched himself from the seat like a loaded catapult and charged up the balcony's central aisle.

"Nay, lad, slow thisen down or you'll crack your 'ead open," Miss Jackson admonished, as Fred flew past her and up the stairs.

By the time Fred had got downstairs and back up the projection room spiral staircase, the intermission was nearly over, and Mr Moores was preparing to start the main feature. The ticking and whirring of the projector's machinery had filled the room with an almost comforting heady mix of acetone, carbon dust and warm oil that greeted him along with Mr Moores.

"Hello, Fred, you just made it in time."

"In time for what?" said Fred, getting his breath back from the run-up the staircase.

"Well, seeing as though you were so enamoured with the projectors last time you came here, I thought you'd like to start the film. Come over here, and I'll show you what to do."

Mr Moores explained how to "lace-up" the film. He showed Fred the route the film took as it threaded through the projector.

"Now you have a go," he encouraged.

Fred followed the course he had been shown and pulled the film down from the top reel.

"Now, clip it into the bottom reel … that's it, Fred."

Mr Moores checked Fred's handiwork making sure there was just the right amount of slack in the film as it passed through the projector.

"Ee, lad, you're a natural. We'll make you into a projectionist in no time. Now if you'd like to start the film?"

Fred felt both excited and nervous at the prospect. He looked out of the same porthole window that he had seen Mr Moores looking from and saw the audience all waiting for the film to start. He could see Lavender and Alice on the front row next to his empty seat.

"I'll turn the lights down and put the sound on, you can turn this knob here. It will bump the carbon rods together and arc the electricity to create the light, then when I say 'Go' you start the projector by moving that yellow lever. Once the film has counted down, and the first picture gets to the gate, you can open the shutter by pushing this yellow button. Are you ready?"

Fred took a gulp. "OK, ready when you are, I think," Fred replied, with more than a little trepidation.

Before having any time to worry, he twisted the knob Mr Moores had shown him on the big projector, and with an electric pffttzz, the carbon rods connected inside between an arc of brilliant, blue-white light. Shortly afterwards, the chandeliers started to dim.

"GO!" said Mr Moores.

Fred moved the yellow leaver, and the projector came to life, with its familiar rhythmic chatter pulling the film through the sprockets and the film gate. 08, 07, 06, 05, 04, 03, - - - then when the first picture hit the gate he pushed the shutter open, and with triumphant splendour, the screen lit up, and the curtains opened.

"Wow, that was brilliant!" exclaimed Fred, with a combination of pride, satisfaction and slight breathlessness.

"Well done, lad, now you get yourself off to your seat and enjoy the film," Mr Moores replied, with a smile.

Fred headed back down the spiral staircase in quick time and into the foyer. He could see Miss Jackson already making a large pot of tea for the rest of the cinema staff through the kitchen door.

"Mind how you go up them stairs, Fred Keighley," she shouted from the kitchen, to which Fred slowed himself to a deliberate one step at a time pace up the balcony staircase. The doors were closed when he got to the top, as were the curtains on the inside, preventing light from entering the auditorium. He pulled open one of the doors and moved back the curtain to enter. A large, powerful hand suddenly gripped his wrist from within the darkness and pulled him in until he was caught in the curtains. The hand was attached to a tall man who was also entangled behind him in the curtains. Fred was in such a state of shock that he froze. It was as if his brain was running at a million miles an hour and was disconnected from his body. As much as he wanted to shout and run, he couldn't.

Then he felt another hand move over his mouth from behind and lips press against his ear. He could hear and smell the breath of his assailant as he spoke, a putrid mix of whisky, cigarettes and onions.

"See here, sonny, don't even think about uttering so much as a gnat's whisper about this if you want to see the sunrise on Saturday. I've been watching you and your little lady friends, and there's something you have that belongs to me."

Fred swallowed the egg-like lump in his throat with a gulp that moved it to sit somewhere near the top of his stomach.

"Bring me the amulet, come to the Cavendish Lane canal bridge at six o'clock tomorrow evening and come alone. Any funny business and you'll regret it. Just nod if you understand."

Fred nodded, breaking his rigidity with an abrupt judder. Immediately, in a swirl of the curtains Fred was released from the man's grip, and in disorientation he fell against the wall with relief. At this point, Miss Jackson was at the foot of the stairs and about to return to her position of work. She had a cup of tea in one hand, and knitting bag in the other, as Fred's assailant bounded down the staircase in haste, bumping clumsily into her and sending hot tea sloshing out of her mug and across the foyer floor.

"What the blazes!" she yelled as the man that she had been watching only half an hour earlier flew out of the front door with coat flapping in his wake.

Fred gathered himself together and made his way down the dimly lit aisle and back to his seat at the front of the balcony.

"You took your time, Fred, where were you? We had started to get worried," Lavender remarked with some concern.

Fred was still in shock and gazed blankly at the images flickering before him on the vast screen.

"Err, just up in the projection room," he replied dismissively, with an automatic avoidance of the preceding events.

But Lavender and Alice were already engrossed in the story, and neither had any inkling of anything untoward happening.

Though the three friends sat there watching the film, only Lavender and Alice actually saw it. For the entire duration, Fred remained lost, deep in spiralling, catastrophising thoughts of what may happen and the dilemma of what he should or should not do. Should he tell the girls, should he tell his dad, should he ignore it or just meet the man tomorrow evening and give him one of the amulets? Then Fred remembered, he actually had an amulet in his pocket when the man grabbed him, he could have let him have it right there. He would have been able to forget about the whole thing. For an hour and a half Fred sat there thinking, yet as the final credits began rolling, it barely felt like a few minutes. Then, as if to provide relief, the chandeliers above gradually illuminated the audience. As they did so, the light they brought somehow seemed to lessen the weight of the burden Fred was feeling.

There was no rush to get up from their seats, as they would be going home with Alice's grandfather, who was always the last to leave. Hence, the three friends sat there for a while, Alice and Lavender chatting and giggling, Fred listened quietly.

"What's up with you, Fred, you're quiet, didn't you enjoy the film?" asked Alice, trying to get him to join in the conversation.

A little unsure of what to say, he was stuck for words.

"I err ..." he stammered and stopped.

"'I er' what," said Alice, goading him a little in jest.

"I didn't see it!" he blurted out in annoyance.

"What do you mean you didn't see it? Of course you did, you were right here with us," Alice continued.

"No, you don't understand," he objected, and then explained, "I mean something happened right before I got back to my seat, and I just couldn't concentrate after that."

He paused for a moment and then sensing Alice's lack of patience, he continued, "You know that creepy man we saw when we first came into the cinema?"

The girls nodded, their expressions dropping with a sudden degree of seriousness.

"Well, he grabbed me and threatened me when I came back from the projection room. He told me to meet him under the Cavendish Lane canal bridge at 6.00 pm tomorrow and give him the amulet – or else!"

"Or else what? He was a real creep, we should fix him," said Alice, with a "Gung-ho" fist punch to the back of her seat.

"We need to be careful, Alice, this fella sounds dangerous, but you're right, we can't just let him get away with threatening Fred. More interestingly, I'm wondering why this fella is so hell-bent on getting the amulet. After school tomorrow, let's meet at Alice's house, then from there we can go to the canal bridge."

A creak of wood behind them broke the conversation as Mr Moores opened the projection room porthole and shouted down.

"Come on, you three. I'm switching the lights off now. Haven't you got homes to go to!"

The children reluctantly got out of their seats, and by the time they had reached the top of the aisle, the lights had dimmed to black, and the now empty void of the auditorium was in darkness except for a chink of light from the staircase.

As he reached the doorway and curtains where he had been accosted Fred paused and stuttered, "It sure is spooky in here in the dark."

"Did I tell you about the cinema gho …" Lavender quickly interrupted Alice.

"Don't start on that now, Alice, you'll have Fred shaking in his boots with your tales of ghosts and whatnot."

"Yeah, I think I've had enough for one day, Alice," said Fred in agreement.

He put his hand in his pocket and pulled out the amulet to hand to Lavender.

"Here, you take it," he said, passing it to her with a sense of relief.

It wasn't long before Miss Jackson, Mrs Chamberlain and Miss Hughes said their goodbyes and left Mr Moores and Willy Sutton to lock the cinema.

"Here's the car keys children. Go and get in the back while we lock up," Alice's grandfather instructed.

Lavender, Fred and Alice stepped outside into what was now a real peasouper of a fog though still infused with the blue and red glow from the neon sign. As they opened the car doors and got into the back of Willy Sutton's Austin Maxi, the foggy air suddenly turned to grey as the lights turned off. Alice's grandfather did his final check of the cinema doors and then made his way to the car.

"Right, you three, let's get you home," he said, pulling out the choke and starting the engine. "Did you enjoy the film?" he continued.

"We did, Grandad. I loved Wilbur most of all. Do you think Mum would let me have a pig?" Alice asked, hopefully.

"Best ask her, love, but I wouldn't count your chickens," Willy replied.

"You've got chickens, and you want a pig as well!" Fred quipped, with a sudden lightening of mood.

The jovial conversation continued until Fred and Lavender had been deposited at Pear Tree Cottage and they both got out of the car into the fog.

"See you in the morning, you two" Alice called from the front seat.

"Yeah, meet you at the park before school," Fred replied.

The curtains twitched open inside the small bay window as Lavender opened the front gate, and behind the glass Lavender could see Delius's nose poking through the gap. The front door opened illuminating the path.

Grandma waved from the doorstep, "Thank you, Willy," she called, and then closed out the fog and the eyes that were watching from the shadows of the working men's club.

"Can we just wait here until we've seen Fred gets home OK?" asked Alice, with some concern for his safety.

"Aye, lass, we can," her grandad replied.

They watched until Fred had turned the corner and then they drove off.

Chapter Twelve

Manasseh Snowzell

Before he met his wife Suzannah, Manasseh Snowzell was a less than pleasant man. Given his start in life, this was no surprise. At the age of eleven, his father was convicted and imprisoned for the murder of his mother while in an inebriated stupor. A fight had broken out in broad daylight outside their home over what was a simple piece of tattered paper. The paper had a riddle on it that his mother had kept secret from her husband and became the only maternal possession Manasseh had.

His mother's death rendered Manasseh a lost and lonely soul, and whilst he no longer had to contend with the regular abuse and thrashing he received from his drunken father, his unfortunate childhood turned decidedly worse when he was subsequently placed into a workhouse administrated by a ruthless master. The latter regularly meted out punishments of the most humiliating and horrific forms.

By the time Manasseh was seventeen, those who knew him would have struggled to believe that this mean, cold and wholly selfish individual could possibly change so categorically through the love of a woman. Still, somehow he did, and the world for a few years was a better place for it. After the miraculous and welcome change in his demeanour, it was nothing short of devastating then to witness the relapse into his previously unpleasant character.

The person who had become so well presented and proud, descended to even greater depths of his shadowy former self in a moment, with a single ill-considered, but well-intentioned act. Even the softer features of his previously handsome face distorted into dark creases, angles and a furrowed brow. His cheeks that before were framed well by a jolly and friendly mutton chop beard were now somewhat sunken, carpeted with differing degrees of greying stubble, making his appearance not dissimilar to a drunkard or vagrant.

After marrying, Manasseh had become a historian of some repute in the city of York, and a keen gardener with excellent knowledge of flora and fauna. He was happy beyond words in the marriage to his beautiful wife, who in many ways, both in personality and appearance, would have been a close sister to his own mother. Suzannah had her own interesting family history, though she was only partially aware of the importance of it. What she did know was that the remnants of her ancestors' lives were contained safely in a chest that had been handed down through the generations.

The chest had originally belonged to a relative of Suzannah's; the captain of a ship named "The White Lion" between 1643 and 1645. It was now storage for the most precious of her family's possessions, including a silver amulet, a curious black book that contained historical details of the captain, a drawing of a cottage and, most precious of all, an ornate golden case that held a lock of hair with a description of the place it was found between two distinctive giant boulders. Manasseh was fascinated by the sea chest's contents and in particular the descriptions within the book of the case and the legendary Amulets of Brigantia. After further research, he concluded that the gold case must be the purse that originally held the lost amulets, of which there were seven.

Each Amulet was described and drawn in detail as follows:
The Amulet of Dreams
The Amulet of Union
The Amulet of Courage
The Amulet of the Nameless
The Amulet of Now
The Amulet of Love

The Amulet of Meaning

The silver amulet was a strange anomaly though, it did not match the description of any of the amulets in the book. Still, over the years that followed, Manasseh became increasingly fixated upon the amulet, and kept it close to him at all times, believing it was a powerful force that would bring him wealth and happiness and lead him to greater discoveries. However, the turn of events that proceeded to occur after possessing it did not seem to bear out his beliefs.

Together, Manasseh and Suzannah had a daughter Eliza. When Eliza was just three years old, Suzannah fell pregnant again and developed dropsy in her third trimester. Her swelling became so bad that in a fit of desperation Manasseh decided to prepare a home remedy of foxglove from his garden. Unfortunately, his treatment did not have the desired effect. It instead tragically caused the eight-month pregnant Suzannah to suffer a violent heart attack. Manasseh was inconsolable and riddled with guilt. Traumatised by the death of Suzannah and his unborn child and left alone to raise Eliza with only the support of Suzannah's mother.

Manasseh and Eliza's home was in a wooden-framed medieval house on a narrow winding street in the centre of York known as The Cringles. His mother-in-law lived alone on the opposite side of the lane where the houses became closer to one another the higher up they went. At the third story windows it was possible to shake hands or pass objects across the street with ease, they were so near to each other. In the period of grief and loneliness following his wife's devastating death, Manasseh remained fixated on the amulet he now possessed, and the supernatural history of the area and its inhabitants. He had kept Suzannah's clothes, shoes and a lock of her hair, that he had cut from her after she died, sleeping with them next to him in bed. In his own desperate and confused mind, from what he had read, Manasseh clung to the elusive hope of reuniting with his departed wife again through the combined power of the amulet, the traversing of the Venetius Stone, wherever that may be, and the lock of Suzannah's hair.

Many years later, it was the death in childbirth of his newly married seventeen-year-old daughter Eliza that was the final soul-shattering occurrence which pushed Manasseh, and any semblance of rational thinking, over the edge. Eliza had fallen pregnant out of wedlock and after a hasty marriage to a young, kind-hearted farmer named Percival Scrubb, the couple lived together in The Cringles until on the 28th of June 1914, Eliza gave birth. Tragically, she traded her life for twin sons Isaac and Elijah and in his grief, Manasseh again took a lock of hair, this time from his daughter. By the autumn Percival was in Flanders, having joined the patriotic fervour and swelling queues of young men to enlist as a soldier. Within a month of arriving in Belgium he was missing in action, evaporated in the bloody mud and fog of war. And so, it was the newborn twins Isaac and Elijah were left with just one carer in the entire world, their tormented, grief-stricken, guilt-ridden grandfather.

During the first few years of Isaac and Elijah's life, Manasseh had become a virtual recluse, hiding himself and the twins away from the world in his crooked house in The Cringles. His financial position deteriorated, forcing him to sell his valuables to pay the bills, including the unusual gold case that still sat in the sea chest. On many occasions as young children, when their hunger was severe, or their crying became too much for Manasseh to bear, he would lock them away in the tiny second-floor bedroom until the torturous noise gave way to morbid silence. Isaac learned that sometimes he would be released if he didn't cry. But Elijah was a sickly child and suffered from perpetual stomach pain resulting in persistent crying for hours on end. Often Manasseh would drift into a fixed empty gaze, only to realise hours later that he had forgotten his grandson was still locked away. It was for this reason that Manasseh favoured Isaac from a very young age, often confiding his irrational notions, in particular ideas that he could somehow reconnect with his departed wife. Elijah, by contrast was punished more harshly and frequently than his brother. In time he came to resent Isaac as well as his grandfather.

The severity of Manasseh's abuse towards Elijah changed unexpectedly one evening after Manasseh had been drinking. Elijah was seven years old and in a moment of brave indignation, had refused to go to bed when his grandfather had demanded it. Manasseh's temper had got the better of him and he launched at Elijah with his hand, only to slip in uncoordinated drunkenness and hit his head on the carved wood sideboard in the front room. Manasseh had descended into a coma that lasted the around the clock and during which he had a series of revelations. The most tormenting of which was his realisation of the foolishness of his belief in the silver amulet and the series of catastrophic events that had occurred since he held it in his possession. When he awoke the following day, he walked through the city to Lendal Bridge and threw the amulet in the river. Manasseh stood for a moment, staring at his reflection in the rippling water beneath. In the pause he had taken, a new determination came over him. He would take Suzannah's lock of hair and weave it with his own. He would find the fabled Amulet of Union and pass through the Venetius Stone to be reunited with his wife. Locally, Manasseh had become infamous due to his obsession with the lost history of the area and an unhealthy desire and failed practice of rekindling Pagan rituals, whilst incorporating his own ideas into their practice. Manasseh had discovered further clues while Isaac and Elijah were at school. One of the most plausible was that, during the Roman invasion, the amulets were hidden, then over time their location forgotten. He had come across drawings and descriptions of ancient settlements on the moors, leading him to seek out these ancient sites where the amulets may lay buried, including an archaeological exploration of a megalithic stone circle, some twenty miles to the west. He discovered and mapped two new monoliths and another stone circle. His passion for this was one of the few things he talked deeply about with Isaac as he got older, who in turn shared a keen interest. Meanwhile, Elijah was either generally ignored or admonished for trivialities, leaving him feeling perpetually on edge, yet desperate for his grandfather's attention.

Despite Manasseh's best efforts, meticulous research and careful map drawing, by the time the twins were thirteen Manasseh reached the end of the line with his historical leads. He had not found so much as a broken piece of pottery on the dozens of sites he had searched. In the subsequent year, he became more despondent, often concluding interactions with bursts of rage.

Everything changed on the eve of Isaac and Elijah's fourteenth birthday, when Manasseh received this hand-delivered letter creating a new line of enquiry for his historical detective work, a letter that would have repercussions that reverberated through the coming decades.

"Thomas Gill
The Turk's Head Inn
Brigden.
Yorkshire.
16th October 1928

Dear Mr Snowzell

I trust you will forgive my unsolicited letter to you on a matter of great mutual interest. I purchased an unusual gold case recently from a collector in York. He had no luck in validating its origins or worth and finally considered it a fake so took my offer to buy it. He told me that he acquired it from you and that you had done a considerable amount of research into the Brigantian people of the North of England, including some crucial discoveries that may help me further my own investigation. I have some information in this regard that you may well find useful. However, I do not wish to disclose too much in writing. If you are agreeable to arranging a meeting to share our knowledge, I would be most happy to catch the train to York and meet you at the railway station at a date and time of your convenience.

Yours sincerely

Thomas Gill"

It was a particularly icy and still morning on the 8th November 1928. The 10.40 am train from Leeds pulled up in the stewing freezing fog of the enormous Victorian station in York. Like the mad laughter of a potion concocting witch, the metal-on-metal screech of wheels against rails rang out. It was accompanied by a spew of vapour and smoke that spilt from the engine as if it were crawling down the sides of a cauldron. Tom stepped out into the swirling disturbed air and walked towards the end of the platform. He could see the yellow glow of the small station café which shone like a beacon through the volume thick air, offering a sanctuary of quiet and warmth. As Tom entered the café and walked to the counter, he carefully noted the establishment's occupants. A middle-aged man and woman in the window seats with a couple of large suitcases, an elderly man sat at the counter with a steaming hot mug of tea. A solitary looking figure tucked away in one of the darker corners, with just a forehead of thinning grey hair visible above a broadsheet newspaper. Tom approached the counter and purchased a mug of tea, and a round of toast then turned towards the single male in the corner. The hands of the man who sat there shook the newspaper with a modest crack to straighten it. As he did so, their eyes locked with an almost indiscernible flicker and an acknowledged union was made. Tom walked over to the table as the man folded his newspaper and put it down on the green leather bench seat beside him. It was the first full view the two had of each other. The man tipped his head down slightly to lower his spectacles, then peered over them without a single change of expression.

"Mr Gill, I presume?"

There was an oily intonation in his whisky-tinged voice accompanied by an air of righteous superiority.

"Mr Snowzell, I presume?" Tom replied, as if to counter the tones he had received.

"Indeed … and at last, we meet," Manasseh confirmed, with barely a visible movement, other than a narrowing of his eyes.

"So, Mr Gill, what is it that is of such great interest to you, and how can you help me?"

"May I sit?" asked Tom, allowing himself an opportunity to pause in consideration of a reply.

Manasseh gestured to the seat opposite him. It was clear to Tom that the man sat in front of him was not the most amenable of characters. He should be careful not to reveal too much before he got to know him. Tom opened the subject with a degree of vagueness.

"I have knowledge of some Brigantian locations of interest around the Brigden area, but there are questions I need answering to narrow down my search. I'm wondering if you have any knowledge or information on the Goddodin moor area that may help?"

"What exactly are you searching for, Mr Gill?" Manasseh asked directly.

The straightforward question cornered Tom.

"I'm not sure I am at liberty to say at this stage, Mr Snowzell," he replied.

"Oh, come now, no need to be so coy, Mr Gill. We both know why we are here and what we are searching for."

There was a long uncomfortable silence as the two men looked intently at one another.

"Well, Mr Gill, are we looking for the same thing?" he continued.

"I believe we may well be," Tom agreed.

"Then let's have it. And, if we are to have it, then what have you to offer me, Mr Gill?"

Tom reached into his inside jacket pocket and pulled out a folded piece of paper.

"This map I have of the area should help us make a start," he said, holding it over the table.

Manasseh went to take it, but Tom pulled it away with a jerk of his hand.

"Not so fast, Mr Snowzell. Before we go any further, I need to see what you can bring to our relationship if I am to trust you."

Manasseh sat up straight on the seat and removed his spectacles, then for the first time, he lifted his head to look straight ahead at Tom.

"I see you mean business, Mr Gill, then perhaps we can work together on this." Manasseh's tone had changed in an instant.

"I too have a map and other research of interest," he continued, reaching for a brown leather case he had on the bench.

Manasseh opened the case and lifted out a well-worn notebook.

"Your toast is going cold, Mr Gill, I suggest you tuck in." Then, opening the notebook at a marked page, he placed it out on the table in front of Tom and continued, "Perhaps now I may cast my eyes over your map?"

Tom opened the map up on the table, and together they fell into silence, pondering the details of what was in front of them.

The nature of Manasseh's research impressed Tom. There was a drawing of the unusual gold case previously owned by him, and of particular interest was the detailed diagrams and sketches depicting the burial sites of the Brigantes. It would be much easier to investigate the area with this. Manasseh watched Tom with interest as he viewed the drawings.

"Do you still have the gold case?" he asked.

"Aye, I do. Why's that?" Tom replied.

Manasseh's eyes lit up for a second. "I'd like to hold it again, one more time," he confessed.

"Aye, it is a beautiful and unusual object, but it's home and in safe keeping, Mr Snowzell," Tom admitted.

What was missing from Manasseh's notes was precisely where the burial ground was. Manasseh was the first to speak as he spotted the burial ground mark on the Goddodin moors.

"This is where we need to start," he said, tapping on the map.

"Start what?" replied Tom, prompting more information.

"Start digging. This, Mr Gill, may well be where we find the lost artefacts of the Brigantes."

Tom could hardly contain his excitement at the prospect of uncovering the amulets that his grandfather had found, then reburied all those years before.

"You mean the amulets, Mr Snowzell?"

Manasseh took a pen from his case and marked an X on the map, then he drew a circle in his own book representing the burial ground.

"That's exactly what I mean, Mr Gill. The Amulets of Brigantia are a lost force of untold power. A power that has not seen the light of day since the Romans invaded our land."

Tom leant back in his seat and took a gulp of tea. "Looks like we have ourselves a partnership then, Mr Snowzell."

Tom looked across at the face in front of him that had now changed so appreciably since he had first cast eyes on him. It was no longer a face of cold cynicism, but one of hope and excitement, yet Tom was still not entirely sure he trusted Manasseh.

"Tell me, how far away do you live from the moors and this spot?" Manasseh asked, tapping the X he had made on the map.

"It's roughly a forty-minute walk from The Turk's Head. What do you have in mind?" Tom replied.

"If I come over next week, first thing in the morning, we can go up to the burial ground together and start an exploratory dig. There's a reasonable chance we will be looking in the right place to find the amulets, or any other Brigantian artefacts, with the information we have. Do you have any hand shovels, Mr Gill?"

"I do and, by the way, please call me Tom."

The two men continued to talk for another hour in the warmth of the station café, growing more enthused and amicable as each minute elapsed, whilst a steady rotation of travellers passed through. Every seat in the café had been taken by the time they had agreed a solid plan to investigate, so it felt like an appropriate time to say goodbye until the following week.

Early in the morning, exactly a week after their meeting in York, Manasseh Snowzell prepared himself a pack of food and drink for his day on the Goddodin moors and wrote out a note for his grandsons informing them of his plans.

It read:

"Isaac and Elijah,
Gone to Brigden. Significant breakthrough on the possible location of the amulets.
Back late."

He had suffered from a broken night's sleep, due in no small part to the discomfort felt from an over-indulgence of whisky, and then later with obsessive thoughts about the day ahead and what he may be able to do if they found the amulets.

He had come to believe his own distorted theory that the Brigantes had developed powers that could bring a person into contact with the dead. Through the elusive amulets and a lock of his wife's hair, he fantasised being reunited with Suzannah.

It was with these ideas running through his mind on the morning of their meeting, that Manasseh stood over the dining table in his tiny front room. If I meet with any objections from him, I need to make sure I do not lose the amulets he thought, I need some form of "insurance". Manasseh was looking at the half-drunk bottle of whisky that still stood on the table from the night before, as a sudden dreadful thought flashed through his brain. An idea he knew was wrong, but nevertheless, he couldn't push away. He reached down into the sideboard behind him, took out his silver hip flask, and then, taking the bottle from the table, he half-filled the flask. Manasseh went out into the dark of the back garden and cut himself a handful of foxglove still growing there. He returned inside, now moving with nervous haste that made his hands shake and his eyes twitch as he prepared the foxglove. He added enough of it to the whisky to render it poisonous then, just as he was about to close the lid of the hip flask, he heard footsteps on the creaking medieval staircase that weaved in an erratic and unplanned fashion through the cold dark house.

"Are you alright, Grandfather?" Elijah said, tentatively as he reached the bottom of the staircase and saw his grandfather in a flustered state.

For a brief moment, a sense of shame washed over Manasseh as he considered the result of his neglect of Elijah. In the same way as the house was unloved and in disrepair, so was Elijah, but irritated by the questioning, he clumsily dropped the lid of the flask on the floor, breaking his sense of remorse. The desire to find what he had been searching for all these years brought an urgency to the moment and he shouted angrily at Elijah.

"Damn you boy! Why are you downstairs so early? Get back upstairs and don't come down until I've gone." Convinced that his grandfather's mood would result in punishment, Elijah dashed back to his bedroom.

However, it was strange that he was so angry at this time in the morning. By the time Elijah had got back to his bed, the low wide front door had slammed behind Manasseh. The slam shook the glass in the windows so violently it ensured Isaac was fully awake.

"What's all the commotion, Elijah?" Isaac said grouchily.

"Grandfather is in a foul mood, and he's gone out somewhere," Elijah replied with relief.

Chapter Thirteen

Maiden Castle

At ten past seven in the morning, Manasseh had reached The
Turk's Head in Brigden and was waiting in the shadowy
concealment of the snicket that ran down its northside. Despite
the hour, many of the town's inhabitants were hidden away in a
hive of activity. He could hear the deafening noise from inside
the nearest mill some three-hundred yards away, humming
through the streets, and black smoke rose from its towering
chimneys, thickening the November air. The bulk of Brigden's
workers, teenage children and all, were already an hour into
their repeating day of arduous drudgery at the three textile
spinning mills. So it was that neither the faint mist from
Manasseh's breath leeching out into the Main Street nor the
sound of his feet on the shining cobbles gave clues to his
presence. He hopped about in a combination of nervous
excitement and the need to keep warm, wrapping and
unwrapping his arms across his upper body to maintain
circulation. Yet, when Tom opened one side of the large double
doors of The Turk's Head and turned to step down towards the
pavement, a warning hit him abruptly, a smell, that to any

other, may have been inappreciable, stung his nose. He knew instantly that Manasseh had already arrived.

For both men, this day finally presented them with the opportunity to realise their visions after years of investigation, hope and focus. Manasseh heard the public house's door close with a deep and solid snap followed by the boot tap of Tom's feet as they transited its stone steps. He pulled up the collar of his overcoat and peered around the corner of the building.

"Good morning, Tom. Are you ready to find some treasure?"

It was the first time Manasseh had used his forename, leaving Tom a little unsettled, though in some ways relieved, at the shift in tone.

"I just need to get the hand shovels from the coal hole, and then we can get on our way," Tom whispered in reply.

The two amateur archaeologists made their way through the dimly lit, narrow back streets of the town and down to the canal. They walked under the bridge and followed the towpath, passing the growing hum and activity of Wades Mill. Some quarter of a mile further along the path, they arrived at the farm that previously belonged to Tom's great-grandfather Tobias and there they stopped by a gate to consult Tom's map. To determine the best way to get up onto the moors, the two men surveyed the fields and drystone walls that lay in front of them. Tom pointed ahead and cleared his voice.

"We need to head up to where that large boulder is near the top of the long field. Then we can follow the beck up to the escarpment and the old Roman road where the moor starts in front of Obadiah," he announced.

Manasseh looked up at the escarpment and the enormous rocky feature on top of the moor. For a split second, he thought he had found the giant boulders drawn in the book from the sea chest, but the thought faded as quickly as it came when he realised the rocky feature was nowhere near the shape it should be.

"Obadiah?" questioned Manasseh.

Tom explained the local significance of Obadiah and its resemblance to a wolf.

"We had better keep an ear out for its howling, my learned friend. Lead on then," Manasseh quipped rather disingenuously.

The light gradually improved as they crossed the wet grass towards the trees. By the time they had reached the escarpment, the sun had broken the watery horizon, casting long shadows of their two figures on the rocks. Scrambling between boulders and natural cliff staircases, they reached the escarpment ledge and undertook a final climb to the top. As they stepped onto the old Roman road that straddled the edge of the heather-dressed moors, Obadiah sat some two hundred yards ahead in proud observation of the valley below. Manasseh consulted his map and scanned the view.

"I see Obadiah in the distance and the trench of Maiden Castle there in front of us. And that must be the burial ground," said Manasseh, pointing vaguely to a rather uninteresting looking plot to the right.

Making their way towards the flat moorland Manasseh had pointed to, Tom was unconvinced they were in the right place until, less than five minutes later, Manasseh abruptly stopped in his tracks. At first, he just stood there, rooted to the spot. Then he looked around at the conflicting vista. The sweeping open moors clashed with the town below with its huddled houses and blackened mills breathing darkness into the air. At this vantage point, the gentle morning breeze still brought with it smoke from the valley that caught the back of his throat. He could sense the cold soft ground underneath his feet calling to him with a roaring voice so deep that it echoed in his stomach as if it were a lion in a cave.

Tom broke the quiet air, "What a view, such a contrast between the moors and the dale it's no wonder the Brigantes chose this position to bury their dead, don't you think?"

There was no movement or response from Manasseh for quite some time. Within his riveted body, in every increasing second that passed, he could feel his departed wife's presence. He could smell her pale skin and soft golden hair; he could hear her voice calling him near, and then as he looked down at the ground by his feet, he could see the winter sky-blue of her bright eyes looking into his mind. Manasseh's fist clenched tight around the lock of Suzannah's hair that he had secreted away in his coat pocket; then, with a deliberate and swift movement, he lifted his right foot high and stamped hard on the ground beneath.

"Here … We must start here," he exclaimed with absolute conviction.

Tom looked bemused by Manasseh's confidence in what was such a nondescript place. There were no outstanding features, no landmarks, or other identifying characteristics to prompt even the slightest notion that this particular spot was the place to start digging.

"What makes you so sure we should start here," Tom questioned.

Manasseh turned slowly to look almost mournfully into Tom's eyes and replied with absolute conviction, "Trust me, I can feel it in the very marrow of my bones."

Before they could start digging, it took a solid half an hour to remove a section of heather, some six feet square around the place that Manasseh had stood. The soft layers of earth could be removed with relative ease once this was done, until they gave way to the harder ground beneath. By one o'clock they had dug a sizeable trench with two steps down, but their pace had slowed as shovels started to hit more pebbles and rocks in the lower section. It seemed an appropriate time to rest a while and eat, they agreed. Tom pointed out a decent-sized flat rock near the escarpment that jutted out over the dale below, making a suitable resting spot to eat their lunch.

While they were eating Manasseh fell silent and took out a well-thumbed notebook from his coat pocket. He began to read from a separate tattered piece of browning paper placed inside. Tom noticed that his eyes glazed over, and his mind seemed to become lost amongst its words. Sensing a personal emotional reaction to what it contained, he decided to remain silent rather than make any commentary. Instead, he tried to surreptitiously read the carefully scribed words, unfortunately with little success as Manasseh closed the notebook and returned it to his pocket.

"When we have finished today, you must show me the gold case before I go home," Manasseh insisted, quite suddenly.

Tom felt somewhat taken aback by his abrupt statement. He paused to think for a moment, rubbing the line of his eyebrow with his finger.

"I dare say," he offered.

The two men continued to sit together, speculating on what they may find and sharing a well-earned rest. After half an hour, with little notice, the wind changed to a northerly direction, and the sky turned an ominous grey.

"It looks like we're in for some bad weather, I think we had better call it a day," remarked Tom disappointedly.

Manasseh sensed an opportunity to continue on his own and claim anything of worth for himself.

"Well, Tom, you turn in if you like, I think I'll go back and carry on for a while, seeing as though I've come all this way."

Tom considered his position for a moment.

"Nay, I'll not leave you here on your own, Manasseh. Anyroad, a drop of rain never hurt anyone," he replied with stoic determination.

It was a clarifying realisation to Manasseh that Tom was not going to be a pushover. Despite his mild manner, he clearly had a steely resolve when something was of importance to him. Manasseh also contemplated the situation for a moment and, with eyes turning a darker shade of black, he reached into his overcoat pocket, pulling out his silver hip flask. The rain started to fall as Manasseh unscrewed the lid of the flask and offered it to Tom.

"Here, take a swig of this. If we're going to carry on in the rain, best warm our innards up."

Tom reached for the flask and put it to his lips. He hesitated for a moment as the whisky vapour hit his nostrils and then passed it back without taking a sip.

"It might be cold and wet, but I'll wait until I get home for a wee dram."

Manasseh put the lid back on and returned the flask to his pocket.

"If you're not then I'll not either," Manasseh replied.

By the time they neared the trench, the rain was coming down by the bucketload. The two amateur archaeologists were being whipped and lashed by an increasing wind that would not have been out of place on the bow of a North Sea fishing boat in winter. But, although the weather had dampened their clothing, it did not seem to have dampened their spirits. They both took off their soaking overcoats, threw them on the heather and rolled up their shirt sleeves as they took the final few steps to the trench. Still, as they stood in their sodden boots at the edge of their mornings' work, they could see it was already a foot deep in water at the bottom, and the sides were starting to slip down into the increasingly muddy hole. They stood on the edge, silent and disillusioned, with the rain falling unrelentingly on them as they peered into the trench. Then silently, as if some greater power had taken pity on their broken faces, the ground gave way along the opposite edge revealing the faintest glint of shining metal in the mud. Tom blinked twice, checking on his own vision as he looked across at the sodden wall of earth. Then without further hesitation, he jumped into the rising muddy water, ploughing his hand shovel into the ground below the object to prevent it from slipping into the developing quagmire. His feet were lodged firmly in the bottom of the trench as he scraped away the wet, muddy soil to reveal what appeared to be a tarnished coin. Manasseh was still stood on the edge of the trench with a shovel in hand.

He shouted down to Tom as the wind lashed his face, "What is it? … Is it the amulet, Tom? TOM!"

Tom put his hands into the water and rubbed the object to remove the mud. It seemed to split in half down its edge to become two coins as the water softened the dirt. He lifted his hands from the water, revealing an amulet in each hand, no longer tarnished, but shining bright gold in the grey air. Tom looked up at Manasseh in excitement but instantly saw he now had an empty look in his eyes. His demeanour had changed entirely. The wind seemed to shift direction and brought with it a growing, deep, howling moan. A sound so unearthly that although he had never heard it before, Tom knew instinctively that it was a warning from Obadiah. Without thought, he put the amulets in his left hand and reached up to Manasseh with his right arm.

"Looks like we have two, Manasseh, give me a hand up will you, my feet are well and truly stuck."

Manasseh's eyes narrowed as he stared down at Tom's short body, submerging deeper in the flooding water as the howling grew louder.

"Pass me the amulets first, I need to see them," he replied, with a coldness that chilled Tom beyond his already shivering frame.

Tom could see Manasseh's intent in his mind's eye as he squeezed the amulets tighter in his left hand. Manasseh wanted the amulets only for himself, and once he had them, he would take aim to slay Tom in the mud with a swing of his own hand shovel.

Tom lowered his right arm and replaced it with his left, opening his palm to reveal the amulets to Manasseh.

"You're a good man, Mr Gill," shouted Manasseh, against the howling wind. As his hand reached down from his pocket to take the amulets, Suzannah's lock of hair was pulled out with it and whipped into the air. "But I'm no fool," Tom said, closing his hand tightly around the amulets.

The golden lock of hair flew around Manasseh and then away in front of his eyes, sending him into a spin of panic. He lost his balance and slipped in the mud falling backwards into the trench with Tom. Manasseh's head fell hard on an exposed angular rock releasing a single red line of blood that silently drained from his nose and in that very moment the howling stopped. His eyes flickered and rolled back into his head, and the wet November sky gave way to Suzannah's face smiling softly in his waning brain.

"Come this way," she whispered.

In a fit of panic, Tom managed to pull his feet out of his bogged-down boots and scramble out of the trench. It was a blessed relief. For a moment he sat on a tuft of heather, allowing the nightmarish visions of being consumed in the muddy earth to dissipate. The salty sweat trickling into his mouth interrupted his dazed recovery. He reached down to check Manasseh for signs of life, grabbing his collar to keep his head above the water but it was no use, his body was limp. Tom's fingers maintained their claw-like lock on Manasseh's collar for some time until slowly, the wet and mud relieved the weight of his lifeless body into the water. Tom had been too preoccupied until this moment to notice how cold he was, despite the freezing weather. His barefoot drenched body though was now shaking uncontrollably with bone-chilling shock, and in desperation he reached down once more into the water and pulled off Manasseh's boots, claiming them for his own feet despite their ungainly size. Struggling to look down into the hole at the crumpled broken figure, his stomach turned, and a wave of sweat flushed his body. The vision before him was too much to bear, and without warning, he retched and heaved his barely digested lunch. Tom composed himself once more. Then, in a mechanical action, he took hold of the hand shovel and set about filling the hole back up, first with rocks to weigh down the body, and then soil to conceal the offensive sight from view.

By the time he had completed his grim task, Tom was covered in mud and numb, both of emotions and the cold. He staggered over to his sodden overcoat that had been cast off earlier and started to put it on. As he grappled with the heavy coat in the squally air, a vision of Manasseh flashed before his eyes. He was curled up, contorted on the heather beside him, moaning into the wind. Instinctively he went to run, but then stopped and turned to look again. It was just Manasseh's discarded coat. What if someone were to find it? I must dispose of it, he thought.

Before starting back to Brigden, he carefully took the amulets from his trouser pocket, placed them in a small leather pouch, and into a concealed pocket he had made in his own overcoat, then bent down to pick up Manasseh's.

The walk back down the escarpment, over the fields and down to the canal was a blank to Tom. It wasn't until he could see the canal bridge and the mill that his thoughts of explaining himself to Fanny materialised. He looked down at Manasseh's heavy overcoat that rested over his arm and remembered the notebook he had been looking through as they sat having their lunch. He decided to check the pockets for any other identifying features. There was a notebook; a wallet, empty but for a train ticket, and the hip flask of whisky Manasseh had offered him. He removed Manasseh's possessions and threw the coat into the murky waters of the canal along with the wallet before putting the flask into his front pocket and opening the notebook to check the contents. Besides the separate piece of tattered paper that Manasseh had been reading earlier, the book only contained some sketches of plants and other doodles and certainly nothing of interest. Tom threw the notebook into the darkening waters to join the coat and wallet, then paused to hunch over in protection from the rain, he read the tattered piece of paper.

"This is the place thou comes from,
And the old moon shone long ago,
Thereupon fair Maiden's castle,
Peace did reign without a foe.

Together, seven made all content,
'Til invaders divided their gain.
Disguised with shining stones they came,
Our perfect vale obtained.

On horses' wings, they rode to us,

By the hundreds, red and gold.

Alas, they took our peace and plenty,

But they could not take our souls.

But though many moons will surely pass,

The seven, together, still are true.

Content can still be found in them,

When they are restored to thee.

Take heed my offspring to this rhyme,

Thy future blessings rest in time.

Though I shall not chance to see,

Ye still may find thy blessings be."

Tom struggled to think in any coherent way about what he was reading. His immediate situation now interrupted any other consideration; what story would he tell his wife? The fearful thoughts that his deadly crime would be discovered had his heart racing and mind exploding. He put the paper in his secret pocket along with the amulets and then feeling the flask in the front pocket, he pulled it out and removed the lid. His hands were shaking as he lifted it to his lips and threw back his head to empty the contents down his narrowing gullet, then as if casting off the burden of what he had done, he slung the flask as far along the canal as he could and cried out into the louring air. He could feel his throat burn as he continued his way along the towpath. Within a hundred yards Tom became increasingly breathless, his veins tingled and throbbed in their extremities. Suddenly he clutched his tightening chest and collapsed onto the ground. Laying on the wet path, his lower legs capped off in Manasseh's oversized boots, half-submerged in a puddle of muddy water. His body twisted then seized. As rigid and hot as an iron rod hammered in a forging heat, he became riddled with crushing pain for a few long minutes. Then as he gazed up at the rain falling towards his eyes, he exhaled for the last time. His body relaxed, and he surrendered himself to the next life.

Chapter Fourteen

Ye Olde Moon Inne.

Walking up the path to the front door of Pear Tree Cottage,
Lavender was still pondering the earlier frightening encounter
Fred had with the sinister man in the cinema. But as she
entered the cottage, her thoughts shifted to the familiar cherry
tobacco aroma of grandad's pipe that drifted from the study.
The smell accompanied that of the fire, making it immediately
apparent to her that he was home again, and all was well with
the world. She turned to look into the small room. Next to the
bookcase full of wisdom, the reading chair in the corner was
occupied with a flat cap on the left armrest and grandad's
polished bald head resting against the winged side. He seemed
to be asleep with his right hand propped up on the other chair
arm and pipe held loosely to his mouth. Lavender went to go
into the study, but grandma gently grabbed her arm.

"Best not disturb him, lass, he's bin on't road since
early morning, and he'll be jiggered, you'll see him tomorrow
though so don't fret thisen," said grandma, softly. "Now come
into the kitchen, and we'll make a cup of cocoa, and you can
tell me all about the film," she continued.

It had been a long and eventful day, and so it wasn't long before Lavender started to yawn in readiness for her soft bed. Delius stretched himself out on Lavender's lap, then jumped down on to the kitchen floor and slinked towards the stairs in knowing anticipation.

He casually glanced behind to look at Lavender, as if to say, "Come on then, what are you waiting for?"

"Go on then, lass, get thisen up t'bed," grandma prompted and continued, "I'll be up to tuck you in shortly."

After changing into her pyjamas, Lavender took the amulet from her dress pocket and placed it in the box on her bedside table with the other amulet. It was blissful to lay there for a while in her big double bed, looking up at the ancient beams that striped the sloping ceiling. She reached over and turned out the bedside lamp leaving just the usual chink of light wedging its way through the doorway. As she lay there, she started to think more about dealing with Fred's threat from the man at the cinema. But in the semi-darkness of the bedroom, Lavender's thoughts spiralled and twisted in her mind for what seemed like hours with no real solution. She was just about to turn on the lamp in frustration when she heard the stairs creaking and shortly after her grandma's head popped in through the doorway.

She paused a moment to listen, and then realising Lavender was still awake called out, "Goodnight, God bless."

"Night night, Grandma," she replied quietly.

Delius slinked out of the bedroom, and the door closed, shutting out the light.

As the darkness deepened, Lavender started to think again.

I wonder, she thought, *if the amulets may help me with this, after all, they must have some use if so many people have been searching for them.*

She turned and reached into the dark for the box on the bedside table and opened it, taking the amulets out and holding them together in her clenched palm. Instantly, her body felt loaded with a heavy weight that sunk her comfortingly deep into the mattress. The feeling of security was supported by a scent, held so precious and concrete in Lavender's memory, that it transported her instantly to the atmosphere of another time. She opened her eyes with curiosity and an eagerness to visit the scent with her other senses and found herself sat in the rear seat of the Morris Minor, looking into the rearview mirror at her mum's eyes. In the front seat sat her mum, spraying "L'air du Temps" on her wrists. It was her favourite perfume. Lavender was spellbound. Absorbed as deeply in her senses as she was in the mattress. She watched as her mum raised her wrist to her nose and closed her eyes, inhaling the floral spice of the enchanting aroma. Then she took out her lipstick and leant over to see herself in the mirror as she applied the peachy pink to her lips. Lavender noticed the letter from Isaac Scrubb sat on the driver's seat. Assuming that she may be on her way to meet him, she looked out of the windows to check on her surroundings. The car was parked outside a steep grassy mound that she instantly recognised from previous visits. A round tower made of solid off-white stones sat on the hill's top. That's Clifford's Tower, we must be in York, she thought.

As her eyes and brain adjusted to the new surroundings, she saw steam coming from the front of the car. With a little hesitation, Lavender called out. Her mum's eyes flicked a fraction in the mirror to focus on its reflection.

"Mum, it's me, Lavender," she exclaimed in a much louder voice.

Her mum's eyes stayed focused in the same spot for a few seconds and then traced slowly around the car and to her side. Lavender turned her head to see what her mum was looking at. There at the driver's door, her father stood looking smart in a tan-brown and grey-checked sports jacket and carrying a "Yorkshire Post" newspaper.

Lavender banged her open palm hard on the window and called out, "Daddy, Daddy!" but he didn't respond.

Instead, he opened the car door and leant inside to talk to his wife.

"The newsagent told me there's a garage only ten minutes from here, near the train station. He kindly allowed me to use his phone to make a call and they are sending a man out in the next half an hour. I've told him where the car is, and I'll leave the key on the front wheel for him, so we can be on our way to the pub. Hopefully, we won't be too late," he continued, as he got into the car.

"Thank goodness," Mary said with relief, "I don't want this to spoil our honeymoon, now we are actually on our way after all these years."

It was clear to Lavender that she was no more than an observer of her parents. No matter how loud she shouted or how violently she tried to pull and push the back of her dad's seat, her parents were blissfully unaware of her presence. Mary put the lipstick into her handbag and rubbed her top and bottom lips together to massage the colour in.

"Will I do, Alex?" she asked, looking intently into his blue eyes.

"You'll do for me love, but we need to get moving. I'm not sure why you're going to all this effort when we're only going to see some oddball who's clearly after the family jewels," he replied, sceptically.

"You may be right, but there's no harm in being well presented, and at any rate, I've changed my mind, I'm leaving the amulet in the car just in case." Mary paused for a moment with a distant glazed look in her eyes, and then continued, "I just hope we can get a step closer to understanding the history of the amulets. There must be some link to them and the fate Aunt Margaret has told of Lavender and I."

Lavender felt her ears twitch with an alert awakening and she pinched her arm to check she was conscious.

What did Mum just say? she questioned herself.

"I know it's best to do all we can to protect her, but just because your Aunt Margaret sees something appearing on the horizon, doesn't mean it will come true," Alex replied, putting a comforting hand on Mary's.

"I know, you're right. But Aunt Margaret was so specific about this and she has been correct many times before. Why would she worry us if she wasn't sure?" Mary asked.

Lavender started to feel hot, and her head began spinning as she listened to her parents discussing her future.

"It still all seems like some disastrous fairytale to me, Mary, but I agree, we must do all we can to keep her safe, just in case. Pass me the map, I want to check where we are meeting this 'ere fella," Alex asked.

Mary reached into the glovebox, took out the town map and passed it to her husband to ponder.

After a short assessment, Alex looked up from the map. "Right, here you are, Mary," he said, folding the map back up and handing it to his wife.

"If we set off now, we won't be too late, and we should be able to get back to the car before the mechanic finishes," he continued.

They got out of the car, and Alex took the car key off his keyring. He checked no one was looking before placing it on the front driver's side wheel and they started towards the pub in the centre of the city.

At first, Lavender lagged behind, caught in shock and disbelief at what she had heard. Realising she would quickly lose sight of her parents she started to run, automatically shouting "Wait for me!" before remembering no one could hear her.

They wound their way past the medieval city walls. Walls that were first laid by Roman hands, then built upon by

Danish Vikings before their current and stable magnesia limestone incarnation.

Although she had visited many times before, Lavender always felt drawn to gaze in awe at every knotted, twisted beam that supported the topsy-turvy buildings on the way. However, on this occasion, she had an added sense of belonging that travelled up through the ground and into her body. With each step she took, the place became sharper and more vivid than reality, more detailed than she had sensed it before. It wasn't long before they turned near the Minster onto another ancient street and saw the black and gold sign for "Ye Olde Moon Inne" that spanned the buildings from one side of the street to the other.

The spring air was warm and clear, and the streets were filling with the rhythmic heel-clicking throng of pedestrian shoppers, visitors and workers. As Lavender's parents turned into the small alleyway below the sign and through to the courtyard entrance to the pub, the street sounds gave way to a new and growing hum. A cacophony of beer-loosened voices reverberated around the courtyard walls and crescendoed in the tobacco-smoked barroom air. Lavender's perceptions conflicted. A contrast in that her eyes were wide and her senses hyper-alert with such commotion, but at the same time, she felt safe, quiet and untouchable in her own observing, separate view.

Inside the pub was a main crowded barroom and several smaller "snugs" which were quieter. It was into one of these that they entered and took up a seat in a dark corner.

"I'll go and get us a drink and a menu, will you have the usual, Mary?" asked Lavender's dad.

Before Mary had the chance to answer, she noticed a lone figure sat in the opposite shadowy corner of the snug looking directly at her. As their eyes met, the man stood up and spoke, revealing a tall slim figure.

"Afternoon, the name's Isaac Scrubb. Would you by any chance be Mrs Bathwater?"

Mary and Alex squinted in the direction of the voice in front of them, still allowing their eyes to grow accustomed to the inside after the brilliance of the spring sunshine.

"Ahh, good afternoon, sir. Pleased to make your acquaintance, I'm Alex Bathwater, Mary's husband and this is Mary." Alex gestured to his wife and continued, "I'm sorry we are a little late, we have had some car trouble, though fortunately, a mechanic is on his way now to sort it out. I was just about to go to the bar and order drinks, could I get you one?"

Scrubb moved towards the chair opposite Mary, passing a small window that revealed his face clearly for the first time. Lavender was stood between them which meant he came within a few inches of her. As he neared Lavender, she let out a loud gasp as his features came into view. She recognised him immediately as the same man she had seen both in Robert's Park and in the cinema, though younger and a little less unkempt.

"A whisky and a dash of water please," Scrubb answered, as he sat down opposite Mary.

Lavender began to panic, I must warn them he is trouble, I must let them know somehow, she thought desperately, but how?

""Have you walked far from the car?" Scrubb asked, with apparent concern.

"No, not too far. We managed to park up at Clifford's Tower before the radiator boiled over. Anyway, I hope you will forgive me, Mr Scrubb, as I have left the amulet in the car. Having yet to make your acquaintance and given the value it may have, I decided to wait until we got to know each other before I brought it in person."

Mary was quite forthright in her approach to the man and had decided in advance that she would be cautious. She handed over a piece of paper she had used to rub over both sides of the amulet as a record.

"Here, perhaps you would be interested in this rubbing I made of it so that you may see it, if not in the flesh, so to speak."

Scrubb put on a pair of thick, black-framed reading glasses and examined it closely for a moment. He gave out a few noises indicating it was of interest such as umm and ahh and a clicking t, t, t, between his tongue and the roof of his mouth, as he put it closer to his eyes.

"Well, Mr Scrubb, what do you make of it?" Mary asked eagerly.

"It's hundreds of years since an amulet has been recorded so it would be quite miraculous if it was genuine. At any rate I would need to examine it, in the flesh as you say, to alleviate doubt. It does appear possible though that you have one of the Amulets of Brigantia in your possession. In fact, it looks like the Amulet of Union if I am not mistaken. Still, there is no telling from this rubbing if it is just a cheap token, forged to deceive. You will forgive my pessimism, therefore at the prospect of it being genuine." Scrubb removed his glasses as he finished speaking.

Lavender looked on and, with genuine concern for her parents' well-being, she put her arms around her mother's waist, locked them together and tried with all her might to pull her off the seat.

Mary had no doubt that the amulet was genuine. Whilst holding it, the object would glow with a warm radiating light. She would experience feelings and visions she had never had before. Still, despite this knowledge, she kept her own counsel. She had a peculiar feeling about the man that gnawed in her brain, and it said: "leave him well alone."

"I can understand you would be sceptical. Assuming what you say is true, how could anyone know what one of these amulets looked like, never mind whether it was the genuine article?"

Mary was testing Scrubb out and, after performing a slow scan of the room, his eyes turned back to Mary. He cleared his throat with a sound reminiscent of a dry, rusty key trying desperately to open a long since seized lock. Alex's timing was excellent as he returned from the main bar with a pint of best bitter, a whisky and a half a shandy.

"Sounds like you need a little lubrication, Mr Scrubb," Alex said, as he put the drinks down on the table.

Scrubb picked up his glass, rechecked the room and cleared his throat once more before taking a long drink. The whisky must have loosened his vocal cords.

"My grandfather would have been best placed to tell you, Mrs Bathwater, but I'm afraid he is long since passed. However, he left me with all his research on the Brigantes, including some detail on the amulets which allow me to verify its authenticity."

Scrubb was growing somewhat indignant in the tone of his reply.

"Nevertheless, Mr Scrubb, what is it that would prove an amulet to be a genuine Brigantian Amulet?"

Mary was not one to give up on a quest for information, especially from someone she felt could be best described as weaselling in their communication.

"Mrs Bathwater, trust me, my grandfather has had sight of genuine manuscripts from antiquity that describe both the amulets themselves and the manner in which they are used. He made records of the manuscripts whilst they were in the hands of a private collector."

Scrubb's response came with a barely concealed sigh which appeared to indicate an annoyance at the lack of trust in his authority on the matter. Mary looked at Alex, who was midway through a gulp of his beer.

"Perhaps you could explain how the amulets are to be used, as a way of building our mutual trust?" Mary's response with another question made Alex feel a little nervous at the direction the conversation was heading. He was stuck to his spot, his hand raised, with his glass placed to his lips, unable to contribute to the discussion. Her mother's response had also quite transfixed Lavender.When imagining her mother, she had not really thought of her as a determined and confident woman. Rather she was a safe place that she would be able to snuggle into if she felt unsafe. Scrubb sighed and rolled his dark eyes upwards and then down again.

"Listen …" he paused, as a couple of students walked past him on the way to the bar, and then continued, "If you let me see the amulet and take hold of it for a few minutes, then I'll share with you how it should be used."

Alex put his empty glass down on the table with a deliberate clunk and turned to Scrubb.

"If you would allow me a minute to consult with my wife?" he asked.

With a barely noticeable tip of his head on an otherwise expressionless face, Scrubb got up from the table and left the snug without uttering a single word. The manner of his exit was such that neither Alex nor Mary was sure if he was allowing them the requested minute, or if he had simply become tired of the persistence of Mary's approach.

"He was rather brusque, wasn't he? Do you think he's coming back?" said Mary, a little stunned by the odd character they had just met.

"He was definitely peculiar. Either way, I'm sure we'll find out soon enough if he's gone," Alex replied.

Despite Lavender's curiosity with the conversation her parents were having, she was far more inquisitive about the man they had met. After all, he was undoubtedly the villain who had accosted Fred in the back of the cinema and who had made a less than veiled threat if he didn't meet him, with the amulet, under the canal bridge.

For this reason, it was without further hesitation that she followed Scrubb out of the snug and into the main bar. She looked around the crowded and noisy room, at the throng of chattering voices, in search of the tall and striking figure of the man. The man who had moments before been sat with her parents, but now seemed to have disappeared into the busy room, or perhaps left. She weaved her way through the groups of people who stood drinking, engrossed in lively conversation, brushing invisibly past their oblivious bodies, all the while scanning the room for the man. Just as she was about to give up and turn back to the snug, a group of large well-dressed men standing in front of her parted company, revealing Scrubb. He was stood facing a cigarette machine with his back to Lavender. Scrubb pulled on the vending machine's chrome drawer and lifted out a packet of Players No.6 cigarettes and turned around, taking off the cellophane wrapper and opening the lid. For a second, he paused and looked ahead, right through Lavender, who took a moment to observe his features. His lips were purple and thin, crinkled into a broken halo as he drew the thick pub air through the cigarette. As the end glowed, his eyes illuminated in synchronicity as if some realisation had crossed his mind, he stretched his arm out with the open packet towards Lavender.

"Here, Elijah!" he said, offering a cigarette. "We only have a minute. You need to go down to Clifford's Tower car park. A mechanic is working on their car, and the amulet is in it somewhere." Scrubb spoke softly and urgently.

Lavender turned on the spot. Her eyes locked in disbelief at the man in front of her. It was if she were standing between the man and a mirror.

"I'll keep them here as long as I can, so hurry and if the mechanic says anything, just tell him you're Alex Bathwater, and you own the car," Scrubb continued.

Lavender was dumbfounded. The man had an identical brother called Elijah, and they were plotting to steal the amulet. Elijah looked hesitantly at his brother.

"Go on, move it you half-wit," Isaac barked at him.

Elijah jerked into action and immediately made his way towards the door. With little time to think, all her instincts screamed at Lavender to follow Elijah Scrubb back to the car. He carved a pathway through the bar and out into the courtyard.

The bright sunshine blinded Elijah for a moment as he bent down through the low doorway into the courtyard. It gave Lavender a chance to catch up before continuing with increasing pace through the cobbled and winding streets towards Clifford's Tower. He clearly knew the place well, moving without hesitation around the perfectly symmetrical grassy hill that the tower was built upon and into the car park. The Morris Minor came into view, parked with its bonnet open and a small, bald-headed man in green overalls bent over and peering into the engine compartment. Elijah stopped for a moment to catch his breath, putting his hands down on his knees for support and then pulled out a handkerchief from his pocket and mopped the sweat from his brow. He stood up straight again and slowly walked towards the car. In the meantime, Lavender continued to the car, desperate to open the passenger door to get inside and check the glovebox. Still, it was no use, her hand just passed through the chrome handle as if it were not there. Then in sudden realisation, she pushed herself through the door and put her hand into the glovebox to rummage blindly inside for the amulet. It was a futile exercise. She knew the glovebox's contents as she had already seen them. Her hand was just waving about in what felt like a void of emptiness, leaving her feeling powerless and desperate. She looked up through the windscreen to see Scrubb had reached the car and, as he did so, he called out nervously to the mechanic.

"Oh, hello there, I'm Alex Bathwater."

The mechanic jumped several inches off the ground in surprise, and if it had not been for his small stature would have bumped his head hard on the bonnet. He abruptly straightened his posture and turned to face Elijah.

"Oh, you made me jump out of my skin there, Mr Bathwater," he replied.

"I've just had to come back as I realised I left something in the car. How are you getting on with fixing it?" Elijah came across as genuine enough.

"If I don't get too many interruptions, I dare say the car will be ready by teatime!" The mechanic put his head back down under the bonnet and continued his work.

"I won't bother you further then," Elijah replied under his breath and with a sigh of relief.

He opened the driver's door and looked at the suitcases and bags in the back. It would take some time to search through the bags, so he decided to get in the driver's seat and reach over to the glovebox first. He pulled down the door and put his hand inside, pulling out the papers to reveal the amulet at the back. Lavender looked on helpless as he took the amulet from the glovebox and gazed in awe as it started to glow in the palm of his hand. Now he had no doubt this was one of the genuine Brigantian Amulets, lost for over five hundred years, or at least that is what he thought. Elijah started to feel increasingly hot. His body tensed until each muscle locked into cramps of iron. His hands clenching into fists and his eyes bulging almost out of their sockets.

Unknown to Lavender, who sat observing in rigid silence, Scrubb's mind had drifted entirely out of ordinary consciousness. He found himself taken onto a howling windswept moor with the rain lashing on his face. He stood next to his grandfather peering into a deep hole cut into the sodden heather half-submerged in water. He looked at his grandfather's eyes, recognising the intent he had at that moment to strike the man in the hole with the hand shovel he was carrying. Elijah became gripped with fear. He felt like the young child he had been, cowering in the corner of the third-floor room, waiting for a beating, pleading for his grandfather to stop, wishing him dead. Within seconds he was staring at the same amulet that he held tightly in his own hand and witnessing his grandfather's death. Elijah's body became limp.

The tension that had turned his muscles into iron had given way to softness, so lacking in substance that his body felt as though it would melt into the foot well of the car then beyond into the tarmac. In her own stillness, Lavender had watched his body turn limp and then in a sudden apparent fit, he threw the amulet back into the glovebox. He sat there for a moment with a vacant expression until, with no apparent explanation, he reached into his pockets in search of something. Eventually, he pulled out a pen and a serviette and began drawing on the paper in hasty yet systematic precision. Lavender stared at him and then at the serviette. He was barely even looking at the paper as he drew, yet his drawing was a detailed and clear representation of the Brigden area and the surrounding Goddodin moors. In no time at all his appointed task was complete. After discarding the serviette on the seat, he immediately jumped out of the car with a blank expression on his face, and then fled as if his life depended on it. She watched through the open driver's door as he disappeared out of sight, and the mechanic stood aghast as he watched the man running away from the car.

"Well, I'll be damned!" he exclaimed to himself.

Lavender was equally dumbstruck. *What on earth just happened?* she thought to herself and then out of the blue came the answer to a very different question. Two pointy ears and then a head with large green eyes popped up by the door sill and then sprang up on to the seat beside Lavender.

"Delius!" Lavender exclaimed, "So that's where you've come from."

As if to prove his identity, the cat opened its mouth to meow, but no sound came out. He then rubbed his soft face on Lavender's hand and began purring. She closed her eyes for a moment listening with comfort to Delius's deep purring, then opened them to see the filtered orange glow of the streetlight through the curtains of the small back bedroom window of Pear

Tree Cottage, Delius on the pillow beside her sleeping peacefully.

Chapter Fifteen

Canal Bridge

Grandad crept down the stairs as gently as he could, feeling the same stiffness in his bones that the oak beams and floorboards of Pear Tree Cottage expressed, with a crack at this turn and a creak at another. It was a familiar and comforting sound to wake up to. This was the cottage's voice that greeted Lavender each morning grandad was home, a personal welcome as if waking to a whispering parent.

Before opening her eyes, it took a little time to determine what day it was. Even with the familiarity of the sounds, for several minutes she doubted whether it was morning or evening. Lavender felt that so much had happened since going to the pictures the night before; it was more like a week had passed by, not just a night in bed. In her mind, rather than the fading details that softened and blurred with the passage of time, her mother and father's faces were clearer than they had ever been before. She could feel with a growing expanse in her heart that they were not dead and gone, but alive somehow, somewhere and she would always be connected to them. She noticed a now familiar feeling in her hand, the amulets were tingling in her palm, so her first vision of the day was to check their presence. Her eyes focused on them, and she suddenly remembered Fred's meeting with the Scrubb man and the arrangement to go from school to Alice's house where it was only a short distance to the canal bridge. The thought spurred her relaxed body out of the warmth of her soft bed and into action, placing the amulets back in their small box. She was washed, dressed and downstairs at the kitchen table and in no time at all, digging into a boiled egg with enthusiasm. Grandad felt intrigued by her energy and looked up from his newspaper.

"You're eager this morning, lass, are you wanting another ride in the lorry?" grandad asked.

"I don't think I have time today, Grandad, I'm meeting Fred and Alice before school."

"Well, I suppose I'll just have to navigate myself then unless you want a lift?" he replied, with a smile.

"Oh, that would be great, Grandad. I just need to get something from upstairs, and I'll be ready," she answered enthusiastically, jumping up from the kitchen table.

"Ee, that lass is a wick 'un, Arthur," grandma observed.

She had a reflective gaze that conveyed to her husband more than just a simple statement, but a reminiscence of their lost daughter's youthful days.

"She is that, Annie, she is that."

Lavender ran back up the staircase and took the amulet from the safekeeping of the box on her bedside table. She stopped for a second, taking in the details of its symbol and considering briefly whether or not she should be taking it. Her moment of doubt passed as quickly as it came when the amulet's circles appeared to turn in opposite directions. It warmed again in her hand as if to let her intuition know the right thing to do.

Lavender met Fred and Alice as usual on the roundabout in the park opposite Albert Road school, where the air continued to hang thick with a fog that held the whole valley in an ethereal cloud world of horizonless, groundless grey and muffled sound. The fog was so dense that both Lavender and Alice had taken torches with them to school. Had it not been for their intimate knowledge of the town, they would most certainly have got lost in the motionless air.

After Fred's encounter with the strange man the previous night, they had all struggled to sleep with their worrying thoughts running through their minds. But as they sat huddled together on the slowly rotating roundabout, they became eager to share their ideas of what should be done. "In all my years, I've never seen fog this thick before!" announced Fred, as if he were a worldly man of advanced age and experience.

"How old are you, Fred?" said Alice, joking at his statement.

"I won't be getting much older if we can't think of a plan for tonight," Fred replied, maintaining his serious demeanour. "The thing is, last night I dreamed about your parents and the man in the cinema," he continued.

"I don't believe it! So did I. And the Morris Minor and the amulet!" exclaimed Lavender.

"Oh, for goodness sake, I'm feeling a bit left out here. Why do you two always get to do the fun stuff together!" Alice interrupted.

"Well maybe you need to have a hold of the Amulet of Dreams, Alice." Lavender suggested.

"If it means I won't miss out anymore, count me in," Alice replied eagerly.

Fred pushed the roundabout a little with the casual intent of moving the conversation on. The fog swirled a little as it turned.

"So, Fred, tell us about your dream," Lavender enquired.

Well, I was sat with your mum and dad in the snug of "Ye Olde Moon Inne." They discussed what to do about showing someone the amulet when the man who threatened me in the cinema last night came in and sat with them. He was Isaac Scrubb, the man who they had arranged to meet. Your dad told him that they would take him to see the amulet if he could share something of worth regarding the Brigantees. He had quite a smug smile on his face when they agreed, and he brought out an old notebook showing sketches of symbols. They were types of amulets, all with a circle but different patterns in them. He said they held great power separately, but together they could protect a whole nation. He started rambling on about the lost Venetius Stone and that it was supposed to be a hallowed healing place. Your mum had the strangest reaction to what he said next. She went white as a sheet and leant over to whisper something to your dad. For a while they looked at each other and then he gave her a barely noticeable nod."

"What did Isaac say that was so special?" Lavender asked.

Fred paused for a while to search his memory, then when he tried to speak, he stumbled on his words. "Come on,

Fred, this is really important, what did he say?" Lavender repeated urgently.

"He said, 'To open the lock you'll need …' Umm err. Oh no that's not right." Fred's thoughts stumbled again as he spoke.

"You'll need what to open the lock?" Lavender asked, with increasing volume and speed.

Fred's frustration was obvious to Alice. "Shh, Lavender, let him think," she said.

There was a slowing squeak from the roundabout, repeating as if the seconds were ticking by, timing the function of Fred's brain.

"I've got it!" he exclaimed, "To find the key, you'll need two locks, fix them together, and the gate will open."

"But that doesn't make any sense," said Alice in frustration.

"Before I knew it, your mum jumped straight up out of her seat and with wide eyes and an urgent expression said, 'I will go back to the car and fetch the amulet. Alex can wait here with you, Mr Scrubb.' The weird thing was that Snowzell neither did nor said anything, he just sat there calmly with a wry smile on his face. I chased after, trying to follow your mum, but it was no use, I lost her in the narrow streets."

There was a noticeable silence as if all the clocks in the world and everything in it had stopped. Even the roundabout had run out of momentum, and the intermittent squeak it made was now just a memory echoing in the foggy air. Lavender sighed a long, deep sigh. She described the vision she had of her parents encounter in great detail, now with the added dimension of tying together the perspective of Tom's dream.

"I am missing out, aren't I?" said Alice, with a genuine sense of being overlooked.

"Well, as someone observing the situation, what do you make of it?" Lavender asked.

Among her many traits, Alice possessed a sceptical nature and a droll sense of humour. She was also known for her analytical mind, which now appeared to whirr into action as she stared into the fog searching for some eureka moment.

"There are three main things that immediately come to me," Alice announced, but without going further left them hanging in eager anticipation.

Fred and Lavender looked blankly at one another.

"Well, what are they?" they asked in curious union.

"First, we can't be sure which Scrubb brother threatened you, Fred, but it is most likely to be Isaac. I say this because Elijah Scrubb's reaction to holding the amulet in the car doesn't sound great. It suggests to me that whatever happened to him could well happen again. As he ran from the scene and left the amulet, he is unlikely to seek a repeat of the experience. Secondly, whatever happened to Elijah when he held the amulet may happen to his twin brother too. That means Fred probably has little to fear if he meets him, as long as Isaac holds the amulet immediately, so I would place it in his open palm when you give it to him. Third, we must be living in the centre of what was and still is a place of mystical power. The answer must be close by. Just before your parents vanished they must have discovered something important, and it sounds like Isaac Scrubb gave them a clue."

Alice stepped off the roundabout as she finished her clinical analysis and bumped her two contemplative friends from their thoughts with a reminder that school was about to start.

"So, you think I should just meet that horrible Scrubb fella at the canal bridge tonight and give him the amulet then?" said Fred less than enthusiastically.

They started to edge their way across the fog blanketed park.

"We can be there too, can't we, Lavender, and anyway, what's the worst that can happen?" Alice replied calmly.

"I could end up dead in the canal, and he could escape with the amulet. He could even be watching us now," Fred whispered catastrophically.

"We'll be there to save you, Fred, and anyway he's not going to do anything with us all being together," Lavender reassured.

As they continued across the park, they finalised their plans for the meeting.

It wasn't long before they had reached the security of the Belisha beacons that emerged, with alternating flashing, in a faint but reassuring yellow glow at the school crossing.

"Thank goodness it's Friday, we have so much to do this weekend we don't have time for school," said Alice, as they switched off their torches and entered the school gates.

The fog had lifted slightly during the day, but by the time the final school bell rang at 3.45 pm, and the three friends made their way back out of the black iron school gates, it had returned with a vengeance.

"This fog is driving me crazy," said Lavender, as they worked their way along the final stretch of Alice's street.

The row of stone terraced houses stood as straightforward and modest monuments to the generations of mill workers who had previously inhabited them.

"We might be thankful for it tonight, Lav, it may well be a help to us with our plan," said Alice positively.

Alice's mum was waiting for the children when they opened the door

"Hello, you three, I was beginning to get worried you had got lost in this fog. I know it's fish supper tonight, so as I've some freshly baked flapjack that will keep you going."

Mrs Sutton announced her homemade baking enthusiastically while ushering the three of them into the kitchen. They removed their coats and school bags and sat their unencumbered bodies down at the table in the kitchen. There were already three glasses of warm banana-flavoured milkshake waiting.

"How are you getting home tonight, you two?" Mrs Sutton asked Lavender and Fred, a little concerned about the fog.

"Fred and I will walk together. We're both going to the fish shop for supper on the way home," Lavender said, reciting a selected part of the plan that the three of them had concocted.

It would be easy to meet Isacc Scrubb at canal bridge, without anyone knowing, as it was on the way back to the fish shop and Pear Tree Cottage. "Well just you take care in all this fog, anything could be lurking in it, and you'd never know."

Mrs Sutton's words were more accurate than she could have realised. They did little to improve Fred's underlying reluctance to proceed with the plan. He felt a twinge in his stomach, and his knees turned into what felt like raspberry jelly as his imagination flitted between notions of being throttled or thrown in the murky canal.

"Aye, maybe we should get a lift, you can't be too sure," Fred blurted out, with a pale look on his face.

"Are you feeling alright, Fred? You've gone white as a sheet," Mrs Sutton asked with concern.

Lavender and Alice gave Fred a direct stare, clearly designed to get him to rethink his statement.

"Err, I'm alright, Mrs Sutton, I think someone just walked over my grave."

He paused after his reply, as his body gave a head-to-toe shiver, and then he continued with a little more composure and a reinforcing nod from Alice.

"We have our torches with us, and maybe Alice could walk with us as far as the canal, Mrs Sutton?" Fred asked.

Mrs Sutton looked over to Alice, who was in mid-nod and with a mouthful of flapjack.

"You lot are like the three Musketeers aren't you. Go on then but mind your step in this here fog won't you," she instructed maternally.

"We will," they replied in unison, as if living up to Mrs Sutton's musketeer comparison.

After they had finished their drinks and flapjack, the three friends left Mrs Sutton in the kitchen and went to sit on the thick handwoven rug that lay in front of the open fire in the sitting room. Not one of them could even contemplate their normal playful activities or conversations. Instead, they sat together in a semi-circle, gazing into the fire, supposing the events of what may lie ahead. Time seemed to drag between 4.30 pm and 5.30 pm. The minute hand of the mantlepiece clock brushed laboriously by each Roman numeral of its face, and in its final climb to six o'clock, each tick became louder and faster in Fred's ear until it was finally time to be on their way.

"Come on then, you two, we can do this," Alice announced with a motivating call, breaking Fred's tranced stare.

They crossed the doorstep and stepped outside into the air that was just as dense and grey. Beyond the vague shading of a car parked some six feet in front of them, no apparent features of the street could be seen. Only the nearest streetlight gave assistance to guide their direction, with a blotching amber glow.

"Straight there and back mind you, Alice, and Lavender, get your grandma to give me a ring when you get home, let me know you are alright," Mrs Sutton instructed, as they disappeared into the soup.

"OK!" they shouted back together, before pulling up their hoods to keep out the cold and damp.

"I'm not even sure he will come tonight, what with this fog," Fred said with a degree of hopefulness in his voice.

"Well, we must carry on as if he is. Here take the amulet and remember, make sure he gets a hold of it straight away," Lavender replied, passing him the valuable article.

Despite the lack of visibility, it wasn't long before they had reached the long dark steps that led from the road, down the side of the canal bridge, to the towpath. They peered into the dank and foggy stairwell constructed of dark solid stone steps and sandwiched between massive Victorian walls. In the light of the clear morning sky, these same walls appeared with green hues, coated with lichen, liverwort and algae that softened the stone's smog-crusted grit. Still, tonight as their torches flickered over the steps to guide them, it was the feel of the walls that conveyed their structure.

Fred led the way stepping carefully over the damp slippy steps, then stopping halfway down he turned his head around to face the others.

"I feel like I'm entering a bottomless pit to Hell," he whispered.

"Oh, Fred, don't be so dramatic, we've been down these steps a thousand times before and anyway, it's far too cold to be Hell," Alice replied.

Lavender remained quiet. She placed her hand gently on Fred's shoulder, reassuringly encouraging him downwards, deeper into the gloom, whilst at the same time steadying herself from slipping.

Although Lavender hadn't spoken, Fred could hear her thoughts whispering in his mind, *we are together, and together we are strong.* Suddenly, a confident shiver tingled in his neck and spiralled helter-skelter down his spine, then left his body with a satisfying shudder as he cast off the last of his reluctance.

"Let's do this," he said convincingly, and holding the amulet tight in his pocket, he moved forward with a steely resolve.

At the bottom of the steps, the air felt even cooler and moved the fog slowly from under the bridge and across the path towards the children. It allowed some sporadic increases of visibility, burnished by the amber-orange glow of the streetlamps on the road above, at times revealing the arch of the bridge and the towpath underneath.

Lavender and Alice were about to separate, as they had planned to do, when they all briefly noticed a shadow in the fog through the bridge. Without hesitation, Fred gently pushed them back and into hiding in the shrubs and rough ground at the side of the towpath.

"Wait here. I'll be alright," he whispered, with a calm softness.

He pulled his hood down to improve his senses, noticing the muffled slow crunching of footsteps walking towards the bridge. Moving forward towards them, the previous quaking fear that had weakened Fred so easily when contemplating this moment had now evaporated into the mist. As he reached the underside of the bridge, he imagined that his previous doubts would drift in the air and infect his shadowy foe with a paralysing grip.

A voice unmistakable to Fred, echoed under the bridge, amplified by the curving stones into a cavernous bellowing and now accompanied by the silhouetted body of Isaac Scrubb.

"Stop there, sonny! Not another step."

Chapter Sixteen

The Old Sea Chest

A week before he accosted Fred in the Cavendish Picture
House, Isaac Scrubb had abruptly jumped up from his bed
where he had laid incapable of sleep.

Previously that evening, Isaac had gone to bed feeling
very old. His aching bones were causing him a dull,
bothersome pain just from sitting is his armchair.
Consequently, he considered that he would be more
comfortable in bed and therefore retired early for the night. As
he lay in the darkness of his room, the wind outside began to
strengthen, rattling the ill-maintained windows intermittently,
annoying and agitating his mind with each irritating clatter The
whistling air pitched itself through the gaps in the window
frame, like a ghoulish master calling its dog, further stirring his
thoughts into action. Memories drifted back to his
grandfather's mysterious disappearance, and he recalled in
anguish how, in the period after his vanishing, Isaac and his
brother Elijah had searched the house for clues to where his
grandfather may be. In his dressing table drawer, they had
found a large iron key in the shape of a T-bar and as big as the

palm of his hand. His grandmother's clothes and lock of hair that always lay on the bed had gone. He remembered that they had found the address of Thomas Gill in a letter to his grandfather, and this had led Isaac and his brother to go to The Turk's Head Inn in Brigden, searching for more clues. They had sat outside the inn after it had closed that night, listening intently at the large green doors. There was a lady inside talking to herself who they struggled to hear, only catching snippets of words, but enough to raise their interest in the topic and send them running to the rear of the inn when the talking moved further inside. As they reached the lit window of the back of the inn, they were just in time to overhear more clearly some worrying information from within: Thomas had died mysteriously. From that moment, they feared that their grandfather had something to do with his death.

The wind outside became stronger and more erratic, bringing Isaac back to the present moment with quite a jolt. Not only was it whistling and rattling at the windows as though someone was trying to enter, but the curtains were blowing out into the room. Even the walls and roof of the timber-frame house creaked and bent perceptibly.

Isaac's own accumulated discoveries were turning over increasingly fast in his brain. He knew there was an unworldly power in the amulets and that his weak brother had missed the opportunity he had created to take one. He also knew that the most sacred place in all of ancient Brigantia, the Venetius Stone had existed somewhere in Brigden. His grandfather's beliefs remained untested and the most intriguing of these tormented and tantalised; the idea that a lock of hair, weaved with one's own could reunite even a long deceased relative, but where was the lock of his grandmother's hair? Since his grandfather had disappeared the hair had gone, and so too had her clothes.

With an abrupt and frightening clatter, the windows suddenly burst open, banging into the walls and sending the curtains fluttering into the room as a flag on a mast, cracking furiously in a storm. The whistling had stopped, replaced by a force of cold wet air that quite vividly placed Isaac onto what felt like the deck of a galleon ship. A burst of inspiration came over him with the feeling, unlocking previously unconnected memories from the deepest recesses of his mind. He jumped out of bed to close the window and make his way up the narrow staircase of 10 The Cringles. The medieval house had an attic crammed full of ancestral relics: An ecclectic mix of paraphernalia that to Isacc's blinded habitual eye was no more than a conglomeration of junk. Still, now he was seeing it all through a new lens. He began searching amongst the clutter for the old sea chest that was, by his grandfather's account, an heirloom of his grandmother's family. It had languished there, hidden for several decades, undisturbed and forgotten, though now the whole house felt like a ship and seemed to be calling Isaac towards it.

Generations of dust were shaken into the claustrophobic air as Isaac rummaged eagerly through the attic. The dead grey remnants reanimated to drift aimlessly until they eventually rested, silently, on some other dormant article. As his eyes followed the settling dust they were drawn to the back corner of the room where, as if he had discovered buried pirates' treasure, it was revealed.

The sea chest was substantial, measuring about three feet wide, by one and a half feet tall and one and a half feet deep. Made from sheet iron, it was painted in a bronze colour and overlaid with intersecting and reinforcing straps. Isaac paused for a moment to consider what was in front of his eyes.

Why had he not thought of this before? How on earth did it get here? Where did it come from? It must have taken at least three strong men to carry it up the stairs.

He examined the casing for a lever or handle to open it, but he couldn't see one. In the front and centre of the chest was a keyhole and the lid protruded over the side, providing a lip to lift it open. He pulled hard on the lid, but the chest was locked tight.

He had not thought about it for so long, but now the key he had found after his grandfather had vanished was making another appearance in his mind. Surely it must be the one that fits the chest. Without hesitation, he climbed down the staircase and retrieved the key from the sideboard in the front room where he had placed it all those decades ago, waiting to be reacquainted with its rightful lock.

Isaac was quite out of breath by the time he had returned to the chest, but despite the exercise, his bones were no longer aching and his focus was locked entirely on what he may discover.

He knelt on the bare floorboards and pushed the key into the lock. It fitted perfectly. Slowly he turned the key, waiting, listening for a suitably distinct click, but there was nothing. The large key, which in effect became a handle for the chest simply circled in the hole. There was no engagement with a mechanism, no clicking or clunking within. He let go of the key, then in desperation tried turning it the opposite way. Nothing happened. Isaac pulled the key from the lock and stood up in frustration. He didn't understand. The key seemed perfect for the lock, yet it was doing nothing. Maybe the mechanism had failed with age. Could there be another key?

He settled down on the lid of the chest to ponder how to break into it and as he did so, something felt loose under his bottom. He stood up again quickly and examined the lid of the chest, rubbing his hand over a rivet in the centre where he had been sat. The rivet was one of a pattern across the iron straps of the lid. It felt loose and with a little agitation it rotated out to reveal another hole like the one on the front of the chest. Isaac took the key and placed it in the secret hole he had discovered and as before turned it tentatively clockwise. This time though there was a clear engagement in the action. The movement below could be felt with a discernable click through the key as the lid of the chest was released.

It was incredibly heavy and creaked grudgingly as Isaac lifted it open and then gasped in surprise at what was inside, something he had not seen for so long.

He had forgotten exactly what they looked like, but upon seeing them again, Isaac immediately recognised his grandmother's clothes, the same ones that lay next to his grandfather as he slept each night. Taking out the neatly folded clothes, he placed them carefully on the floor beside the chest and continued his search. Next was an assortment of large ships' logs, brown with age and tattered at the edges, as well as other nautical paraphernalia. He took out each item one by one, placing them next to the clothes until he revealed a wooden box that was an exact miniature, in form, of the sea chest. Just like the sea chest, it had a T-bar key in its lid. Even the pattern of straps was carved into the box with the same detail. He lifted the box out, turned the key in the lid and prised it open. Inside was a lock of fading red hair held together with twine and sat on top of a slim black book. He removed the hair and took out the book. As soon as he opened the book cover, the wind stopped outside. The house, which moments before had been alive with rattling and whistling, was still again. Isaac began to read:

"Mother Fortune

Mother Fortune built her home,
Upon that old Venetius Stone.
Bow of ship made strong the frame,
On walls broad thick and steadfast lain.

Pillars now craft the great fireplace
And sick no more traverse the space

Disguised twixt room and chimney back
The lintel stone will never crack

Here she slept on hallowed earth
Old Mother Fortune then gave birth
To triplet sons of mirrored face
Thrice born on lowly fireplace

Then in her prime she began to write
Prophesies that came at dead of night
Of mayhem, madness and darkest grief
Of magic and wonder beyond belief

For thirteen years her sons grew strong
But Mother Fortune then passed on,
And in her place a pear tree tall
Was planted 'gainst the cottage wall

Now all that passing folk may see
Is humble home, no dynasty,
Yet still there lies within its bounds
A force now dormant to be found.

In the year of our Lord 1699

Isaac was transfixed, his eyes glazed over as he reached the last line and then in haste he returned to the beginning and read again, this time out loud, as if hearing the words echo around the attic would make them even more real. He turned the page, revealing a skilled hand-drawn sketch of a cottage with a tree as tall as the roof growing against the front wall, hanging with pears. Immediately it all became clear. The Venetius Stone was still standing and hiding in plain sight. A cottage had been built around it and now disguised it from curious eyes. Was it possible that he had seen the same building? He had visited Brigden many times over the years in search of the illusive stone and to unravel the mystery of his grandfather's disappearance, so knew it well. The picture of the cottage was just too familiar to ignore and resembled in detail the well-known landmark at the centre of the town. But who was Mother Fortune and what were her prophesies? Was she a distant relative? He looked back at the book and turned the next page in the hope of learning more.

"A tale of the soothsayer's dream

Since I lay upon hallowed ground
The ages secrets I have found
In morrow's nature, I clearly dreamt
Too many disasters to lament

The innocent men of ages hast
Spirit upon the world to cast
'Til his boastful mortal frame
Believed the tiger he could tame

And thus now man cannot see
Nature's great ability
The whole is made of counter sides
One of truth and one of lies

Good and bad cannot exist
Without the arm there is no wrist
Gold alone will never reign
Without the silver's lesser vein

And while the will to be a master
Of nature may end in man's disaster
There is a chance that he may see

When he lets go then he is free

But slumber's illusion conceals the way
With false reward the soul will lay
No counterbalance, the scales will tip
To prosperous dungeons, a wealthy whip

A world of soulless blinded men
And shining servants thy could not ken
Through the air man will glide
To unknown lands beyond our tide

And thoughts will flash across the sky
In a twinkling of the eye
Hundreds, thousands hear you talk
Yet to thy neighbours thou does not walk

The struggle of man shall haunt the earth
And every creature that gave birth
'Till wives no more will bear a child
And marriage's lost to lovers wild

Feasts a plenty there will be

But still there's starving bended knee
The seed from which our hands are born
Knows not the path to Hell forlorn

So, heed this warning lest ye forget
And know futures plan is yet to set
There is a chance that ye may see
When ye let go, then ye are free."

And so it was that Isaac failed to sleep at all that night. As the hours of darkness ticked by and his thoughts connected, Isaac formulated a plan. He would revisit Brigden and stake out the cottage for an opportune time when he could break in and see for himself. He had his grandmother's lock of hair from the sea chest that he could tie to his own. If he could only obtain the Amulet of Union, he would have all he needed to traverse the stone.

When the first rays of sunlight clipped the rooftops opposite, piercing the bedroom window, Isaac finally fell asleep. Consequently, it wasn't until the early afternoon that he woke and leapt eagerly out of bed to pursue the intention he had now so clearly formed. After gathering himself a small case of clothes, some important papers, including the black book he had found in the sea chest, and the lock of hair, he phoned ahead to The Turk's Head Inn and booked a room. Within thirty minutes Isaac had made his preparations and stepped outside into The Cringles, closing the door behind him to set off for Brigden.

A peculiar feeling of conviction washed over him as the door wedged firm in its medieval frame, gently rattling the windows. Before him he could see patterns in the cobblestones, reminiscent of footprints in a muddy field. He had not a shred of doubt that they were the impressions left by his grandfather's feet as he left for the final time. Now his footsteps fell on the same cobblestones, treading the exact same steps.

Chapter Seventeen

Return to Brigden

The bustle of Saturday shopping was just about over, and the cold, still winter air had started to thicken with a thin blanket of snow clouds that hinted at a white world to come. Isaac pulled up his coat collar as he walked along Brigden High Street and considered whether he should head straight towards the inn. He had a little time to spare before the bar of the inn opened and so, as it was not far out of his way, he decided to walk past the old cottage with the pear tree before the last of the pale winter light departed.

As he turned the corner onto Bridge Street, the quaint building stood before him like an artist's dream of a fairytale cottage, and the peripheral surroundings blurred away. A low stone wall topped with a half-height white picket fence neatly surrounded the building. The cottage was decorated at the front by the beauty of stripped bare pear tree branches that seemed to call him forward, yet at the same time stopped him dead in his tracks. He pulled out the slim black book and turned the pages to the drawing of a cottage inside. It was an incredible likeness. Despite the fact that the drawing may have been nearly three-hundred years old, the only differences he could see were the size and shape of the pear tree and a new chimney pot with a veiled ribbon of brown smoke slipping up into the sky. Isaac mulled over his plan.

I must get inside and see. I'm so close I can feel it, he thought.

Had it not been for the sudden and rather loud sound of a motorcycle, mounted with an overly round shaped elderly lady, he may well have remained there for some time. But a backfire of the engine as it sped up around the corner shook him from his intentions and sent him into an about turn towards the high street.

By the time he arrived at The Turk's Head Inn, the clouds were lowering into a soft, heavy white blanket that enveloped the whole valley. The lack of sleep from the previous night and the excitement of his discovery had hit him quite suddenly on the last few yards of his journey. It made the warm glow of lights inside the inn quite seducing and offered the prospect of a comfortable rest for Isaac's fatigued body.

For the first time, Isaac noticed the polished brass sign above the inn door which read, "Samuel Gill. Licensed to sell all intoxicating liquor on or off the premises".

As he approached the front doors, a large thick-set man with wavy ginger hair, and a moustache of considerable thickness to match his heavy bones, was lifting the bottom door bolts to open them. He pushed them across to their open position and pulled one door inwards then stood up. In front of him was the tall, grey, dreary looking figure of Isaac Scrubb, adorned with his heavy trench coat that hung upon him like a shabby garment on a coat peg. His face was gaunt and drawn in at the cheeks and framed with long dull hair.

"By 'eck. You're eager aren't you. You're on to me before mi breeches are down!" the man said.

"The name's Scrubb. I have a room booked for a few nights. It's been a long day and I wondered if it was available now?" Isaac replied.

"Aye, I dare say, Mr Scrubb. My name's Sam, I'm t'landlord tha knows. Just give me five minutes to get t'bar open and I'll get our lass to show you up to your room. Would you like a drink first, you look like you need one?" Sam asked, opening the other door and ushering Isaac inside.

"A whisky would be nice, straight," Isaac replied, making his way into the main bar and sitting down on one of the more comfortable seats near the famous Inglenook fire.

The fireplace was an original feature of the inn and well known. Historians had discovered with great interest that, during the time of the dissolution of the monasteries, fleeing monks had used what was a secret tunnel behind it as a hiding place from the King's men. He put his small case on an adjacent chair and gazed into the fire, captivated by his thoughts of its long history, while Sam continued preparing the bar for the evenings business.

"Give me a couple of minutes," Sam replied, though Isaac seemed not to hear him as his face warmed from the radiant heat.

The long fruitless search for the elusive amulets was now preying on Isaacs mind. *If I have finally found the location of the Venetius Stone, what use is it to me without the Amulet of Union?* he thought.

Isaac had been back to Brigden in search of the amulet several years earlier. It had been the day after he met Mary and Alex Bathwater in York, but he had hit a brick wall with their disappearance. No one was at home in their old house on the other side of town and the neighbours had been under the impression that the Bathwaters were away on a belated honeymoon. He had returned again the next month but still there was no sign of them. It was at this point that he had presumed they had left the area altogether and consequently given up his search. Maybe it was worth asking some more questions just in case. Sam came across to him from the bar with a glass of whisky.

"Here you go, Mr Scrubb, I'm sure you're ready for this," he said, handing Isaac the whisky.

"I am that. A blind man would be glad to see it!" Isaac replied, with a wink.

Sam laughed and patted him on the shoulder as he warmed to Isaac's unexpected humour.

"What brings you to Brigden?" Sam asked curiously.

Isaac stared back into the fire for a moment considering the enquiry, then turned and looked up at the landlord.

"I'm seeking the whereabouts of Alex and Mary Bathwater. I don't suppose you know them or where they are living now?"

"There's many a folk around here who'd like to know that I dare say. It were a rum do them goin' missin' an all."

Sam stroked his moustache downwards and then rubbed his hand across his chin as he pondered his own statement.

"So, they didn't move from the area then?" Isaac asked.

"No one knows what 'appened to 'em since they vanished. Their poor little lass Lavender. Losing both her mother and father so mysteriously, what a tragedy. The whole town talked of nothing else for the first year." Sam shook his head, still in a state of disbelief at the thought of it all.

"Do you know where they were last seen?" Isaac asked eagerly.

Sam was curious about Isaacs keen enquiry into the subject and looked him straight in the eyes.

"Why are you so interested then, Mr Scrubb? Did you know them?" he asked bluntly.

For a moment, Isaac became uneasy and hesitated. A feeling passed through his body suggesting that somehow Sam had seen into his mind.

"We had a mutual interest in the Brigantes and shared some information years ago. It would have been nice to catch up," Isaac revealed, in hope of satisfying the enquiry.

"Well, tha'll not get a chance now. They were last seen outside their mother and father's house, where they left the car. It must be six years ago now. Such an odd thing with them supposed to be away on their honeymoon and all."

The front doors swung open with a chilly blast of air from outside, breaking their conversation. Entering with the cold was an elderly gentleman, bent over at a virtual right angle and propped up with a stick.

"Cathy, Albert's here already!"

Sam turned and headed towards the bar calling out to a healthy-looking, middle-aged woman with glowing cheeks and a broad smile who had just popped her head up behind the beer pumps.

"Don't fret thisen, Sam, the mild's primed and ready," she replied.

"You can see why I married her can't you," Sam quipped.

Isaac drew him back to the previous topic.

"Perhaps you could tell me where their parents' house is so I may call in on them," Isaac asked.

"Pear Tree Cottage on Bridge Street. You can't miss it. Oh, and when you're ready to retire, take the door marked "Private" on the left-hand side of the bar and up the staircase. Your room is number two at the front and already made up for you."

It wasn't long before the warm bar started to fill with the lively cackle of voices you would expect on a cold Saturday evening, and within an hour Isaac decided he needed some peace and made his way up to his room for the evening.

In the wee small hours of the morning, when the lively hum of voices and clinking glasses had long since given way to a muffling peaceful winter's night, Isaac broke into a sweat. He had tossed and turned in the unfamiliar inn bed with its cast iron frame and lumpy mattress. The dream he was having was more like a continuation of the previous days thoughts and saw him hiding in the dark shadows on Bridge Street staring at Pear Tree Cottage. In a turn to the left he rolled onto his back pressing into an annoyingly uncomfortable lump that felt about the size of an orange between his shoulder blades. He woke abruptly and the dream dissolved into the cold air of the room leaving him again with cycling anticipating thoughts. After some time, the brilliant moonlight beckoned to him. It was magnified by the pure white snow and reflected through the rooms inadequate curtains.

I may as well go out and see for myself as lay here, he thought.

Navigating his way to the back door of the inn was easier than he had thought it might be. The kitchen was at the rear of the inn with a door leading out into the backyard and alley beyond. Fortunately, the key was in the lock and with an undoing of the bolts, Isaac was soon stood in the alley. The scene was very familiar to him, returning his mind to his last visit with his brother at fourteen years of age. Yet at the same time, the snow added an otherworldliness to it and a sense that this could all be a dream.

There were two ways to get to Bridge Street of similar distance from the inn. The first was along the main road and then to turn into Bridge Street from the square. Via this route, Pear Tree Cottage presented itself directly in front of one's view, just as he had seen it yesterday. The second was to take Fairfax Street, a smaller road whose junction was at the top end of Bridge Street near to Fred Keighley's butcher's shop. Isaac opted to take the Fairfax Street route as it was more discreet, offering narrower ginnels and snickets between buildings that he may hide in. The town was especially peaceful. Decorated with a blanket of fresh snow it was in complete contrast to the previous afternoons dirty bustle of vehicles and shoppers. He made his way past St Paul's Church and up Fairfax, here he turned the corner into Bridge Street and headed towards Pear Tree Cottage at the other end. As Isaac crossed the road just before Fred Keighley's butchers, he caught a flash of movement. Stopping for a moment he saw a tabby cat sat in the snow ahead, halfway between him and the cottage. He was about to continue when a young girl appeared from the gate of the cottage. She stopped to look up and Isaac moved into the shadows watching as she turned to walk towards him.

That must be the Bathwater's daughter Lavender. Whatever is she doing out in the middle of the night and in this weather too? he thought, and then concealing himself further, he moved into the snicket at the side of the butcher's shop and waited.

Before long, he heard footsteps crunching softly in the snow towards him and the sounds of snowballs being thrown up at the butcher's window, followed by a faint groan and a thud. He moved forward a little to peer through the entrance of the snicket and saw a paper aeroplane silently glide down through the clear crisp moonlit air and spiral into Lavender's grasp. As she opened it, Isaac could sense the message it might contain and retreated further into the snicket. Strangely, he felt somewhat cornered. What if the person delivering the aeroplane came downstairs? There was a risk he would be discovered. He had no intention of explaining himself and would have to hide in the snicket.

He moved further into the darkness between the two buildings and came out at the back where a small yard existed for the row of terraced buildings. Turning left into the shadows just in time, he heard Lavender's footsteps moving behind him onto the cold cobblestones of the snicket. Shrouded in the black frame of a rear doorway he secretly listened with pricked-up ears and scheming intent, as the two friends exchanged their freshly dreamed journeys and the potential whereabouts of the amulet.

The following day, Isaac arose just in time to take advantage of the enormous cooked breakfast Cathy had prepared for the inn guests. He was greeted by her welcoming maternal tones as he descended the stairs.

"Now then, Mr Scrubb, I'm just dishing up a full English. Take a seat in the bar, you look like you need a good feed."

He looked across the room at one of the small tables that had been set ready for breakfast with a pot of tea and condiments.

"That's wonderful thank you. I wonder if you happen to know what time the morning service is at St Paul's?" he continued.

"Ten-thirty, you've plenty of time and the vicar is allus late anyway," Cathy replied.

It had been a while since he had eaten anything substantial, grabbing only a curled up British Rail sandwich from the station in York the day before, so the promise of a hearty breakfast was welcome relief for the gurgling void in his stomach. In this moment, the salty smell of fried bacon and crispy-edged, rich black pudding, overlaid with the buttery softness of scrambled eggs was just as satisfying a temptation to his belly as the thought of obtaining the amulet was to his mind. He was not disappointed when the large plate of food was presented before him and spent a leisurely hour savouring his food and reading the Sunday newspaper.

It had been some time since Isaac felt hopeful about much in his life, but this morning as he stepped outside on his way to church, the clear winter sky mirrored his refreshed state of mind. It had the effect of putting a spring in his step and a twinkle in his eyes. All the significant events in his life, whether joyful or painful had led him to this point, converging in an unmistakable culmination of fate.

The meaning of it all was as clear as the blue sky above him and his thoughts began to cycle through his brain in a surge of steely determination: *I'll make sure that within the week's end I'll have what destiny has designed. Nothing will get in my way.*

Chapter Eighteen

The Silver Amulet

Fred stopped as instructed at the entrance to the canal bridge. The silhouetted figure shifted into the darkness towards him.

"You have got it with you?"

The deep voice rumbled from the inners of the bridge, shaking off drops of condensing water from the arched stones. Fred pulled his clenched hand from his pocket and held it out in front of him.

"Here," he said confidently.

Scrubb moved closer and out of the bridges shadow, revealing his face clearly for the first time.

"Good boy. Now give it to me," he instructed, as he reached Fred and held out his hand.

Fred's hand opened, dropping the amulet into Scrubb's waiting grasp. He held his breath. So, it seemed, did Scrubb as he focused his eager eyes on the gold disc that now warmed the cold creases of his palm. Lavender and Alice looked on, waiting motionlessly from the concealed safety of the towpath shrubbery.

Even if he had wanted to, Isaac Scrubb could not have resisted the contraction in his fingers, closing in a vice like grip around the amulet. Unexpectedly, his head began spinning and his conviction faded into helplessness as he saw Fred watching on, mesmerised by the effect that the amulet appeared to have. Scrubb's eyelids fluttered and his eyes turned white as they rolled up into his head, his body collapsing to the floor. For the first time since Scrubb spoke, Fred felt he could move. He looked back to check on his hiding friends and then turned and bent down to the prostrate figure that was beginning to shake uncontrollably on the path. The amulet was still held tightly in Scrubb's grip and started to glow, casting narrow wedges of light between the cracks in his fingers. It was clear to Fred that the amulet was working its magic, Scrubb may have been lying trembling and convulsing on the ground, but his eyes were wide and active behind his eyelids, taking in something no one else, except perhaps his brother, could imagine.

Isaac found himself in his grandfather's bedroom. The room was at the back of 10 The Cringles and he looked down through the window into the rear courtyard below. The room was small and dimly lit by the dreary daylight that struggled to penetrate the modest north-facing window. On the bed in front of him lay a young woman in the later stages of pregnancy. Her face and legs were severely swollen, and she was clearly in some degree of abdominal pain as she rubbed her labouring belly and let out a pained moan. Isaac could see his grandfather Manasseh take cuttings of foxglove in the small courtyard and then look up at the bedroom window. With dread, Isaac caught sight of his troubled face. He was so much younger, and his face possessed an obvious fear. To Isaac it was as though their eyes had briefly met, before Manasseh moved swiftly into the kitchen, disappearing from view. This must be his grandmother, in distress and laid in front of him heavy with child.

Despite feeling uncomfortable in his position, Isaac couldn't help but stare at the woman in front of him, she had a kind face and he felt drawn to her softness. His gaze was broken by the sound of a child in his own bedroom just a few feet away. He made his way across the small room and out to the dark landing to see who was making the sound. The bedroom door was ajar, so he peeked through the gap to look. Kneeling on the floor, a young girl with a beautiful head of copper-streaked blond hair was lining buttons up into patterns on the floorboards while quietly singing a joyful, imagined melody. As Isaac watched, he realised that this must be his own mother, Eliza. Coinciding with the sound of her soft innocent voice, an entirely foreign feeling washed over Isaac's frame sending him weak at the knees. It was a desire to be nurtured and held, a need to be wrapped in maternal arms and have his hair stroked gently, to be sung to and swayed until drifting into a warm, secure sleep. He walked into the bedroom and knelt by the child's side to take in her rosy face and bright eyes. She continued humming her childish composition all the while moving buttons into patterns on the floor, oblivious of Isaac's presence. The buttons were mostly bone and wood in various shades and colours, but Isaac noticed a few metal buttons and then, quite by surprise, a silver coin. Tarnished and dull, but with a similar pattern to the amulet he now held in his hand, there were two circles with what appeared to be the bars of a prison cell overlaid.

Could this be an amulet and if so, why is it silver, not gold?

His thoughts were interrupted by the sound of his youthful grandfather leaping up the winding staircase, three steps at a time and dashing into the bedroom where his grandmother lay.

"I have prepared you a foxglove tonic my dearest one, please take it now." His grandfather spoke with some urgency.

The young Eliza picked up the tarnished amulet and moved it to the centre of the circle of buttons she had made on the floor. Sitting in the centre, it started to shine, the tarnish melting away to a bright white light. In wonder and excitement, Eliza jumped up and ran to her parent's bedroom, but her timing was anything but wondrous. Having taken several large gulps of the tonic, her mother was overcome with extreme nausea. She turned as white as the amulet now was and entered a terrifying fit of convulsions that seemed to last for minutes. Isaac looked on through the doorway between the narrow landing, frozen in horror. Manasseh was desperate, frantic in his vain attempts to reverse the effects of the tonic until his wife, pained and grimacing, clutched Manasseh's hand and uttered her final words.

"Meet me. I'll wait in the sacred place you are searching for, under the Venetius Stone."

Manasseh slumped over her limp body and whispered something in her ear and then, with a quiet automation, picked up a pair of scissors from the dressing table and cut a lock of her golden hair and placed it inside a clean handkerchief. The brilliant glow of the amulet extinguished in synchronised harmony with the passing of Suzannah's life, returned to its tarnished state.

Scrubb's breath steadied. His body stilled itself in apparent exhaustion. His arms flopped to the ground, and his unbuttoned great coat lay open and dishevelled under his body on the towpath.

Fred nudged him a few times with the toe of his shoe, testing his consciousness, but he made no obvious response, so, he turned again to Lavender and Alice and whispered loudly, "He's out of it, come on, now's our chance."

He added a fast gesture with his hands, emphasising the urgency of the moment.

"Come on then, Lav, let's do this," encouraged Alice, making her move on to the towpath.

Fred waited until his two friends had joined him before reaching down to Scrubb's hand. He tentatively pulled back the gnarled bony fingers that had relaxed and half-opened, and in which the amulet now lay visible in the palm. It was a palpable moment. Each one of the children could feel the amulet's presence so intensely that it would have not surprised any of them if it had levitated away from Scrubb's possession of its own magical accord. As Fred pulled back Snowzell's fingers, and his other hand went to take back the amulet, Scrubb's body twitched with a hypnic jerk, catapulting all three children several feet backwards on to the path in a heap of racing heartbeats. Scrubb let out a deep long breath as his limp hand involuntarily discarded the amulet on to the path where he lay. There was no further movement. Alice was the first to pick herself up. She crawled forward and reached into his open coat, eagerly rummaging the pockets for anything of value. Fred picked up the amulet from the ground and placed an old shilling, about the same size as the amulet, in Scrubb's open hand. There was nothing except a set of keys in his coat.

"Try his trousers, Alice," whispered Fred eagerly.

She looked at Scrubb's trousers and then at his gaunt face and sunken eyes that could at any moment pop open.

"I think I'll leave that to you, Fred," she replied, pulling back from Scrubb's body.

Fred knelt in Alices place and reached carefully into his right trouser pocket. It wasn't easy as the cloth had pulled tight under his weight. The smell of stale whisky and unwashed clothes caught the back of Fred's throat as he got close, making him feel quite sick. Gently patting the pocket, he could feel there was something contained in it. He pulled the cloth away a little from under Scubb's leg and managed to carefully get his hand inside, pulling out a carefully folded white cotton handkerchief. Lavender and Alice held their breath as they looked on in anticipation.

"Oh, it's nothing," said Fred in disappointment, pushing the handkerchief back inside the pocket.

"Wait," said Alice, as a sudden and clear image ran through her mind. "There's something inside, I'm sure of it," she continued with absolute certainty.

Fred pulled his hand back out and passed the folded piece of white cotton to Alice.

"Here you are then, Aunt Margaret!" he said jokingly.

Alice unfolded the handkerchief in a deliberate fashion until finally it lay flat on the flagstones edging the canal. Lavender clicked the button on her torch and pointed at the handkerchief and its contents. Laying on the cotton was a lock of golden hair tied with a piece of string.

"It's now't special, just a snipping of someone's hair, that's all," said Fred, as if to justify his previous action of returning the handkerchief to the pocket.

"It must mean something though, Fred, otherwise, why would he be carrying it?" Alice replied.

"Check his other pocket, Fred," Lavender encouraged hopefully.

Fred was feeling a little more emboldened now and quickly moved to the other pocket, patting it down carefully again. There appeared to be something concealed inside that resembled the shape and size of a coin.

Perhaps it's another amulet, thought Fred in a return of his previous excitement.

The girls became aware of a diffused blur of white light that appeared through the other side of the bridge, then a voice from the light stopped them all in their tracks. Lavender switched her torch off quickly.

"Oi, what's going on there?"

The sound echoed against the dark underside stones of the bridge and through the fog, rattling in the children's ears. As it did so, Fred suffered from a moment of hesitation leaving his hand wavering over the pocket. Before he could make a move though, his wrist was grabbed by the abrupt, hard grasp of Scrubb, whose eyes sprang open as if they were on storks. It was a possessed look in his eyes that sent Lavender and Alice backwards again and causing her to drop the torch in fright. The silver shilling fell out of Isaac's hand, onto the stone flags that edged the canal and then rolled, as if in slow motion. In his first moments of waking consciousness, Scrubb along with all three of the children, watched as it wobbled and then toppled with the quietest plink into the murky water. Scrubb's grip loosened as he watched it disappear, leaving Fred to escape his clutches. With a swift dash all three children sprinted off into the fog.

"Are you alright, sir?"

The deep baritone voice came from a rather large figure, elongated by the unmistakable height of a police officer's helmet. The police officer moved his torch beam across the scene in front of him as he spoke.

"Err … yes constable … umm, I think I must have lost my footing in the fog and slipped over."

Scrubb's words were somewhat dazed and confused but also not without a semblance of guilt in their tone.

"What are you doing down here on such an evening, sir?" the police officer asked.

Scrubb pulled himself up to a sitting position and noticed his handkerchief laying open on the ground with the lock of golden hair still sat in the centre.

"I am returning to town to see my grandparents and I … umm … seem to have got lost, constable."

Scrubb had not considered his words before they left his mouth and despite the gloom of the scene, he could tell that the police officer was taken aback by what he had said.

"Well, sir, if you don't mind me saying so, your grandparents must be of a remarkable age to have you as their grandson."

Scrubb stumbled to his feet and placed his hand on the police officer's shoulder for balance.

"Did I say grandparents, constable? I err ... meant to say grandchildren. The fall must have rattled my brain somewhat I think."

Now they were eye-to-eye and Scrubb was standing without aid. The police officer could see that he was not inebriated, despite the faint smell of whisky.

"What's your name, sir?" the police officer asked.

"Scrubb, Elijah Scrubb," he replied.

"Well, Mr Scrubb. Best you be on your way and carefully mind. I don't want to be collecting any bodies from the towpath tonight if that's alright with you."

Scrubb bent down, picked up his handkerchief from the ground and carefully folded it back up.

"Err ... Thank you, constable. Goodnight."

Isaac started to walk off, but the police officer's resounding voice halted him in his tracks.

"Aren't you forgetting something, Mr Scrubb?"

Isaac stopped with his back to the police officer as a momentary doubt crept into his mind.

What on earth has he figured out? he thought.

Isaac turned around and faced the imposing figure before him.

"Your torch, sir, you must have dropped it," the police officer said, holding Lavender's torch out to him.

Isaac let out a long-held breath in relief.

"Ah thank you, constable. Goodnight," he replied, heading towards the shadows.

Back at the top of the bridge, Fred and Lavender tried hard to insist they should walk Alice to her front door, but she was adamant they go on their way.

"I'll be fine. We have a good head start and there's no way he will be able to catch up with me before I get home. Anyway, it would mean you have to double back on your walk and then you might pass him again. Best to get going now."

Alice's reply made complete sense.

"OK, let's meet up tomorrow at my house," Lavender suggested quickly.

Having said their goodbyes, Lavender and Fred continued their planned route home, relieved by their narrow escape and ecstatic by their success.

Chapter Nineteen

The Venetius Stone

Once he had regained composure, Isaac picked up his pace and
in no time at all had caught up with Lavender and Fred. By the
time they were turning into Fairfax Street, he was close enough
to see their lively figures and hear their animated conversation
in the fog ahead, though he was careful to move quietly and not
to alert them to his presence. They were talking about getting
fish and chips, which explained the less direct route they were
taking home. Isaac paused for a moment to consider his plan
and then left them to go their way while he continued along the
main road, turning into the square and then Bridge Street. Pear
Tree Cottage presented itself as a vague, grey-orange oil
painting, illuminated insufficiently by the streetlamp opposite.

In a mysterious twist of fate, as it came into view the
front door opened almost as if a waiting inhabitant had seen
him coming and was inviting Isaac to enter. The doorway cast a
welcoming light into the dark foggy night before the emerging
silhouette of a woman stepped outside and bent down to put
something under the doormat, then disappeared again as the
door closed. He stood still again and waited, deliberating his

intentions and watching as she briskly headed left along Bridge Street. Everything was aligning, with the exception of his possession of the Amulet of Dreams. Still, he could not squander this fortuitous moment.

He must grab the opportunity while he could and enter the cottage. Would it really contain the Venetius Stone? If it did, he could always come back later when he had the amulet.

Crossing the road to the cottage, Isaac checked to his left and then right, more with his ears than his eyes. The fog made a good cover for his nefarious act and as far as he could tell, all was clear. The white picket gate squeaked as if to warn of an intruder approaching, sending a nervous shiver down his spine, even though he was sure the cottage was empty. At the doorstep he pulled out the torch he had picked up at the canal and switched it on. In the firm belief that the key had been put there, he lifted the doormat, pointing the beam of light onto the stone flags underneath. He was not disappointed and, without delay, he placed the key in the lock and opened the door. If it had not been for Delius leaping from his slumber on the raised warm plinth by the side of the fire, Isaac's rapidly pumping heart may have started to settle. As it was though, having the cat launch itself towards Isaac and then fly with determined urgency between his legs and out of the open door, had the effect of sending his heart into race mode and his body into a spin. The torch he was holding flew out of his hand as he did so and rolled under the piano. Before he could even catch a breath and close the door behind him, he looked ahead to see the fireplace itself. The size and shape of the pillars and lintel were indeed unusual, not only in their size which matched the details his grandfather Manasseh had described, but also in their shape. He was mesmerised.

This must be it, he thought as he approached the fire and reached up to put his hand on the curved lintel stone.

It was warm, heated into life by the glowing logs beneath that had settled themselves into pockets of yellow-white-orange caves. As he moved his hand across the stone, he sensed the memories it somehow held and then he noticed an unnatural pattern in its texture. Puzzled, he stood back for a moment and changed the angle of his gaze. The faint relief of worn-down carved writing could be seen from a particular angle. He carefully traced the letters and numbers it contained: Anno Domini 1647.

Isaac let out a deep sigh of recognition and considered his discovery.

I've found the stone, he thought. *It must have been a part of my grandmother's family and I never knew.*

He stood back again to get a full view of the stones and the room itself. The low ceiling held so solidly with bygone black oak beams and adorned with shining horse brasses. The polished piano at the end of the room that sat open and ready to play. He put his hands in his pocket and felt the lock of hair he had found in the sea chest. A sudden feeling of a deep connection took over his entire body. The vision of his grandmother lay dying on her bed returned to his mind.

There are so many questions I wish I could ask her, he thought, removing the hair to look at it.

For a while he stood there, twisting the hair in his hand and questioning whether the colour of the hair matched that of his memory, then with no self-control he tied it tight to his own hair. His whole body now seemed possessed. He was conscious of everything around him, yet unable to suppress the feeling that was drawing him towards the fire as the embers softly hissed and shifted their burning weight. As he got nearer to the fire, he became aware of a slowly approaching noise beyond the walls of the cottage. It was indiscernible at first, then unmistakable as the heavy wheels and deep engine of a lorry that sent ripples of vibration through the ground as it pulled up outside. Almost immediately the engine stopped, followed by a door slamming. Isaac was stood so close to the fire by now that the wool singed on his overcoat stinging his nostrils. Instinctively, he peeled off his coat, dropping it to the hearth, but he only felt the heat more intensely. Despite the unnatural action, he couldn't stop himself moving his head forward until it went under the lintel and over the fire.

It was at this very moment that Arthur Tilly charged through the open front door and into the cottage, bringing with him curling wisps of the foggy night air. In front of his eyes the vision of this tall slim figure of a man leaning over the fire stunned Arthur for a split second.

"What the blazes are you doing, man?" he exclaimed.

Isaac turned his head and looked directly at Arthur. He had an innocent look in his eyes and a smile on his gaunt face that beggared belief.

"You can't stop me; I have found my destiny," Isaac replied in a loud whisper.

Arthur could foresee the bizarre man burning in the flames of his own fireplace and, without hesitation, rushed ahead to pull him away from his impending doom. As Arthur grabbed him by the arms and began to pull at his deceptive weight, a sudden blast of white heat ripped through their bodies and sent them spinning into the fire.

For a while they were in a state of shock and weightless disorientation. Neither was sure how long it took, but gradually the spinning slowed, and they became aware they weren't in the fireplace anymore. Arthur released his grip on Isaac's arms as he began to feel less fearful. He could feel his heart slow from the pounding rhythm it had sustained during the whoosh of noise and heat that engulfed them. Instead, it was now synchronising to a new subtle sound that started with the delicate tone of a harpsichord followed by the plucking of violin strings moving repeatedly in upward progressions of four notes. Somehow, he knew, without any defining evidence, that he was drifting in-between time and space. It was a state of absolute peace and calm, a feeling that came with a sense that he was ethereal. His journey, wherever it may be going, was accompanied now by increasing layers of violins bowed in rising and falling harmonies. Even though his eyes were closed, the light surrounding him was so brilliant that it seemed as though he was gazing directly at the sun on a mid-summer day.

I wonder if I've died, he thought, then, just as he had grown accustomed to the feeling of serenity he was experiencing, the spinning and music came to a stop and the brightness he had been floating through crashed into a pitch-silent tunnel of darkness.

Chapter Twenty

Fish and Chips

For Lavender and Fred, Friday was the traditional night for a
fish supper. They would often go to one another's houses after
school, and then later, walk the short distance to Fairfax
Fisheries.

Despite it being a regular occurrence, buying a meal
from the fish and chip shop always felt like a special treat.
Tonight would be no exception, though they had arranged to
collect the food on their way home from Alice's instead.

"I'm hungry" said Fred as they turned where a row of
cottages were set back on Fairfax Street. Fred started to pick up
his pace. "I'm having scraps with mine, I think I've earned
them," he continued.

The cottages had long gardens at the front and there was
not much to distinguish Fairfax Fisheries from the rest of the
cottages except that it was at the end of the row and had a
driveway down the side which ran parallel with the garden. It
was here that customers would most often queue while waiting
to place their orders. There was a discreet "Fairfax Fisheries"
sign that hung out from the side wall near the back. The simple

sign illuminated the driveway, otherwise, if you were a stranger passing by, you would most likely miss it altogether. A small group of people could be seen queuing in the fog by virtue of the light from the shop doorway. Lavender and Fred moved towards the end of the queue nearer to the sound of simmering beef dripping spitting in the fryers and the wrapping of fish suppers in yesterday's newspaper.

They had barely been stood waiting more than a few minutes when Lavender felt something pressing softly against her leg and looked down to see what it was. Delius had arrived on schedule to greet them as if to remind them not to forget a little extra fish, just for him.

"How did you know we were here?" Lavender asked, as she bent down to stroke his arching back and slinking body.

"I dare say he just got fed up with waiting for us and set off on his ..."

Grandma came up behind them, interrupting Fred.

"There you are, you two, Oh and Delius has sneaked out too! I was beginning to wonder where you'd both got to. What's taken you so long?"

Lavender and Fred looked at each other and then back at grandma.

"Nowt," they answered in unison.

"It's just this fog," Fred continued, in an attempt to explain their lateness.

"Well seeing as though I'm here, I might as well wait with you," grandma replied.

Inside the fish shop, Charlie and Archie North were busy preparing the food in their usual well-practised style. The two brothers had taken over from their father after the war and despite it being nearly thirty years later, nothing had really changed. They both wore white jackets and had balding shiny heads and small slight bodies, probably on account of their seemingly never-ending movement. Charlie made appearances less often as he prepared the batter, fish and potatoes in the shed in the back garden. He would come in through the back door to give Archie large stainless-steel buckets of chips and batter to fry, then take the empty ones back out to refill.

Grandma called out to Archie as soon as her head was inside the doorway, "Put us a special in will you, love."

"I take it your Arthur's home then," Archie replied across the top of the fryer.

"He will be by the time I get home, love, he's just on his way back from Birmingham," grandma replied with a smile.

"Grandad will be home?" Lavender asked eagerly to confirm.

"He will, and he's home all weekend as well, lass."

Archie's wife, Mavis served them from behind the fryers. In contrast to her husband, Mavis was a more rotund, sturdy figure, with a particularly red face and a mass of curly black hair.

"Fish and chips three times and the special please, Mavis," grandma asked politely.

"Can I have scraps wi mine please?" Fred asked quickly.

"And me too!" Lavender added.

"Will that be all, Annie?" Mavis asked.

Delius pushed up against grandma's leg extra hard and she looked down.

"Oh, and if you have any bits for Delius, I'm sure he'd be grateful," grandma asked.

Mavis looked down at the cat circling the feet below.

"We can't let your Delius go without a treat now, can we?" she replied.

Lavender was walking at double speed as they left the glow of Fairfax Fisheries and into the fog.

"Come on. We need to get home quick. I can't wait to see Grandad and it's so freezing out here, those fish and chips will be cold before we get back," Lavender said.

"It's OK, Lav, I've stuffed them inside my coat to keep warm," Fred reassured her, as he supported the warm and precious package with his hands, like an expectant mother hugging her round belly.

"Just mind your step, Lavender, and don't go charging off, you'll end up tripping and breaking your neck," grandma advised with a typically catastrophic turn of phrase.

Delius, as usual, had already bounded ahead in enthusiastic anticipation of supper, so it was unexpected when they saw him come back towards them halfway down Bridge Street. Instinctively, she knew that something wasn't quite right.

"What's to do?" said Lavender, as Delius materialised out of the fog and opened his mouth with a silent meow.

Lavender, Fred and grandma looked at one another with the same thought: *Whatever it is, we are about to find out.*

Within another few yards, the shape of the cottage started to emerge from the fog. Strangely, grandad's lorry was parked outside. It was strange because whenever grandad was home, he would never choose to park his lorry anywhere except in the barn and without doubt, not outside the cottage where it was near a junction, especially in the fog.

"Whatever's going on 'ere?" exclaimed grandma with some concern, as the vision of the cottage became clearer and they could see that the front gate was open.

The front door was ajar too and shed a narrow glow of light outside and on to the path.

"What the devil is he playing at leaving his lorry there and the front door open," she continued.

Delius got to the front gate and stopped by the post to peer curiously at the doorway.

"Happen he's forgotten his keys to the barn," grandma said, in an attempt to rationalise the unusual scene.

Lavender walked ahead down the path towards the front door and stopped. The cottage was eerily quiet. It was the kind of silence that has a constant high pitch to it that only appears in the ear when there is nothing else to muffle it. Grandma and Fred caught up with Lavender at the doorstep, then, just as they were about to enter, the sound of a high-pitched bell tinkled from inside. Grandma put her hand on Lavender's shoulder and took in a hesitant breath.

"Did you hear that?" she asked, Fred didn't hear anything, but Lavender heard it too and stood very still to listen.

The high-pitched tinkling sounded again.

"I hear it, Grandma!" Lavender announced.

"I don't know what you're talking about," said Fred feeling left out.

"I recognise that bell ... but I haven't heard it in years. Arthur, Arthur!" She called out with a frightening tone and then moved in front of Lavender to walk through the open doorway.

The key, she noticed, was sat in the lock, confirming her instinct that something was wrong. Inside, the cold foggy air had replaced the usual warmth of the front room and the fire was no longer alive and glowing, but instead a grey smouldering pile of ash. Lavender and Fred followed behind.

"What on earth!" grandma exclaimed in shock, as the three of them stood and gasped as they took in the scene.

Slinking in behind them, Delius tentatively approached the discarded coat that lay. in an undignified heap, on the floor. "That's not Grandad's coat," Lavender observed.

Delius sniffed at the pocket and then plodded over to the wall at the side of the fireplace and jumped on grandad's rocking chair. They all stood in bewilderment for a moment, watching Delius. He was sat on the chair staring at the whitewashed stone, on which hung three small brass bells. With an abrupt jolt from her gaze, grandma walked over to Delius and unhooked the top bell from the wall and gently shook it. It rang out with a soft round tone. She put it back on the wall and took off the middle bell and repeated her action. Again, there was a similar medium pitched soft tone a couple of notes higher than the first bell. Neither were the same as the ringing they had heard at the doorstep. She replaced the middle bell, then unhooked the lower bell, turning to Lavender and Fred as she did so and shaking it hard. It was silent, there was no clapper to sound the bell.

"I knew it couldn't be that, we must have been hearing things," she said to the two stunned children.

"Wait, Grandma," said Lavender, rushing into the kitchen and coming back with a spoon from the cutlery draw. "Hit it with this."

Grandma took the spoon and gently tapped the inside of the bell lip. It rang out magically with the exact tone and pitch they had heard at the doorstep a few moments previously. Grandma clutched the bell to her chest and bent over.

"It's your Grandad my dear," she said sobbing.

"What do you mean, Grandma?" Lavender asked in confusion.

"This was his bell; he's had it since he was a little 'un and the clapper came off years ago. I allus said we should get it fixed, but he just laughed and said you can do that when I'm gone and ring it when you want a chat."

With that, tears began to flow from her eyes like a stream.

"I don't understand, Grandma. Where do you think Grandad is?" Lavender asked, now with tears streaming down her own face.

"That's just it my dear, I don't know. But I have the same feeling I had when your mother and father disappeared."

As they were talking, Fred noticed a narrow beam of light that had no right to be there, shining from under the piano. He went over to the piano and crouched down onto his hands and knees to investigate. Slowly he edged his hand underneath and extended his fingers out to reach the source of the light and pull it out.

"How on earth did your torch get here, Lav?" he said with disbelief, then continued, "Someone else has been here and by the looks of things I know who."

He walked over to the coat and examined it.

"Look here!" he said, pulling out the ancient black book and opening the pages to see. "There's a sketch of your cottage and summat about Mother Fortune, whatever or whoever she is," he continued.

Grandma sat up straight in the rocking chair.

"Did you say Mother Fortune? Well, I'll be … and you reckon you know who has been here do you? I think I'd better call the police station, but before they get here, you two had better tell me what you know," grandma instructed in a surprising shift in demeanour.

"First though, I need a cup of tea. You put the kettle on, lass, and I'll make the call," grandma continued, as she went over to the phone and started to dial.

It always struck Fred as peculiar that no matter what disaster may unfold, adults seemed to find solace in drinking tea, whereas he found food a much more satisfying comfort.

Lavender and Fred went to the kitchen and made the tea; within a few minutes, grandma had made the call and joined them at the kitchen table. Fred was patting the warm package of fish and chips that was still securely held under his coat.

"Do you mind if I have my fish and chips? I'm starving," he asked sheepishly.

"Nay, lad, of course not, but I couldn't stomach them right now. I'm afraid they'd be going down in lumps," Annie replied.

Within a few minutes Fred was devouring the best part of two portions, as they sat at the kitchen table drinking tea and discussing the previous week's events. Like her grandma, Lavender's appetite had also evaporated, though as they talked, she started to feel that somehow everything was happening for a reason. She picked at the food, alternating between placing an odd chip in her own mouth with feeding pieces of fish to Delius, who in contrast, sat in ecstasy under the table.

By the time the food was finished, the astonishing circumstances that transpired over the week had been revealed. They sat, for what seemed to the children to be an uncomfortable amount of time afterwards, in silence as grandma pondered the news. This may have continued for longer, had it not been for the arrival of a young police officer whose assertive knock on the front door broke the silence and sparked the three of them into action.

"You two, stay in here while I talk to the police officer."

Chapter Twenty-One

The Special Place on the Moor

In the early hours of the following morning, Annie had left her restless bed and her sleeping granddaughter and gone downstairs to sit in Arthur's rocking chair by the fire. In the darkest hours she had been wrestling with the intrigue of the contents of the black book and the revelation that was Mother Fortune. The name Fortune was familiar to Annie, and of particular interest, because it was Aunt Margaret's name when she was born. A maiden name which held such importance to her that she had reverted back to it when her husband died. Could it possibly be true that she was related to Mother Fortune of 1647?

She stared intermittently at the brass bell on the wall waiting for it to ring with some kind of answer, writhing in her emotions and regurgitating the information that Lavender and Fred had confided. It had been decided that no mention of Isaac Scrubb would be made to the young police constable who arrived shortly after Annie's call to the station, and who dutifully noted the details. What good would it do to tell him? There was nothing the police could do, but they did need to know he was missing, just as Mary and Alex were missing. She had managed to keep her silence for all the intervening years since her daughter and son-in-law's disappearance, but now it would be impossible not to confide what she knew about them to Lavender.

As she sat thinking in the wee small hours, Annie remembered how, from a young age, Mary had a keen interest in local history and a deep connection with it. Maybe it was the tales that she and her own mother had told Mary of bygone days and curious or eccentric ancestors. Perhaps it was her hometown, full of historical buildings with stories that connected to her family, including her own childhood cottage. Whatever it was that made Mary so inquisitive of the past, her sense of belonging to the land was realised one particular day while visiting Aunt Margaret. It was the day Annie first received the warning from Margaret about Mary and her first-born child.

For as long as Annie could remember, Mary had been intrigued by Aunt Margaret. She was an unusual oddity who seemed to know things before anyone could possibly know them. When Mary was only a little older than Lavender was now, they had visited Margaret at her small end of terrace house on the edge of the moors. It was a warm, late summer afternoon and the adults sat out in the garden in their deck chairs, eating egg and cress sandwiches and drinking Margaret's special tea. It was a blend of Earl Grey and lapsang souchong, drunk from fine bone-china cups. As they chatted, Margaret noticed that Mary was unable to settle.

"Have you got ants in your pants, lass?" she called to her, as she danced around the flower beds and walked precariously along the drystone garden walls.

Mary jumped down from the wall, half-eaten sandwich in hand, and laughed loudly as she wriggled and mimicked the sensation of having a nest of ants crawling around her body.

"Now then. I have a challenge for you, Mary, if you're ready for it," Margaret said with intrigue.

"What is it, Aunt Margaret? I can do it whatever it is," Mary announced with confidence still hopping around the lawn.

"Go over the stile and on to the moors and I want you to find your special place," Margaret instructed, pointing her trusty black cane towards the open ground.

"What do you mean my special place, Aunt Margaret?" Mary questioned as she continued to hop, now just on one foot.

"I mean that somewhere out there on the moor is your special place, you must go and find it," Margaret answered, with no greater degree of elaboration than before.

Mary looked bewildered.

"But, Aunt Margaret, how will I know it is my special place?" Mary questioned.

"Your whole body will know. You will feel that you are entirely at peace when you reach the right place on the moor. Now go on, off you go, lass, it's out there somewhere," Margaret finished.

Mary climbed the stile over the drystone wall at the back of the garden and launched herself on to the moors. Every so often she would come back to the garden with a sense of frustration at not finding her special place and repeatedly, after a little encouragement, she would return to the moor looking for a boulder that was good enough to feel right to sit on, or a clearing in the heather soft enough that might be the elusive spot. But despite this, each time she stopped, she would feel more annoyed that there was just nothing outstanding about it. This went on for some hours, with Mary growing more and more frustrated with each flitting stride. By nine o'clock, the sky was beginning to turn a warmer shade of yellow on the horizon, and grandma and grandad felt enough was enough with Margaret's little game.

"Oh, it's not a game, Annie. Mary will discover summat very important, mark my words," she announced soberly.

On the moor, Mary had come to a point where she was tired of searching for her peaceful feeling, and she sat down on a closely grazed piece of grass near a bilberry bush. At first, she didn't notice the bilberries, being that they were so small, but then in her stillness she saw there was quite a harvest to be had. As she was tired and dry in the mouth, Mary decided to sample a bilberry. It was sweet and tangy and acidic, all in one tiny little purple ball and left a stain on her fingers. She pulled a few more bilberries from the wiry little shrub and lay down on the grass to look up at the sky and sample the growing depth of her attention. The air was still and quiet, except for the faint buzz of insects that were employed in pollinating splendour around her. She noticed a particularly fat, hairy caterpillar crawl onto the back of her hand before curling up as if it were going to sleep, and all at once she felt at peace. Her searching had stopped, and her mind was still. A wave of contentment washed over her entire body and with it, in that moment, something incredible changed. She was the sky and the ground and the insects and the soft bilberry, all at the same time.

This, she thought, *is the spot.*

Meanwhile, Aunt Margaret had fallen into a trance as Mary laid on her special place on the moors. Annie and Arthur were taken quite by surprise with Margaret's change. They had not experienced this before and there didn't seem to be anything in particular that caused it. One minute they were talking about Mary and the next, Margaret fell silent, her eyes locked in a distant gaze towards the horizon.

Then she spoke, slowly and softly in riddled verse, "I have a message; summat I must tell thee, though don't be afraid when you hear it. Your daughter's future is caught in the past, and there she must go to leave you aghast. A daughter of her own she'll leave behind, to search for summat not yet brought to mind. The child has a fever risen from the earth that strikes on the thirteenth year of her birth and though it seems that death may be bound, for her an elixir cure may be found."

At the time, both Arthur and Annie had dismissed Aunt Margaret's words, though they returned with untarnished clarity when Mary and Alex disappeared. The relevance of Aunt Margaret's character was too important to dismiss. She knew much more than she let know and the question was, could she help? Now, in the middle of the darkest of nights, Margaret's words had returned again, repeating in Annie's brain until finally she drifted into sleep.

A light morning breeze in the twilight hours dissolved the lingering fog and ushered in a crystal-clear dawn just as an opening of the eyes relieves a nightmare, but rather than bringing the soothing realisation that all had been a bad dream, Annie woke to the reality that Arthur was not just away on a long trip in his lorry, but somewhere she could not imagine. She pulled herself up from the chair and stretched her neck in clicking circles to relieve the stiffness that had set in.

"Oh, Arthur, whatever has happened. Are you with our Mary?" she asked the bell on the wall. It didn't reply.

While they had waited for the police to arrive, Annie had rekindled the fire and kept it going well through the night. Not only was it needed to warm the cottage, but somehow for her, it kept everything alive. Now, the fire had shifted and settled into a comfortable mound of greying coals that rested lightly until Annie gave them a riddle with the poker to revive them and put a large log on the glowing embers. She turned and walked to the kitchen to make a cup of tea, but instead became hypnotised by the sky that was shedding the last of its night-time mystery. She listened to the lack of creaking timbers. The quiet was pronounced, as if it too was listening, waiting for her to speak.

Again, she called out, "Arthur, what shall I do?"

Her words rang out into the stillness and then, ever so gently there was a tinkling of the bell from the front room. Annie's heart skipped a beat.

"Arthur, is that you? ... Should I call Aunt Margaret?"

Instantly, the bell rang out again and this time in a constant ring until Annie had to grab it from the wall. She went to the phone in the study, hesitating for a moment. It was still early. Perhaps she should wait a little before calling. Before she had time to dial, she became aware of the sound of a familiar motorcycle engine echoing between the drystone walls of the road into Brigden and realised, with little doubt, that Margaret was already on her way.

Chapter Twenty-Two

A Distant Relative

"Come on, lass, it's time to get up," grandma spoke softly into
Lavender's ear, and as gently as she could, lovingly rubbed the
top of her arms to carry her into the cold reality of the day.

Lavender's eyes opened just enough to see the blurred
outline of the room and her grandma. She closed them again,
creased tightly in denial.

"Don't fret thisen, lass; everything will be alright … in
time. We have a visitor coming, and she'll be here any minute.
Get thisen up and dressed, and we can talk things through
downstairs."

Lavender didn't answer. She squeezed her eyes closed
until grandma left the bedroom, then once she could hear the
staircase creak, she tentatively opened them and crept out of
bed. She walked over to the window and peeked outside,
squinting at the bright, clear air.

As if to eliminate any doubt of the previous night's
events, she could see grandad's lorry still parked right outside.
While she was looking at it, she noticed a shape move inside
the lorry cabin. Lavender momentarily caught her breath, then

in dismay realised that it was just Delius who had somehow got inside and jumped up onto the dashboard. She stared at the lorry in disbelief. It can't be there.

Surely it is all just another dream, she thought, but it was plain enough to see.

A thousand and one thoughts bounced around her brain at the sight of it, but her attention shifted with the sound of Aunt Margaret's motorcycle, and then shortly afterwards it came into view at the junction of the main road, with a billowing line of blue exhaust fumes dispersing in its wake.

In the time between Aunt Margaret dismounting her incongruous transport, and knocking on the door of Pear Tree Cottage, Lavender had dressed, whizzed down the narrow staircase and was waiting impatiently for what appeared to be an important meeting.

"Come in, Marg, door's open," grandma announced eagerly.

Aunt Margaret entered, removing her helmet with a customary shake of her head that sent her jowls wobbling in their typically independent fashion.

"Ee it's a fresh 'un out there this morning, Annie. I'm right pleased to see you've got the fire going well." She paused, her eyes glazing over momentarily as she looked at the fireplace, then they shifted back to Annie. "Now then, Annie. I believe you might need a little help locating a lost article," Margaret continued, with a deliberately light and vague turn of phrase.

"It's alright, Marg, Lavender knows Arthur is missing. Actually, Fred, Alice and Lavender probably know more than me about the situation," Annie replied with a resigned transparency.

Aunt Margaret looked at Lavender, "Alright then lass, you'd better tell me what you know," she asked.

Lavender hesitated.

"Go on, Lavender, it's alright, you can tell her," grandma added with a reassuring arm around her.

Aunt Margaret listened carefully to Lavender's description of the previous week's events. At first the words dripped reluctantly from her lips, but by the climax of the story they had reached a torrent of both excitement and fear.

"Is this all my fault?" Lavender finished, sobbing tearfully with her head burrowed deep into her grandma's chest.

"Nay, lass, it certainly is not. Now listen here, make no mistake about it, there is hope. But I need to explain a few things that most ordinary folk would not understand," Aunt Margaret replied.

Lavender composed herself a little as Aunt Margaret continued.

"First things first, let me explain how I fit in to this curious sequence of events. It all started long ago. Pear Tree Cottage was built by a distant relative of ours in 1647. His surname was Fortune, as is mine. You see my dear, we are part of the same family, many generations ago mind."

Aunt Margaret walked over to the fireplace lintel and reached up to rub her hand over the stone.

"Come, lass."

She beckoned Lavender with her finger as she spoke.

"If you stand to the side and look at the stone from here, you can see faintly carved letters marking when the cottage was built. He was the captain of a ship, and on his travels he heard legends of an ancient race of men who created a hallowed place in this area. He came here to discover this for himself and never left, falling in love with a mysterious maiden and choosing to make this spot his home. The maiden became known locally as Mother Fortune after they were married and the house was built. Years later she started to make increasingly dramatic prophesies that nearly always transpired.

She first predicted the birth of her own triplet sons, and then more ominously foresaw the Great Plague of London in 1665 and the Great fire of London of 1666. The prophesy of the Great fire was the last record there is of her."

"I've heard of Mother Fortune. Isn't she quite famous?" Lavender blurted out excitedly.

"Aye, lass, she is. But what happened to her is a mystery. They were dark old days make no mistake and anything could have happened. Regardless though they didn't destroy her gift, the wise old mother of our families was more powerful than anyone could imagine. Since then, every so often a female descendent of Mother Fortune, on her thirteenth birthday, becomes a soothsayer. I have this gift of seeing visions of the future and I see that you too will also have it in time."

As she spoke, Aunt Margaret looked deep into Lavender's eyes and put the sausage like fingers of her rather plump hand on Lavender's head.

"You mean I will have special powers when I am older?" Lavender said excitedly.

"There's not a person amongst us that doesn't have special powers, my dear, therefore the question is not whether a person has those powers, but whether they have access to use them."

Lavender put her hand on the pillar at the side of the fire and closed her eyes. The stone was strong and slightly warm. Solid and unshakeable as if it was melded to the core of the Earth. She searched through each of her senses for a sign that Aunt Margaret's words could be true.

Just as if Aunt Margaret could see into her mind, she spoke softly to her.

"In time you will see, but not now. You must learn how to stop searching and allow yourself to be, my dear."

Annie, who had been riveted in dropped-jaw silence during Margaret's revelation, cleared her throat.

"I'm agog, Marg. All this history you never shared. I allus knew there was summat different about you and that we were related in some way. How come you never told me, especially when our Mary vanished?"

Marg looked wistfully into the fire for a moment and then back at Annie.

"Would you have believed me if I had, Annie?" she replied.

"Maybe not. Regardless, what can we do now? How can you help get my Arthur back when you couldn't help with Mary and Alex?" Annie said tersely.

Marg looked back again at the fire and continued.

"The stone is the gateway to people in the past, Annie, but it requires a key to unlock it. That key is a strand of hair, tied with your own hair, that belongs to the person you wish to see. Now a soothsayer cannot travel to the past, for their eyes lay firmly on the future, and so we have several problems to fathom if we are to see your Arthur again. First, we need to know who this Isaac Scrubb was determined to see? Next, we would have to find a strand of hair from that person? Finally, we would need to decide who to send in order to bring back your husband."

"Can't Grandad just come back himself?" said Lavender, in a burst of inspired hope.

"I'm afraid not, my dear, unless he has a strand of hair from one of us. No, someone will have to take him a lock of hair so that he can return. I can't go because I am a soothsayer and I believe that you are unable to go as you will be a soothsayer too, even though you are not yet thirteen. If we could answer the question of who he has gone to, would you go Annie?"

Annie's jaw had dropped, and her eyes widened as if she had witnessed an impossible circus stunt.

"Err, not on your Nellie, Marg. There's no chance I will be leaving Lavender here on her own, no matter what. She's lost too many of her family already," Annie answered indignantly.

"Well, who then?" Lavender questioned.

No sooner had Lavender asked her question, than there was a Tap, Ta, Ta, Tap, Tap … Tap, Tap on the front door. It was still early in the morning and most definitely too early for visitors.

"Who in heaven's name is that at this time in the morning?" Annie said in exasperation.

"I think we might be about to find out the answer to Lavender's question." Margaret said, as if she already knew the answer.

Chapter Twenty-Three

Fred's Dream

For Fred, the previous evening had left him with conflicting
emotions. Something had changed inside him while he was
walking so nervously down the steps to the canal. On one hand
he felt a sense of strength in the courage he had summoned up
to meet with Isaac Scrubb. It was a feeling of invincibility; that
he could now cope with whatever was thrown at him. Yet on
the other hand he felt quite powerless, unable to do anything to
help his lifelong friend and her grandparents. After the police
officer had left Pear Tree Cottage, and he reluctantly said
goodnight and walked the short distance home, these were the
incompatible thoughts that passed through his mind, obscuring
the straightforward view he had of himself, just as the stagnant
fog obscured the street in front of him.

As he reached the entrance to the snicket at the side of
his father's shop, the faint glow of light from the windows at
the rear of the houses guided him to the back door of his home.

"Is that you, son?" his mum called out, as Fred entered
the kitchen through the back door and shut the fog out. "You're
later than I thought. What kept you?" she continued.

It was a familiar greeting from his mum, who had the most incredible knack of worrying about anything and everything and was known to become quite nervous when alone, or out of her normal surroundings. In Fred's mind though, Cynthia Keighley was a typical mum. Her face was delicate and pretty, and her hugs were soft and comfortable, like being wrapped in scented pillows. Her fair hair seemed to bounce as she walked with the shoulder-length curls dancing to their own silent tune. As usual, she was apron clad and homely, and sometimes a little smothering. But that didn't matter, as long as one of his friends wasn't there to see.

Normally Fred would have been ready with his reason for the delay, otherwise even a misplaced hint of secrecy would have brought about a re-run of the Spanish Inquisition. But his mind had been so deep in thought that he hadn't considered being questioned by his mum. He didn't want to go over the events of the evening again, however, both his mum and dad would know soon enough that Lavender's grandfather had gone missing.

I might as well tell them now, he thought.

"You probably won't believe me when I tell you, Mum," he answered, as casually as he could while he walked through the kitchen and into the sitting room.

His mum put down the blanket she was crocheting and looked up.

"Well … Try us out and we'll see," she replied.

His father joined in too, without glancing from the "Spot the Ball" competition he had been mulling over for the last hour.

"Go on then, son, what's happened that's so unbelievable?"

Fred peeled his coat off and threw it on the back of the sofa.

"Err, you can hang that up where it belongs if you don't mind," his mum prompted.

Fred picked the coat up and walked back into the kitchen to hang it in the cloak cupboard by the back door, pleased he had a few moments to think about where to begin with his version of the evening's events. He returned to sit beside his mum.

"Well, you see …" he began, and continued with a particularly long preamble that sent both his mum and dad into a vague stare and a desire to finally get to the point.

By the time he eventually revealed the mysterious disappearance of Arthur Bathwater, Fred's mum and dad felt rather deflated by the revelation and appeared to dismiss it out of hand. His dad sighed and finally shifted his gaze from the "Spot the Ball" competition.

"Nay, lad, there'll be a rational explanation, I'm sure of it. Anyroad, I'm catching up with Arthur in The Turk's Head after work tomorrow, I'm sure we'll have a good laugh about it then."

He spoke in a "matter of fact" way, returning his focus to the newspaper. If it had not been for his mum interrupting his indignant feelings, Fred would have been arguing his case profusely, but fortunately she spoke out before he could.

"Come here and give me a hug," she said, opening her arms deliberately wide to offer a soothing cuddle. "There, there, Fred. It'll all come out in the wash."

Once he had got over the fact that his parents hadn't taken him seriously, Fred decided that it was probably just as well, besides, "Dad's Army" was about to start on the telly and it would help take his mind off everything before he went to bed.

Fred had quite forgotten the amulet in his pocket until he got undressed and threw his trousers on the chair in the corner. The precious article fell onto the carpet and headed, as if deliberately, in his direction. He bent down and picked it up, feeling it warm in his hands, remembering that only a few short hours before, he had taken it from Isaac Scrubb's limp hand as he lay on the path by the canal. As he looked at it, a wave of heaviness quite abruptly passed through him sending him climbing into bed to relieve his weight. His hand clenched firmly around the amulet as he sank deeply, like a stone in a lake, into the soft mattress. At the same time as his body was sinking, his mind seemed to rise and separate until he could no longer feel the weight of his material self. As the ceiling appeared closer and closer he turned to look down on himself laying on the bed motionless and heavy below.

For a few seconds he questioned if he was dying. A rush of fear compounded his sense of mortality, yanking him down towards his body below, yet he resisted the pull due to an intense curiosity, until the feeling ebbed away. Slowly, he became aware his perception was of passing through the ceiling and then the roof, up past the chimney and through the curling smoke and the diminishing layers of fog that petered out into a bright star-filled sky above.

It was as if he were flying peacefully across the fog blanketed landscape. The houses in the vale below were shrouded in the still, foggy air, with only wisps of smoke hinting at their presence. On the higher ground over the moors the air was clearing, and as he climbed higher Fred could see the vale beyond the moors and further to the chimneys of the slowly decaying textile mills that poked their stacks, monumentally, into the clear air. Fred began to feel a pull onwards to the vast, flat vale of York and the ground began to rush beneath him. Within no time at all, he had reached the heart of the vale and the walls at the ancient city's gates. He flew over the silent winding streets, and then down around the three towers of the Minster. As he circled the high walls, his eyes were drawn to the faces of the gargoyles and statues keeping watch over the empty streets below. This variety of mythical beasts and statuesque figures with their weather-worn faces, started to twitch and wink at him from its walls. Eyes were tracking him like a crowd following a runner on a stadium track, and mouths started to move in the gargoyle stones, clicking their tongues in their contorted faces. Fred began to feel as though he was approaching the winning line of a race as the spectators started calling, first with vague and mumbling voices, then with encouraging words, that crescendoed into shouts and yells. Passing the south-east corner of the central tower, an especially deep, loud male voice rang out from a seated statue. Fred made a double-take as he flew by. It had a striking resemblance to Malcolm Majors, sat on a throne with a deerstalker hat for a crown, a hymn book in one hand and a sceptre in the other. As he passed, it reached out and pointed with its sceptre over Petergate towards The Cringles.

"Keep going, Fred, you can do it. Number ten, number ten, down there."

Fred swooped across the rooftops and descended as softly as a guided parachute through the crooked angles of number ten and into the attic.

Without disturbing a single speck of dust, he landed directly on the corner of what appeared to be an old sea chest. The strangest thing that he noticed was not the mysterious and magical nature of his journey and what appeared to be happening, or the impossibility of it all. It was that he now knew, beyond any shadow of doubt, that he was being guided by his spirit, and that it was all perfectly natural. He didn't need to fear, he didn't even need to know, he just had to trust in his spirit completely and it would guide him to what he needed.

Fred put his hands through the sea chest lid, sensing the fibres of the wood and minerals of the iron it was made from, until they gave way to the space inside. There, his fingers started to trace the contents like a blind boy, sweeping slowly and dismissively over the items until they came to a single long thread of hair. As he touched the hair, he envisioned it belonged to a beautiful young woman. She was standing with her back towards him in a grassy clearing in front of Pear Tree Cottage. There were none of the other nearby buildings surrounding it, nor the street or the pavement he would walk down to his own house. As he looked in awe at the shining beauty of the woman's head of long and wavy, flame-red hair, she turned to face him. Her face was oddly familiar, as if they had met previously, yet frustratingly he couldn't think who she was. Her alabaster skin was clear, and her eyes were pale green and smiled at him in such a way that he could hear the words in her mind.

"Hello, Fred. You have my hair; I see your intention is to find me," she seemed to say.

There was not a shadow of doubt in his mind that this woman and the message she was sending to him was genuine, and as if she was reading his own mind the words continued.

"You see this is true, now go and return to the girl who shares my spirit. She is waiting for you."

Fred didn't want to leave. The feeling he had was beyond anything he could have imagined before. He felt so utterly at peace that the thought of leaving was tragic, yet he knew he couldn't stay, and the moment he acknowledged it was finite, he was pulled instantly and unexpectedly back into his body.

For some time, Fred just lay there in complete stillness, feeling his material presence again and mourning the sense of belonging and peace he had miraculously encountered. The amulet in his hand felt cold now, and as he focused on it he started to move, placing it on his bedside table, with a new reverence for the power it had.

Chapter Twenty-Four

The Last Strand

Tap, Ta, Ta, Tap, Tap … Tap, Tap. The knocks came for a second time, prompting Lavender to rush across the room and open the front door to Fred's smiling face.

As it was Saturday morning, Fred had been up early helping his mum as she made pork pies for the shop. Fred Keighley's pork pies were famous for miles around, and were especially popular with walkers and day trippers, who stopped on the way to the Yorkshire Dales to grab a hot one for their travels. They were colloquially better known as "chin dribblers" and were usually difficult not to consume within a hundred yards of the shop while they were still warm. The delicious juices would then run from the soft inside as the teeth cracked through the crispy edge of the casing.

"Hi, Lavender," Fred announced, in an especially positive tone, whilst thrusting a brown paper bag of the warm pies towards her. "My dad's sent me round with these for you." He paused as he noticed he could be overheard by Aunt Margaret standing close by, then continued in a whisper, "Actually, I've something important to tell you."

Lavender turned to look around at her grandma and Aunt Margaret causing Fred's eyes to widen, and the corners of his mouth to drop, as if he was anticipating imminent pain. Lavender turned back to face him, then winked, and nodded reassuringly to come in.

"It's OK, lad, you can tell us all if it's really important," Aunt Margaret announced in her usual forthright manner.

Fred stepped inside, immediately sensing the timing of his arrival was like that of a court waiting for the key witness. Aunt Margaret ushered him in to a central spot near the fire in a more subtle tone.

"Come over here and wait while we get a seat for you, then we can listen carefully to whatever it is that's brought you round so excitedly. Lavender, go and get that stool of your great-grandad Augustus's from the kitchen for Fred to sit on, will you?"

While Fred stood with his back to the fire, waiting for Lavender to return with the stool, he felt like an awkward exhibit in some bizarre display. He was also a little bemused by the attention that was being placed on him and the fact that Aunt Margaret seemed to already know why he was there, and it wasn't because of the pork pies. Lavender returned with the old oak stool that used for the annual trim of her locks and placed it next to him. Aunt Margaret patted the seat as a prompt but before he had a chance to sit, Delius jumped down from his fireside home and launched himself up on to the stool.

"Not you, you daft cat," grandma said, with a wafting of her hands.

Delius just sat there and stared at her with a nonchalant expression. Fred picked Delius up, sat down on the stool and put him on his lap, stroking his soft tabby fur. He purred approvingly.

Grandma sat down in the rocking chair and Lavender perched on the window seat, waiting eagerly for Aunt Margaret who was clearly holding court.

"Right, young man, you have something exciting and really important on your mind. This is about Arthur's disappearance, isn't it?"

Fred was still a little apprehensive about revealing his news. The details of his experience were as clear in his mind as any memory he had, he was certain they were not some kind of hallucination or dream. Yet who would believe such a thing.

"Would you care to divulge what is so crucial?" Aunt Margaret prodded him out of his pensive silence.

"It sounds so farfetched when I think about it that I'm not sure you will believe me," he confessed nervously.

"Well, Fred Keighley, I believe you, and to prove it I'm going to hazard a guess as to what it might be," she continued.

"Go on then," Fred answered keenly.

"You are here to tell us that you had a very strange experience after you went home last night. That you travelled somewhere beyond your physical body, and that on your journey, you discovered something that may help us find Arthur. Am I right?"

Fred was momentarily gobsmacked.

"You are right. And actually, I don't care whether anyone believes me or not, I'm more sure about what happened than I am about sitting here right now," he confessed.

"Will you tell us then what it is you are so sure about, Fred?" Lavender chirped in from the window seat.

Fred shuffled his bottom on the stool and straightened his back.

"OK then …" he started, then realising he needed a bigger breath he stopped to inhale deeply.

He began again, "I did travel last night, all the way to York and the home of Isaac Scrubb. Curiously, I was drawn to the place, as if something else had decided where I should go. When I got there, I found myself sitting on an old sea chest and inside it was a single strand of hair that spoke to me. The woman it belongs to is connected to you in spirit Lavender, she told me I must go to her."

Lavender gasped in awe as Fred's words left his lips. She pointed to great-grandad Augustus's carved symbol on the old stool that had started to change shape.

"Look," she exclaimed, "It's moving."

Aunt Margaret stepped towards Fred and put her hands on his shoulders.

"Well, lad, it looks like you're just what we need. You've allus wanted a ride on a motorbike, haven't you?"

Aunt Margaret wasn't asking a question though, she was organising the recovery of the only link to get to the past, and Arthur, that they knew of. With Aunt Margaret's hands still resting firmly on his shoulders, Fred gave a series of clear nods expressing his agreement to the suggestion. Annie stood up from the chair and spoke with some concern at the prospect.

"This is all well and good, Marg, but don't you think we should have a word with Cynthia first to make sure she's alright with it?"

"I'll go and ask my dad, he won't mind, but my mum 'ud make a right fuss if she knew," Fred said.

"No, no, no. I'm not happy about that, if you're going, then your mum needs to know," Annie answered firmly.

"Right then, come on, lad, let's have you," Aunt Margaret said, springing into action and picking her helmet up as she walked towards the door.

Fred and Delius followed dutifully.

"We'll go and explain our mission then tha's not hiding 'owt," Margaret announced assertively.

Being well prepared for a pillion passenger, on the back of her motorbike, Aunt Margaret had a spare helmet ready. Lavender and grandma watched with bewilderment from the window seat as Fred put the helmet on and the unlikely couple rode off the short distance to Fred Keighley's butcher's shop with Delius in hot pursuit.

"Well, I'll be. Did that happen, lass?" grandma exclaimed.

Lavender didn't say a word. She just stared out of the window and thought *I want to go too.*

"You wait here, lad, and I'll go and have a word with your mum. Won't be long," Aunt Margaret instructed as she dismounted, pulled her cane from the holster on the side of the motorcycle, and left Fred to move onto the front of the seat and twist the throttle, imagining he was flying around a racetrack at high speed.

Aunt Margaret certainly looked a vision of eccentricity as she disappeared down the snicket striding out with her rotund figure, walking cane, and topped off with her motorcycle helmet. She reached the butcher's kitchen and walked in. It was a separate private building in the rear yard behind the shop, especially for preparing the pies and cuts of meat. Fred's mum was still busy cleaning up after the pie making activities of the morning and turned with surprise when Margaret announced a cheery "Good morning, Cynthia," as she entered the building.

"Oooh, you gave me the fright of my life, Margaret," Cynthia said, in a wavering high-pitched, fragile voice.

"I'm sorry, Cynthia, I didn't mean to startle, just wondered if I could have a quick word," Margaret said calmly.

"Whatever about?" Cynthia asked nervously, still visibly shaking from the surprise she had received.

"I have some important business to attend to in York and I need your son's help. The only thing is, we'll be travelling there on my motorcycle. Is that's alright with you Cynthia?" Margaret asked.

"Oh dear, I don't really know. What if something happens to you on the way? Cynthia's voice dithered with apprehension.

"You don't mind taking hold of my cane while I remove my helmet, do you?" Margaret said, thrusting the ornamental black stick towards Cynthia's wavering hand.

"Err no," Cynthia warbled feebly as she reluctantly took the cane.

But no sooner had she felt the cold shiny wood touch her hand, with its ornate patterned slivers of mother-of-pearl, than Cynthia's hand steadied and her arm felt less like jelly. By the time Margaret had removed her helmet, Cynthia had straightened her body into a pose more reminiscent of a soldier on parade and her nervousness had evaporated entirely.

"Right my dear, I'm here to say I have important business in York and I need your son's help. We'll be travelling there on my motorcycle, if that's alright with you, Cynthia, and I promise I'll fetch him back safe and sound." Margaret's jowls shook enthusiastically as she spoke, which from Cynthia's perspective reinforced the importance of the proposed trip.

"In that case, I've no objection Margaret. It sounds important and I'm sure Fred will look after you," Cynthia replied.

An hour later, they had arrived in York and were walking across the well-worn cobbled stones of The Cringles in pursuit of Fred's vision. It was busy with the cacophony of Saturday morning activity from the nearby outdoor market square that spilt into the streets leading to it. The vibrant atmosphere carried the tempting smells of freshly baked breads and pastries and the sounds of stall holders tunefully broadcasting and competing in ever decreasing prices on their latest goods, "Not twelve pounds, not ten pounds, not even nine pounds."

With a raised voice against the hum of activity, Aunt Margaret called out to Fred, "Is this it?"

She squeezed through the bottleneck of pedestrians that funnelled towards the narrow end of the street and braced herself against the crooked frame of the house. Fred was already there waiting, having weaselled his way more easily through the throng, to sit perched on the deep windowsill that was barely a foot and a half up from the pavement.

"Aye, this is it," Fred said.

Aunt Margaret stopped and closed her eyes for an exceptionally long time as she faced the door. It almost looked to Fred as if she was meditating, but unknown to him, a series of disturbing visions were flashing incoherently through her mind.

Sensing a great deal of pain and anguish from behind the doorway, she lifted her cane and tapped vigorously on the medieval timbers. The precarious glass rattled loosely in the putty. For what felt like far too long, they waited for an answer. Fred cupped his hands to the window to peer inside.

"There's someone home, I can see a light on in the back. Knock again so they can hear," he suggested.

But instead, Aunt Margaret stood quite still, rolling her hand across the shiny top of her cane.

"Shh," she said calmly.

Fred continued to peer into the house, observing the lit area for signs of life until eventually there was a movement of shadows. He breathed in sharply, holding his breath for a second as the familiar silhouette of a man revealed itself and transported his mind back to the encounter with Isaac Scrubb under the canal bridge. He couldn't be sure, but the figure appeared to turn and face him, making Fred jump from his position at the window to a less conspicuous pose by the door with Aunt Margaret.

"Here he comes," she said casually, as if she knew precisely what was going to happen.

As he opened the door, it didn't go unnoticed by Fred that even though Elijah Scrubb was unquestionably Isaac's twin, his features carried a softer element to them, which seemed to conceal an underlying pain. Elijah stooped down a little to see under the low door frame, which also gave him an air of humility, and he looked around the street first, as though he was checking for prying eyes, and then looked at Margaret.

"Hello?" he said, as his eyes returned nervously to scan the street beyond.

"I think you know why we are here, Mr Scrubb." Margaret said, trying to make eye contact.

He avoided her eyes and replied, "If it's Isaac you're after, you've got the wrong brother."

"We are not here to see Isaac, but we are here to find where he has gone," Margaret replied.

Elijah looked at the two unlikely pair in front of him. They didn't look a threat in any shape or form, but he was clearly nervous about something. He stood aside from the doorway and ushered them in urgently.

"You'd best come in," he said, and closed the door quickly behind them, muffling the street noise to a dull drone.

Stepping into the house was like arriving in a different century. An orange glow from the street, dimly lit the main room through the cottage window. At the back of the room a wedge of light from the kitchen beyond drew the eye towards it, but also made the corners of the room darker.

"Mr Scrubb, thank you for allowing us to talk with you about your brother," Margaret started.

Elijah recoiled slightly at the reference to his brother.

"Who are you, and what do you want with him?" Elijah asked pointedly.

"This is Fred Keighley and I'm Margaret Fortune. We've come from Brigden where we believe your brother was before he vanished."

"Vanished … Did you say vanished?" By the tone of his voice, Elijah seemed more elated than upset at the news.

"I did. It appears he has, and the reason we are so interested is that he's disappeared along with the grandfather of this young man's friend. You don't seem too distressed by the news, Mr Scrubb."

Elijah stood quite still for a moment; his eyes fixed on the hefty, ornately carved sideboard.

"Mr Scrubb, are you alright?" Margaret put her hand on his elbow as she spoke, nudging him gently from his thoughts.

"Are you quite sure it's my brother that disappeared?" he asked.

"We believe so. He left his coat behind. Fred had seen him earlier in the evening he disappeared and recognised the long grey great coat he had been wearing, and …"

Fred interrupted Aunt Margaret to finish her sentence, "And I know it's your brother because you look the same."

"You'd better come into the kitchen and sit down," Elijah said, as he led the way into the back of the house.

Compared to the front of the house, the kitchen was warm and cosy. It had a cream Aga cooker radiating comforting heat and a large solid oak table in the centre that looked to be as old as the house itself.

Elijah pulled out a chair at the table for Margaret to sit and offered them both a cup of tea.

"What was the nature of you seeing my brother, young man?" Elijah asked, as he finished filling the kettle and lifted the cover on the Aga hot plate.

Fred bowed his head for a moment and looked at the floor.

What should I say? Can I trust this man?

He was in a quandary of how to respond and turned to look at Aunt Margaret for some divine intervention. Aunt Margaret cleared her throat interrupting the question.

"Why do you think he was meeting with Fred?" she asked.

Elijah paused a moment, pressing the kettle hard against the heat of the hot plate and then turning it. "I'm not like my brother, apart from my looks of course, and I'm certainly not obsessed with trying to find these amulets, in fact, I want nothing to do with them. They finished off my grandfather and they've probably finished off my brother too. I reckon that's why you're here now and that's why you met Isaac." Elijah appeared genuine enough.

Aunt Margaret looked over to Fred and nodded almost imperceptibly, just enough to indicate, it was ok to speak up.

"He threatened that if I didn't meet him and bring him the amulet, that I would not live to see this morning."

After he had spoken, Fred immediately felt a sense of relief, and then almost straight afterwards worried that he had said too much. Now that Elijah knows he had an amulet, what would he do?

Fred's expression must have given his concerns away to Elijah.

I can see you're worried, but no need to fret thisen young man. There's an opposite to everything in this life and I'm quite contrary to my brother. Bad means there must be good, knowing sadness means that there must be a chance of happiness, losing something means you must have had something. You can't have one without the other. In the case of my brother, you can see I am the opposite of him because of how he is. Now let's have a cup of tea and talk about what we can do to help find your friends grandfather."

Elijah spooned two heaped teaspoons of Earl Grey, and two heaped teaspoons of lapsang souchong tea, into a large brown teapot and poured the boiling water into the pot from an exaggerated height. It sent the unique atomised aromas around the kitchen.

"That's a striking combination," Aunt Margaret remarked with intrigue.

For the first time in her life, she had come across someone else who used this personal blend.

"Aye well opposites go together you see, so it's normal for me."

Over the course of the next half an hour, their conversation began to reveal more similarities and coincidences that seemed to draw Margaret and Elijah closer together. Their paths had crossed, unknown to them, on many occasions before and it now seemed that finally fate had achieved its goal. Meanwhile Fred was beginning to get restless and feeling sidelined by their conversation.

When will they get to the point, he thought, as they exchanged stories in search of more evidence of their hitherto unknown connection.

Fred interrupted clumsily, "You have an old sea chest in the attic. Can I go and look through it?" he declared.

Elijah was at a critical point in trying to recall his memories and gave a slightly irritated point towards an open doorway in the opposite wall.

"Aye. Up the stairs until you can't get any further," he said, before continuing his thoughts.

Fred didn't need any more permission than that to go. Without the slightest hesitation he sprang from his place at the table and made for the staircase. On his way up, he couldn't help but slow down to take in the curious meandering crookedness. The house was more crooked than anywhere Fred had been before. The floors were sloping in different directions and not a single wall appeared to be built straight or square. The windows were in the most peculiar places and even some of the doorways started a third of the way up the walls. On the narrow landing between the bedrooms, he slowed down further as he approached an old oil painting on the wall. It was a portrait of a young woman with the most piercing pale green eyes that appeared, for a split second to be following him. If it had not been for the fact that the face was an uncanny resemblance to the vision he had seen in the night, Fred would have been more than happy to race past it. But the likeness was so striking he was drawn to stop and check on the detail. There was something else about her face too, he felt a deeper familiarity as if he already knew the woman, yet he had not seen her before. Fred turned his head, forcing himself away from what was a mesmerising stare, to continue along the landing and then through a small doorway, the bottom of which was oddly a step-height up from the floor.

The wooden stairs spiralled, coming out into a loft that had a small window built into the roof. After his vivid experience in the dark of the night, the room looked a little different to how he remembered. Streams of light filled the space, and as he walked through the room, the dust was disturbed around him, in a slow animated dance.

Nevertheless, the sea chest sat in proof of his recollection, and it was with a magnetic pull that he found himself almost floating towards it and lifting open the lid.

Sure enough, a long single strand of hair was waiting for him inside, and with great reverence, he carefully picked it up between his thumb and forefinger and held it up to the sunlight. It had the palest tone of ginger that lit up as if it were smiling at the freedom of the air and silently spoke to his mind.

"There you are, now what do you think I offer you?" it seemed to say.

As he ran down the stairs, bursting with excitement at his discovery, he didn't notice that the painting he had been so mesmerised by had changed completely. Not only did the hair mean that he now had a chance to go wherever Lavender's grandad went, but that the visit he had to York last night was not just some bizarre illusion, it really happened. He almost crashed into the kitchen table as he came to an abrupt halt in front of Aunt Margaret and Elijah, who were still engrossed in conversation.

"I take it you were successful young man?" said Elijah in distraction.

Fred held up the strand of hair proudly, "Here. This is it. Do you have something I can put in in?" he asked.

Elijah got up from the table and went through to the front room to rummage in the sideboard. Within a few moments he came back, handing Fred an empty cotton reel.

"Here you are, wrap it around this," he said.

Fred slotted an end of the hair into the top of the reel and wound it around until it was wrapped entirely and then slotted the other end in the top of the reel again.

"Look, you can see the colour quite clearly now. It's the same colour as the woman's hair I saw last night," he said.

Margaret stood up from the table to look, then turned to Elijah.

"Well, it has been lovely to meet you, but we must go now. I have to return this young man to his parents as promised," she said, then looked him directly in the eyes and raised her index finger ominously close to him. "You take heed now of what I've said, and you'll come to no harm," she concluded.

"Will I see you again?" Elijah replied.

Margaret said nothing until she got to the door and stepped outside.

"I have no doubt."

Chapter Twenty-Five

Passing the Waterfall

From the moment Fred and Aunt Margaret left, Lavender sat watching at the window seat with wide longing eyes, and for a while she didn't say anything. Grandma knew instinctively that it was best to leave her to her thoughts. There was a growing procession of people passing by as she sat there, pedestrians walking to the right, empty handed and coming back from the shops laden with bags and pulling tartan shopping trolleys. By 11.30 am, there seemed to be a sudden increase in men walking back from Fred Keighley's butcher's shop in mid-devouring of warm pork pies and heading towards the pub.

"I feel like I should be with them, Grandma," Lavender said, pressing her head against the cold window.

"They'll be a while yet tha knows so how about we go and get some fresh air lass, it might make us feel a bit better," grandma suggested.

It was a suggestion to herself too, that Annie had made in the midst of her own quiet struggle. She didn't really want to go out. At home she felt closer to her husband and going out she might meet someone in the street, a friend perhaps who might ask about Arthur. But nevertheless, it seemed like the best thing to do.

"We could go through the fields and up Hargill to the waterfall. By the time we get back they should be on their way home," she added.

Lavender pulled her face away from the glass and gave a reluctant smile, "OK, Grandma, let's go."

The walk was a good idea. The first breath of expansive, fresh air felt like a reconnection to the world. A reminder that life continued, despite the absence of husband and grandfather.

"I'll have to get someone to move your grandad's lorry, we can't leave it where it is for who knows how long," grandma said, as they walked past it and around the corner.

The little lane at the side of the cottage led up a gradual incline towards drystone-wall-framed fields and the woods that followed the beck up stream until it reached the base of the waterfall at Hargill. It was a walk that Lavender and her grandmother had done many times before and in all seasons, so they both knew it well. As they approached the small wooden footbridge that spanned the beck in front of the cascading water, it was a surprise when grandma began to divulge an interesting story about the waterfall, that she had never cared to mention before.

"There's that much water coming downstream after all the snow we've had, you can't see it at all can you?" grandma remarked, as if Lavender had full knowledge of what she was talking about.

"See what, Grandma?" Lavender replied, somewhat confused.

"The witches cave of course. I thought you knew about it," grandma answered, with a little surprise and a raised voice as she fought with the noise of the water.

She stood quite still on the little bridge, looking intently at the thundering water as it crashed into the pool at the bottom and then turned back to Lavender. Lavender responded with a blank expression and shook her head.

"Well, lass," grandma started loudly, "Behind the waterfall is a hidden cave and sometimes when the water flows slower, especially during the summer, you can see glimpses of the cave behind. They say that in olden days, it was a safe refuge for witches and no one else could enter. If anyone tried to pass the waterfall to get into the cave, they would seize up and slowly turn to stone. In the pool of water beneath the waterfall, the stones are said to be made of the broken bodies of all who tried in vain to enter."

The spray in the air was cold and had started to seep through their outer layers, so they moved ahead across the bridge and along the meandering path that led down the embankment at the other side and back home to complete the circuit.

"Have you ever tried to go in the cave, Grandma?" Lavender asked as she looked back at the waterfall below.

"Nay, lass, you don't see me turning to stone and falling in the water, do you?" she replied.

Lavender wasn't sure how serious grandma was and spent the rest of the walk back home wondering just how true the story of the cave was.

Their timing couldn't have been better, the fog was starting to return as Lavender and grandma turned the corner back onto Bridge Street and were walking the last couple of hundred yards to Pear Tree Cottage. Aunt Margaret's motorcycle rattled passed them and parked up behind grandad's lorry. Lavender couldn't contain herself and switched immediately from her previously meandering pace to a sprint. She arrived as Aunt Margaret and her excited pillion passenger had dismounted and were removing their helmets.

"Well, did you have any luck?" she asked eagerly.

In nonchalant splendour, Delius sat watching from the top of the stone gate post, casting his droll eyes over the scene as if he was reviewing what he already knew. Fred's beaming face was all she needed to see, and he nodded vigorously in assurance.

"Come on, we all need to get inside, this fog is getting worse. We'll tell you everything we know soon enough," Aunt Margaret instructed.

It wasn't long before they were all sat around the kitchen table eating the warmed pork pies and drinking hot cups of tea, Fred pulled out the cotton reel with the strand of hair wrapped tightly around it and the four of them discussed the visit to Elijah Scrubb and The Cringles.

"What shall we do now?" said Annie, as Fred finished recounting his part of the tale.

"Now it's up to you Fred. We need you to go and fetch Grandad … if you're up to it!" Lavender goaded.

"Ee, I'm not so sure, Lavender. What about his poor mum and dad, they're going to be fretting more than any parent has a right to," Annie said with concern.

"We'll see about that," said Margaret, standing up from the table and putting the last piece of pie into her ample cheeks.

Margaret walked through into the front room and stood looking at the fire, which was in need of a log or two to revive the dying embers. She placed a couple of nicely shaped lumps of wood across the middle of the fire and went to sit down. The four of them sat in silence as the flames rekindled. Annie, Lavender and Fred observing Margaret, and Margaret watching the fire, listening to the cracking and spitting of the wood in the flames.

"Well, Marg, what do you see?" asked Annie, impatiently interrupting her look of concentration.

Marg slowly moved her finger to her lips.

"Shh," she whispered in reply, and returned her stare to the fire for a while, before her eyelids fluttered and closed.

Suddenly, she called out in urgency, "Fear not my dears, I see a clock ticking in the fire, and a rope woven from Lavender's hair that binds this 'ere young lad to his place in time!"

She slumped back in the chair with her arms draped loosely at her side. Lavender, Fred and Annie looked at each other in wide-eyed confusion and shook their heads.

"Whatever does she mean?" Fred asked doubtfully.

Lavender and her grandma shrugged their shoulders in unison. Abruptly, Margaret opened her eyes wide.

"It means that you must have a lock of hair cut from someone you trust, if you want to return without being missed. When you return to the Venetius Stone, bear the lock of hair to bring you home. Now then lad, are you ready to go and rescue Mr Tilly?" she added.

Fred looked at Lavender, as if for some kind of approval. She looked back in a manner that indicated to Fred exactly what she was thinking. "You'd better go and get the scissors, Mrs Tilly," Fred instructed.

Chapter Twenty-Six

Captain Fortune

To Arthur, Isaac and Fred, the experience of moving through the fireplace was unworldly, until that is, they appeared on the other side of it. The sensation of floating and spinning in white, light brightness had given way quite abruptly to a contrasting, dark stillness. From here they each languished for a while as the movement and light in their heads stopped and dimmed. Eventually, they picked themselves up and walked through what felt like a long empty tunnel until they appeared in a place that they seemed to know, yet at the same time was quite different to anywhere they had been before. The opening they came to stand in was at the other side of the Venetius Stone. It was positioned in an oval meadow, filled with tall grass and wildflowers, and surrounded by trees at the back and sides that were older, taller and thicker in limbs than they had ever seen before. The atmosphere was so peaceful and the air so clear and heady with scent, that they each felt as though they had arrived in a version of heaven. In front of them was a river that meandered into the valley, guiding the eye into the distance where the familiar moors above Brigden appeared in their ordinary glory. Coming from further along the river was the soothing sound of falling water, and wood shifting and creaking at a watermill on the opposite riverbank, with its large wheel turning gracefully, churning the rumbling stones inside. The sight was quite surreal to them all, to such an extent that they had not yet acknowledged one another or that they were together and had accompanied each other on their journey. A large booming voice behind them broke their gazes.

"What thee be doin' round these parts, passing through my land, you ungainly set of travellers?"

They turned around to face the voice and in doing so crossed glances with one another before their eyes caught the stone through which they had just arrived.

In front of their new position was Pear Tree Cottage in a state of construction. There was a tall, heavy-set man with a tanned complexion and an impressive brown beard. Two younger, slimmer men on the other side of the building were carrying stones towards him. The walls were only partially complete and taking advantage of the Venetius Stone as a fire surround, the chimney had been started to be built against it. The tanned man had an impressive presence, even from this distance. He wore a leather sleeveless jacket that showed off his thick strong arms, and his hands seemed to be the size of shovels as they scooped up a large stone and placed it into the wall near the back of the cottage. Neither Arthur or Isaac was able to speak and stood quite still and dumbfounded by the reality of their situation. It was Fred who answered with a confidence and courage incongruent to his years.

"My name is Fred, Fred Keighley, and I'm here to …" Fred stopped mid-sentence, realising what he was about to say would probably seem ridiculous.

"What's wrong with thee. The cat got yer tongue?" The man laughed raucously as he spoke breaking Isaac from his frozen state and sending him dashing across the clearing to the woods.

Fred and the man watched Isaac's sudden departure with surprise and then Fred replied, "I've come to talk with the lady that lives here."

The words just came out of Fred's mouth without him even thinking, but they made no sense to the man, who placed the large stone down on the wall and started over towards them.

"What's wrong wi yer fellow traveller?" he said, as Isaac hastily disappeared into the concealment of the trees and the man approached the Venetius Stone.

"What's wrong wi you that you keep asking all these questions?" Fred replied belligerently.

The man stared at Fred, looking even more ominous to the two of them as the reality of his impressive frame came within striking distance. Arthur put a hand on Fred's shoulder to steady himself from the dizziness and disorientation he was still feeling. To Fred it felt like a signal to temper his attitude as the man's gaze fixed and his eyes sharpened in focus towards him. Then he let out a deep and resounding belly laugh that seemed to shake the ground he was stood on.

"Haha haha haaaa," he bellowed, bending over to clutch his stomach as he laughed, and the two other man joined in.

Fred was not amused, but Arthur felt somewhat relieved.

"There's no one that lives here yet. Have you got eyes in that head of yours? Can you not see the walls not finished and the roof has yet to go up?" the man replied.

Fred felt he was getting drawn in to defend himself, forgetting for a second the whole reason he was here was to get Arthur back to his wife and granddaughter.

"I do have eyes thank you. I was meaning the lady who's going to live here," Fred replied.

The man looked equally puzzled and intrigued. Arthur gripped Fred's shoulder tightly and guided him to turn around while speaking softly in his ear.

"Come on, lad, let's leave it for now. We'll give these men some peace."

They started to move away from the scene and wade their way through the knee-high grass towards the river and the watermill.

"We'll be in 'The Priest's Inn' tonight if you have a mind to tell me more about the lady. Just ask for Captain Fortune," the man shouted out to them as they walked away.

Arthur turned back to look, holding up his arm in acknowledgement.

"Right, lad. I think you'd better tell me why and how on earth you got here?" Arthur asked, as they picked up their pace across the meadow.

"Isacc Scrubb is the name of the man you came with. Lavender found the ancient amulet that her mum had, and Scrubb has been trying to get it. We know he had discovered that the arch of the fireplace at Pear Tree Cottage is a sacred place built by the Brigantes thousands of years ago. He had drawings of it in an old book that he left behind in his coat when he travelled through the fireplace. The thing is though, to go through the fireplace, you need to hold a hair from the head of the person you want to see. Isaac must have had a hair from someone who lived when Pear Tree Cottage was being built."

Fred paused for a moment to catch his breath.

"Nay, lad, you mean this is 1647? It can't be. All I did was try and stop that daft burglar from throwing himself on the fire and then I thought I'd knocked mi sen out," said Arthur in disbelief.

Reaching the banks of the river, they found a pair of large smooth rocks near some large weeping willows that made favourable places to sit and contemplate their circumstances.

"Sit thisen down, lad, I need to get mi 'ead around this," Arthur suggested, pointing to the rocks.

The weather was pleasant and the sun, high above, felt warm on their backs as they sat watching the clear water flow smoothly at this section of the river. It reflected the blue sky and the occasional light cloud that drifted in a carefree dream above.

"Whenever this is, it's a summer's day I'd say," Arthur observed, giving himself confirmation that this was not a concussion he was experiencing.

Fred continued to tell Arthur his tale, "I'm here to bring you back to Annie and Lavender. You see, it's a long story but Aunt Margaret and I found a single strand of hair in the same place Isaac did. The same hair that brought him here. I have a feeling it is from a distant relative of Annie and Lavender's and also of Aunt Margaret's. Her name is Mother Fortune, and it looks like she was the first to live in Pear Tree Cottage." Arthur interrupted Fred when he heard the name, "Wait. Mother Fortune you say? The great lump of a man building our cottage is called Captain Fortune. That surely can't be a coincidence can it?" he said.

"Definitely not. Anyway, all that is what brought me to be with you when I stepped into the fireplace," Fred concluded.

They both sat for a while contemplating the situation and gazing into the gently flowing water. Eventually Fred started to feel a need to move, and he stood up and went down to a wide arc of pebbles that followed the riverbank below. He picked up smooth flat pebbles and skimmed them across the river. When he had had enough, he bent down and scooped up several cups full of water with his hands to quench his thirst.

"This is the best water I've ever tasted," he said, as the cool quenching softness slipped down his eager throat.

Arthur remained on the rock, rubbing his bristly chin with his oil-ingrained fingers, and furrowing his brow in puzzlement.

I'll wake up in a minute, he thought to himself.

But nothing happened.

"Ok, if you're right then how are we going to get back?" Arthur called out.

Fred put his hand into his pocket and pulled out the lock of Lavender's hair, holding it up in the air. It glistened with hues of red and gold in the sun.

"Look. We cut it from Lavender just before I went through the fireplace. It should take us back to that same time."

"I hope you're right, but I don't think it's safe to go to the cottage while there's someone there. We'll wait until they've gone before we go back," Arthur advised, before shifting himself to lay down on a soft piece of ground in the shade of the willow.

"Suddenly, I'm feeling very tired. I'm just going to shut my eyes for a few moments," he said.

Fred was starting to feel tired too. He stood for a while surveying the area and breathing in the beauty with all his senses and then lay down near Arthur under the tree. The intoxicating fragrance of the air and the strobing sunlight filtered through the leaves above made his head feel light and his eyelids heavy. It felt like a long time ago that he had woken in his own bed and so much had happened since then. In seconds he closed his eyes and relinquished his mind to the lure of the moment.

The river curved downstream beyond the watermill where, on a steeper grassy bank at the start of the curve, there was a packhorse bridge with a single high arch spanning the river. There were a dozen or so stone buildings scattered there, and Isaac had run off in this direction to cross the bridge and watch and wait in safety. He had not arrived in the time he intended, and it was clear that connecting to his grandmother somehow was not going to happen. Instead, he found himself quite unprepared for his situation.

Eventually, Isaac found his way to the watermill and stood hiding against the safety of the side wall. It felt warm in the direct sunlight, and he basked in it, his eyes closed listening to the falling water and the grinding stones inside.

For a while he relaxed. The stunned feeling and then the rush to get away from the situation prevented him thinking clearly what to do. Now he started to calm. He opened his eyes and looked across the river where he had a clear view of Arthur and Fred walking through the tall grass and wildflowers towards the glistening smooth water only a short distance from him. Isaac was baffled.

I wonder how the young lad got here, he thought, as the stones Fred was skipping over the water left their rings of expanding ripples.

But when Fred held up the lock of hair in the sunlight for Arthur to see, he realised it was possible that Fred had come to rescue Arthur. Isaac contemplated the situation. He was in a time he didn't intend to be in. What use would it be for him to be here if he couldn't get back? He must return to his own time and if he could get hold of it, the lock of hair Fred had may provide the means. When he saw them lay down under a tall weeping willow tree and appear to go to sleep, he felt that fate had bestowed on him the chance to return.

Arthur's sleep was filled with a tormenting dream. Standing in the front room of Pear Tree Cottage, he could see his wife and granddaughter at the front door looking distressed at the situation and fearful of what may have happened to him, yet despite knowing the feeling all too well with the disappearance of his own daughter and son-in-law, he could not comfort them. He called out to Annie, but she didn't hear him. He looked around the room, searching for a way to let her know he was there. For a reason he couldn't fathom, the small brass bell from his childhood hanging on the wall stood out to him and he remembered it had no clapper. As he did so it rang twice like an echo from his infant days. He turned to look at his wife, but his attention shifted dramatically as he suddenly felt the presence of others. There were noises of men talking and a horse neighing and snorting. The sound of unfamiliar voices echoed in his mind, and he opened his eyes to see where they came from. On the water in front of him and from horses and cart behind him they were real enough. As he accustomed himself to the scene, he realised that he was in close proximity to the delivery of large wooden timber beams from a boat on the river. Three men were on the boat and another leading a tall sturdy horse, black except for its white fetlocks, that stood out like painted arrows of brilliant white. It had a shaggy mane that cascaded forward rebelliously as it pulled the boat on a long rope along the riverbank.

Arthur quietly leant over and nudged Fred gently on his shoulder to wake him, but rather than coming around unnoticed, Fred sat bolt upright, thrusting his arms out parallel to the ground announcing, "Just like that!"

The great black horse reared up in surprise at the sight of Fred springing from under the willow causing a sudden movement that jerked the boat from its slow glide across the water, sending it directly into the path of the pebbled riverbank, grounding it unceremoniously in the shallow waters of the riverbed. Across the open meadow, Captain Fortune and his two labourers were leading a horse and cart towards the river as they heard the crunch of the boat grounding. His bellowing voice drew Arthur and Fred's attention towards him.

"Ahoy there!" he shouted. "Seems we have ourselves a couple of pairs of hands to help us with our cargo."

He was looking directly at Arthur and Fred. There was a moment of frozen animation before Arthur stood up and spoke.

"Happy to help if we can. Are those timbers for the building?" he asked, reaching down to give Fred an encouraging hand.

"Aye. They're from mi old ship "The White Lion" bless her wooden 'eart. She ran aground in a storm last winter that wrecked her too much for the mending. Lost a few faithful souls that rum night. So now her old timbers will not shiver again, they're ready for a new vessel, that cottage I'm building o'er yonder. Come on now, all hands to the decks, hahaaha and there'll be a jug o' ale for thee when the sun goes down."

As Arthur and Fred tentatively made their way towards the boat, a scrawny specimen of a man jumped down from the grounded vessel while another two men of equal physique remained on the boat.

"Aye aye, Captain. Are you ready for a back breaking haul?" he shouted out.

"Come on now, Parson, many hands make light work o'it. We'll have them in place afore thee know it," the captain replied.

The huge black oak timber beams were indeed a back breaking weight to bear. They smelled of the salty sea and were as hard as iron, and it seemed as heavy too. With the aid of the horses, rope and the combined strength of eight men and one boy, they worked together to haul them from the boat. Time after time they repeated the route across the meadow, transporting the beams on the cart for the last hundred yards and stopping at the river each time to quench their thirst. The sun was starting to lower in the sky and the now warm, comforted earth basked in the accumulation of the afternoon heat. Placed at the cottage, the well-travelled oak was waiting to be erected into it's final resting place, along with the eight hungry labourers who were sat propped against the stone walls.

Fred had found his own special spot under the Venetius Stone and there, in the glow of the late afternoon sun, everyone was quiet, eyes closed and faces content, absorbed in the gentleness of the air.

As he sat in the radiant splendour, Fred observed the tranquillity. It was almost unrecognisable from the industrialised winter of Brigden he had somehow travelled from. Before him, the meadow was a ballroom of waltzing summer insects and gently bending cornflowers that he had only known as grey streets and repeating rows of terraced houses. While he considered the vast differences, the figure of a young woman appeared from the trees at the edge of the meadow, walking along the river line until she was near the moored boat. She was some distance away, yet he could make out her beauty and the striking colour of her red hair, that flowed like flames all the way down her back. The colour reminded him of Lavender's, leading him to instinctively reach into his pocket to feel for her lock of hair, but it was missing. In panic he turned out both pockets of his trousers, yet they were empty, sending his mind into a frenzy and with it his body too. He launched himself unthinkingly from his position and out across the meadow, retracing the cart tracks, and his own steps, that had cut a well-trodden track from the riverbank.

Chapter Twenty-Seven

Olicana

By the time Arthur, Captain Fortune and the rest of the men realised he had gone, Fred was halfway to the river and quickly approaching the young woman who had sparked the discovery of his loss. She couldn't help but see him, erratically scanning the ground and the trampled grass and cornflowers that marked their afternoons work. She paused silently to wait for his anticipated arrival. As soon as he approached close enough that she wouldn't need to raise her voice, she spoke to him.

"You're looking for something very important, I see. Can I help you with your search?"

Her voice was calm and soothing to his mind, like the cool water of the river, that had been so thirst quenching to his body. He stopped, immediately, captivated not just by her loveliness and grace, but because he recognised her from his vision of the painting at number 10 The Cringles. He gazed, entranced into her pale green eyes. The woman moved toward his stationary body, reaching out her hand to touch his with her slender, pale fingers.

"I'm Olicana. Tell me, who are you and what are we to find?" she asked.

"I'm Fred Keighley and I've lost a lock of hair, the same colour as your own, which is very precious to me. I'm stuck here and if I don't get it back I'll never be able to return home."

His reply came with a returning feeling of panic. She was still holding his hand as he spoke.

"All will be well my dear, remember to fear not." She squeezed his hand gently. Now, tell me when and where did you last have sight of it?"

Feeling a trust in her presence, Fred thought for a moment.

"Right by those rocks near the willow trees at the riverbank. I was showing it to my friend's grandfather, and then right afterwards we both fell asleep."

Back across the meadow at the cottage, Parson spotted Fred who appeared to be holding hands with the flame-haired woman.

In teasing laughter, Parson announced his discovery, "Aye, Aye. I fear your dreams of love with the red-haired maiden are lost to a mere boy, Captain! Maybe your days of being a fine catch are over, what do you say lads?"

All the men looked out towards the river to see. Little Pip, one of the cheekier younger labourers from the cottage, who was particularly scrawny, added to Parson's tormenting.

"Well, the lad may be young but he's striking in his stature. Happen I'm in with a chance with the sight of your longing, Captain, it seems she prefers a nimbler fella than thee."

All the goading was turning the captain's usually jovial demeanour into one of seething irritation, putting Arthur on edge, and distracting him from observing Fred and the young woman.

Captain Fortune had spent the last two months of that unusually warm summer in a growing state of besottedness. Twice a day at least, the young woman would appear within his view as he and his labourers built the cottage. Gracefully, she would move across the meadow drawing his eye and then, following the river up to the bridge, she would mystically disappear. Later in the afternoon she would come back again, lightly treading a similar path. He had made enquiries in the village of whom she was and where she lived but all he discovered was that her name was Olicana and that she came from the moors. Recently there had been several occasions when they had spoken, but each time, Fortune's boisterous personality had become lodged in his throat, leaving him feeling lost in unfamiliar territory. His awkwardness in this had not gone unnoticed by his young labourers and in the last week, feeling the need to explain himself, he had confessed his blossoming feelings of love for the woman.

At this moment, Arthur intuitively felt the captain's embarrassment. It was a feeling that spurred him to rise from his resting place against the wall and walk over to him. As he did so he noticed the blood rising in the captain's forehead.

"I have something to show you, come with me," Arthur invited, guiding him from his position of unwelcome attention.

The captain followed Arthur to the back of the cottage where Arthur stopped and looked him directly in the eyes. He pulled out his wallet from his trouser pocket and opened it up to the captain. Arthur removed a small black and white photograph of Annie that he had carried with him since 1940. The edges were dog eared and well handled.

"See here. This is a picture of my wife Annie from around the time I first met her."

The captain was intrigued. Looking at the remarkable detail, the picture was more lifelike than any painting he had seen before. The face on the photograph was serene, clear and bright, with deep, dark entrancing eyes. Her hair was sleek, straight and black, cut in a 1920's bob haircut that framed her face to perfection.

"You see, Captain Fortune, back then I was as tongue-tied as you are now. I couldn't get a word out, though I longed to speak to her every time I passed her in the street or leaving church on a Sunday. I thought, she's too perfect for the likes of me, and with that my mouth would dry up and my tongue would feel like a lump in my throat."

Captain Fortune stared at the picture of young Annie and then turned to Arthur.

"Well, I can see why you'd think that, she hath the face of an Egyptian Goddess. How did you ever become married, sir?" he asked curiously.

"Well, it was all because of a Terry's Chocolate Orange," Arthur recalled, then, realising the nonsense his words must have meant, he clarified, "Have you heard of chocolate Captain?"

"Aye, I've had a taste of the drink in London only last year. It was a surprising tonic," he replied.

"Chocolate has been made into all sorts of sweet things where I come from, you wouldn't believe the variety. It's even combined with the flavour of orange and shaped so it looks like the fruit. One day I had visited her mother's shop and bought one of these chocolate oranges and then as I turned around, I saw the beautiful Annie right before me and in a nervous mesmerism, I dropped it on the floor. It split open in front of us, Annie and I bent down at the same time to pick it up and bumped heads. I was so dazed, embarrassed and concerned about her that I offered her a piece of the chocolate in compensation. We just laughed at one another and the rest, as they say, is history."

Arthur's story gave Fortune a sudden bout of courage, changing his entire demeanour. He straightened his posture, then with a hefty pat on Arthurs back that knocked an uncomfortable amount of air from of his lungs, Fortune announced he would go to greet Olicana.

He walked off around the cottage walls towards the open meadow, but to his dismay, Olicana and Fred had disappeared.

Meanwhile, Olicana and Fred searched the area under the willow trees for the lock of Lavender's hair, but Olicana's intuition told her that this was a futile exercise. As they scoured the surrounding grass and rocks, Fred explained the circumstances of his arrival in this place with Lavender's grandfather and the unsavoury character that was Isaac Scrubb.

"He gave me the heebie-jeebies that man, I wouldn't trust him as far as I could throw him," Fred said, as the encounters he had with him replayed in his mind.

Olicana's sensed another set of eyes watching and her attention was drawn to the opposite side of the river. She traced the riverbank as far as the bridge and caught sight of the slim figure of a man walking surreptitiously across towards the village on the other side.

"Would that dubious character on the bridge be the unpleasant man you refer to as Isaac Scrubb?" she asked.

Fred looked towards the bridge, instantly recognising his tall thin frame and distinctive posture.

"It is, miss, it is," he replied.

"Then we must follow him. I sense he hath taken your precious locks to satisfy his own ends."

It was at a fair pace that Isaac made his way over the unmade road and through the small collection of mismatched stone buildings that made up the village. Olicana and Fred followed behind him in covert pursuit and growing interest as to the direction he was taking. The lack of houses, other manmade features, and the wealth of trees that covered the land confused Fred's bearings. Even the canal didn't exist and perhaps most surreal of all was that his own home was gone, yet he didn't feel lost. The permanent features of the landscape were more prominent and recognisable to his eye than before. As they continued out across the higher ground towards the moors, they stopped to hide for a while by a copse, just before the open incline of land that bordered the escarpment at the moors edge, and the striking rocky feature that was Obadiah.

"It looks like he's heading towards Obadiah. Do you know the legend of Obadiah?" asked Olicana, pointing to the prominent feature on the Goddodin moors.

Fred watched Isaac making his way on to the rocky ravine at the start of the escarpment and noticed an obvious difference to the rocks.

"I do know the legend and I can see Obadiah, but it looks odd to me that there is a boulder beneath him," he remarked.

"But if you know the legend, then you would know that is the sheep Obadiah caught in his jaw," Olicana replied.

"Ah, that explains it," said Fred, as he realised the change. "In time the sheep will escape Obadiah's grip and make its way down the escarpment. In the time I come from, only Obadiah remains on the moor."

Unaware that he was being followed, Isaac scrambled up the last steep part of the escarpment with his heart thumping hard in his chest.

While Isaac had been waiting to make a move on Fred and steal the lock of hair from Fred's sleeping body, he had passed the time surveying the area. It was the sight of the huge boulders high on the moors that were a prophetic sign to him, unexpectedly adjusting his priorities. Before he tried to get back to his own time, he had a chance to retrieve one of the illusive amulets. The sight of Obadiah and the sheep was an absolute match of the records his grandfather had kept. In these records, a place like this was identified where the Brigantes hid an amulet from the invading Romans. On its own, Obadiah was just a shadow of the drawings he was so familiar with, but with the other boulder wedged in Obadiah's jaw, there could be no doubt that this was one of the places he, and his grandfather before him, had been so desperately looking for. Finally, Isaac disappeared over the escarpment and onto the purple-heather carpet of the moorland, his eagerness was spurring his ageing body beyond its comfortable limits as the sight of the huge boulders stood only one hundred yards across the heather. From this distance the wolf appeared to smile at him, but then the closer he got to it, the more he doubted its apparent friendliness. He reached the base of the huge dark grey boulders and placed his hands flat on the weathered surface, sensing it as if feeling for the pulse of a wounded animal. In parts, the seams in the stone were like the hair of the wolf, yet the texture of the adjoining stone was quite different. He peered into the cracks between the rocks, searching the dark inaccessible grooves. There would be no chance of retrieving anything that may be deposited here. Isaac pulled himself up onto a foot hole that was the open jaw of Obadiah. From here he continued to investigate the dark crevices of the rock further and as he did so, the sun, descending towards the distant horizon behind, pierced a narrow pinpoint of light between wolf and sheep and into his eye. Blinded for a moment, he squinted, forcing him to consider the reality of the situation. If his grandfather's records were to be believed, as the Brigantes fled Maiden Castle and crossed the moors, the amulet was placed here between wolf and sheep. But even if it was, he had little hope of getting it. Nevertheless, his doubts were surpassed by an urge to know more, so he pressed on to gain a better view, climbing upwards onto the rocky nose of Obadiah.

From here the vantage point offered a clearer view of the gaps between the two, one of which was a wedge of space that could accommodate a fully grown man, albeit at a snug fit.

Could the amulet be sitting at the bottom of the hole? Isaac contemplated his chances of successfully getting into the wedge and then out again.

It would be much simpler if I had a smaller younger body, he thought.

By now Olicana and Fred had reached the top of the escarpment and were crossing the heather towards Obadiah and the sheep. They arrived at the deep ditch that formed the outer edge of Maiden Castle. It was a rough circle of considerable size and offered them a place to stop and crouch down in concealment to observe. Fred knew this was the remains of Maiden Castle though he wasn't entirely sure what it was.

"He must be on the other side of the rocks. What do you intend to do?" Fred enquired with some concern.

"I hath my means. You wait here below the cover of the heather and leave it to me," she replied.

Olicana was a nimble young woman and unlike Isaac, it wasn't long before she had reached Obadiah and made her ascent onto his nose, where she came face to face with Isaac Scrubb. Like most who first encountered Olicana, Isaac was stunned into a frozen pose. It wasn't only her striking features that were so captivating; the vibrant colour of her hair and eyes contrasted in an other-worldly manner with her pale skin, but her very presence had occurred almost magically to him as if she were an apparition. He was sat, with his legs dangling into the wedge-shaped void, jaw dropped and mouth agog. She approached him gracefully, her head held high with her hair flowing and fluttering in a strengthening breeze that lifted the scent of heather from the moors. Isaac was entranced, as golden threads of her flaming hair, shimmered in the setting sun.

She spoke assertively, extending her arms out to him and opening her hand.

"You have taken something of mine and now, Isaac Scrubb, it is time to return it."

Isaac's eyes glazed over, lost in the flickering locks of her fiery hair. Who was this unearthly vision before him and how did she know his name? She tilted her head down towards him, her pupils narrowing in the sunlight and wind as she focused the power of her request and pushed her hand a fraction further toward him. His eyes flicked back into the reality of the moment, and he automatically reached down into his pocket, pulling out the lock of hair and holding it up in front of himself. For a second, a single thread caught the sunlight, just as Olicana's had, and then it extinguished, dulling as the sun dropped behind the horizon. He shifted his body, turning on the ledge to get up, but as the rising movement ensued, it sent a wave of light-headedness over him, buckling his knees beneath and weakening his grip. The lock of hair lifted silently into the air, carried high up and over the escarpment and the dale below. In a desperate reach to catch it Isaac tumbled, awkwardly trapping himself halfway down the narrowing gap. There were audible bone crunching cracks as his body hit the rocks followed by a pained cry and a long silence. Olicana peered down at Isaacs contorted body that had started to moan and then turned to look back for Fred hiding in the heather. She waved her arms high in the air, gesturing and calling for him until he made his way to join her on the rock, then turned back to call down to Isaac.

"Can you move at all?" she asked.

He tilted his head back so that she could now just see the whites of his eyes.

"I think I've broken my shoulder," he groaned, as he made a futile effort to adjust his body.

Olicana made her way to the other side of the gap to obtain a better view of his position. The narrowing wedge Isaac had fallen into seemed to open up lower down into what appeared to be an enclosed space. He may well have dropped into this dark hole if he had not fallen towards the back of the rocks and lodged himself between the two.

She lowered herself into the gap and reached down to Isaac.

"Give me your hand," she offered.

In Isaac's mind he lifted his arms up towards this mystical woman, but physically, they did little more than twitch, increasing the pain in his chest as he drew breath. Olicana manoeuvred herself to the side of him straddling the larger gap and hole beneath. She could see his body was stuck at the lower torso and his legs were dangling in the void beneath. It was clear that getting him out would require someone to pull from the top and push from the bottom.

"Where are you, Olicana?" Fred shouted from the base of the giant boulders.

"Up here Fred. Isaac is trapped in the rocks. Quickly, go and fetch help!"

Chapter Twenty-Eight

Help!

Captain Fortune gazed out across the empty meadow, resigning himself to what he had come to expect. Each time he summoned up the courage, Olicana seemed to disappear, denying him the chance to develop an acquaintance. For a while he stood staring into the distant Goddodin moors. It was an impossible hope that he might see her on the horizon, but nevertheless he studied it intensely.

"Has anyone seen Fred?" Arthur called out, with the first hint of panic breaking Fortune's stare.

"It seems they have both gone," Fortune declared in resignation.

"What do you mean gone? They must be somewhere nearby," Arthur questioned.

Little Pip chirped in again with his ill-timed humour. "They've run off together over the bridge, never to be seen again. I saw them looking quite the proper couple, I did."

Arthur's panic did not diminish at Little Pip's observations.

"Come, Captain, we have to spread out and search the area, we must find the lad," Arthur encouraged, but his words did little to motivate the recumbent men.

"Leave them be, old man. They're ready for a hearty meal and a jug or two o'ale in The Priest's Inn, not a wild goose chase around the village. Your lad will return when he's good and ready," Parson advised.

There was chatter from the rest of the men, now roused out of their relaxation. Hungry after a hard day's work, they added to the conversation with a restless need for sustenance.

"A group of empty bellies and dry throats I see before me. I can taste the roasting hog already. Come men, let's be makin' tracks," the captain announced, then started out across the meadow to the inn.

The men quickly joined him leaving Arthur trailing behind, torn with what he should do. He paused for a moment and thought. What if I'm not here and Fred comes back. The daylight will be gone soon. Still, with increasing distance, Arthur followed the men until they had crossed the pack horse bridge and reached The Priest's Inn. It was a building he had frequented most of his adult life, though he knew it not as The Priest's Inn, but as The Turk's Head. The irony didn't escape Arthur. Here he was, exactly where he would normally be on an early Saturday evening, but today he wasn't meeting Fred Keighley Senior as he finished his day at his butcher's shop, he was with a group of strangers in a village that was a world away from his own.

Inside the inn, the surroundings and furniture were rudimentary; natural stone walls and flagged floors, wooden benches and large tables, but the Inglenook fireplace that was such a famous feature of The Turk's Head stood much the same as usual. Arthur found himself becoming rather sombre as he saw it, his mind drifting to the many happy evenings where he had stood by the open fire with a pint of best bitter and the welcome ear of a good friend, that now seemed so lost. Captain Fortune noticed Arthur's vacant eyes and with blunt address he slapped him hard across the back.

"Fear not, my ancient traveller, when his belly tells him, your young companion will be back. Meantime fill your own with ale while you smell the cracklin' hog on the spit."

Arthur's stomach was indeed in need of nourishment and his hunger seemed the most immediate necessity to address. He took his share of bread and cheese, roasted meat and cabbage with the rest of the men, then washing it down with a jar of ale. Feeling replete, he made for the door and sat on a low wall opposite the inn in the hope of catching sight of Fred.

He watched the slow shadows stretch over the landscape as the summer sun descended. He listened to the muffled merry voices inside the inn contrasting with the calm satisfied air that heaved gently, satiated from a day of sunshine, just as he was from the wholesome food that lingered savourly in his mouth. If it were not for Fred's disappearance with the striking young woman, he would feel as content as the land before him. Half an hour passed by, and the deepening blue sky turned orange over the moors and then to indigo and adding to the beauty, a harvest moon rising as the sun set, cast enough light to navigate the fields.

When the first faint hint of Venus pricked the evening canvas overhead, the door of the inn creaked open and Captain Fortune strode over towards the wall. Arthur made no movement. His eyes closed in an attempt to flee the manifestation of such a vivid dream. For a while the captain sat on the wall in silence taking in the expanding cosmos overhead.

"A sailor's best friend these jewels in the sky. Always moving, forever repeating."

His words were so fitting, they repeated in Arthur's mind. Was he and everything else just like the stars, cycling the universe and forever returning?

Beyond the outer buildings of the village, the rising sound of feet and shins running through a grassy meadow interrupted Arthur's thoughts.

He sprang to his feet in sudden interest, striding out towards what was now a distinct figure with panting breath, heading towards them.

Realising with interest the sense of urgency with which the approaching person possessed, Fortune jumped up from the wall as well to join Arthur. Within seconds they could soon see the youthful pace belonged to the panicked and breathless Fred Keighley.

"Hey there ... Please, help me. Help!" he gasped as he drew closer, almost flying past them before coming to a screeching halt.

"Whatever's the matter, Fred?" Arthur asked in a combination of relief and concern.

Fred bent over resting his hands on his knees and gasping for breath.

His words were hindered by his need for air. "It's Isaac, Isaac Scrubb ... and Lavender's hair."

Fred straightened his back as he grimaced at the urgent breath entering his lungs.

"What of him and the hair?" Arthur looked mystified as he asked.

"He took Lavender's hair from me while we were sleeping and then went up to the moor and Obadiah."

Arthur's confused look unexpectedly turned to a wry smile. "So, you followed him up onto the moors to retrieve Lavender's hair, did you?" Arthur checked.

"Aye, we did. Me and the red-haired woman, Olicana, but that's not all. Isaac fell down inside Obadiah and he's gone and got himself stuck in the great wolf's belly." Fred elaborated what he knew and the sense of importance in which Olicana had asked for help.

"Is the fair maiden Olicana with Scrubb?" Fortune enquired with urgency.

"Aye she is," Fred replied.

Fortune's face lit up in the silver beams of moonlight as he grabbed Fred by the arm and pulled him back towards the direction he had been.

"Come, let us find this wretched soul that lies in Obadiah's stony bowels, and make safe the bonnie lass that dares to save a thief."

Beyond the village, Arthur struggled to keep up with the two pairs of younger legs that strode out into the open fields.

"Wait for me. I can't keep up wi' thee," he called.

But their pace increased further as Fortune led the way.

"Wait by the inn for us old man, thy breath is shorter, and thy body slows us down. I'll look after the lad, do not fret," the captain called back.

Arthur stopped to catch his breath, then called out in frustration. "Wait … come back. I have summat to tell you … Wait! He doesn't have Lavender's hair. Wait!"

It was too late. In a blink of the eye they were gone, two quickening silhouettes vanishing over a stile in a drystone wall. Isaac Scrubb had lost all sense of feeling in the lower half of his body, as with each increasing minute, his weight seemed to lock him deeper in the gap. He was cold with shock and his growing quietness was concerning Olicana. She attempted to reassure him and keep him warm, manoeuvring herself carefully over the large hole to be near him.

"Hold on, sir, help will arrive soon, and we will have you released from your fast."

Isaac's eyes acknowledged her words, but he didn't otherwise reply. It was dark in their concealed trap, the low-slung moonbeams hadn't reached into the depths of it, leaving Isaac to contemplate the thought that his end was nigh. He strained his eyes to see the outline of Olicana's features, filling in the gaps from his memory of the woman's face in the painting he lived with from his earliest moments, the portrait that hung in the hallway of the landing in number 10 The Cringles. He began to speak, but in what was now no more than a whisper, his lungs rattling a little in his chest after every few words.

"Listen ye here … my reckoning has come … Between these stones … lays an amulet … More ancient than the Romans … More precious … than the King's crown. Find it … and …"

Isaac's words petered away until the breath that carried them, would barely flutter the downy barbs of a dove's feather. Olicana placed her ear against his dry lips and listened. There was nothing, and then, as if in a last sigh of relief, his soul released itself from its bitter prison with a "haaaaaaaaaaaaaaaa." And the wind lifted across the moors and down through the narrow cracks in the rocks to sweep up the remains of the day.

Captain Fortune and Fred Keighley were nearing the top of the escarpment when the wind picked up. The horizon before them an evolving view of the conspicuous rocks that appeared to emerge from the ground as they reached the top. They looked towards the great rocks of Obadiah and the sheep, and the strengthening wind hit them in the face. Olicana had climbed back to the top of the rock and stood in striking pose on its summit, her red hair in silver relief and blowing in the breeze. Fred felt an unwelcome icy shiver pass through his body as they moved towards her, and the ground began to tremble, rattling the stones and scree on the slope they had climbed.

"Olicana, we are coming," Fortune called out into the wind, waving his arms high in the air.

They weren't sure if she had turned to see them, but in that moment the trembling earth gave a final shudder and the giant rock of Obadiah let go of his sheep and tumbled from his grip and rolled, rumbling towards the valley below. Olicana appeared to plunge into the moors, letting out a piercing scream that ended in silence and sent the two rescuers into a sprint towards her.

Chapter Twenty-Nine

Revelations

On the uncovered earth, beside the remaining giant rock of Obadiah, Olicana lay unconscious, draped over the broken body of Isaac Scrubb. It was a vision that halted Fred's hope and left him rooted to the spot, trembling in shock. Fortune sped on ahead. On approaching Olicana, he knelt at her side, hesitating to act, as he gazed in awe of her quiet beauty, her luminous pale skin in the moonlight, her fine features and tangled red hair, her eyes peacefully closed.

He sighed thankfully as he saw her chest gently rising and falling, then bent his head down to get closer to her ear.

"Olicana! Depart not this earthly plane afore I have truly known thee," he whispered.

She blinked, revealing his face to her watering vision; his eyes that were cast loving upon her.

"Be afraid not. Ye are safe, let me take thee home," he offered.

Olicana's cheeks raised slightly, turning the corners of her mouth into a fragile smile. Carefully, Fortune slid his strong arms underneath her body, lifting her light frame up to his chest. Her weight surrendered to him.

Alone now on the ground, Isaac Scrubb's body lay abandoned, as if clumsily hidden under a discarded coat. Fred approached the site where he lay and stared at the body of the man who had led him to this place for the pursuit of something important, an amulet perhaps, whose power he had no real understanding of. What a shabby hollow vision of the man who had taken Lavender's hair and that now prevented his return home. The earth shuddered a little more underneath his lifeless bones and drawn grey skin shattering him into dust, leaving only his limp clothes and empty boots.

Fred knelt to the great coat where Isaac had lain, lifting it off the ground in disbelief, searching for the body of this peculiar man. Only his ragged trousers and shirt lay uninhabited underneath.

"The devil hath taken his soul, young Fred. Away! We must get this young maiden to the village to rest," said Fortune.

Fred kicked Isaac's clothes on the ground, sending them unceremoniously into a new heap along with a night-time cloud of dust. As he turned and started walking away, Olicana felt an invisible pull in her body, back to the stone. It became so strong that she felt as though she was a fish caught in a net.

"Wait," she said, wriggling in Fortune's arms, "The ground speaks to me. Thou must search. There, where we fell."

She pointed to the naked earth scorched by Isaac's shattered body.

Even with the full moon, it was difficult to see with any clear definition, but nevertheless Fred got down on his hands and knees.

"It's hard to see down here. It might help to know what I am searching for?" he questioned.

"Ye will know if ye finds it," Olicana continued, unsure of the reason for her feeling, but certain they could not leave until a thorough investigation had occurred.

Fortune sat down on a large tuft of spongy heather, still holding her in his arms, her body resting against him, though with enough strength to stretch her head around and off his shoulders to strain at a view of Fred.

"Make haste then, lad, 'tis what the fair maiden desires."

Fred dug at the ground with his bare hands. It was soft and easy to move at the bottom of the hole between the rocks of Obadiah and the sheep. Before long he felt a warming sensation beneath his hands. It was a feeling that he recognised from holding the amulet back at home, a feeling that brought with it a sense of other worldliness. Olicana and Fortune watched as Fred's digging became more frantic at the sensation, and then he stopped. A few seconds later he raised his arm into the air and stared in silence and disbelief at the object in front of him. It was the intricate gold case he had found hidden in the church organ.

"What do ye have there, my little ship mate? Pirates treasure?"

Not willing to let Olicana from his safe keeping, Captain Fortune stood up with her as he spoke and moved towards Fred.

"I think it's much older than pirate's treasure, and more valuable," Fred answered.

"Bring it here for a closer look then," Olicana instructed.

Fred placed the case in her hand. Immediately her fingers tingled at the touch of it, her mind sensed something beyond the shining metal, its deep ancestry and powerful heritage.

"Come now," the captain announced and started walking before he had finished speaking. "Time we should be moving on and return to the village. The old man is waiting for thee, and we shall see more clearly this treasure thou hath uncovered," he continued.

Olicana handed the case back to Fred, leaving him momentarily in awe, lost in thought at their discovery.

The walk back to the inn felt surprisingly quick to them all. The multitude of thoughts Fred had distracted his attention for much of the journey. So too did the need to scan the fields, hedgerows and drystone walls, all in the remote chance of finding the lock of hair that had been carried high on the wind. But his eyes would return again and again to the golden case, rechecking it in the silver moonlight. For the most part, Olicana drifted in and out of consciousness, and even though his arms started to feel like the weight and stiffness of cannon barrels, Captain Fortune relished each step of the way while he held her in his protective grasp.

So, it was in many ways a disappointment to him when she eventually woke fully at the entrance to the village and declared. "I can walk, sir, thank you. Please set me down."

With reluctance Fortune lowered her down to walk under her own strength, at the same time breathing an incongruent sigh of relief. As he did so, she smiled at him. It was a smile that a few short hours ago he could only have dreamed of receiving.

Soon, they turned a corner on the rough road, opening up an inviting view of Brigden's sparse scattering of buildings, including the welcome glow of light and distant muffled voices of raucous activity at the inn, that now acted like a beacon to their weary feet.

Opposite the inn and still waiting, Arthur had remained rooted to his spot on the wall, eventually falling asleep in a most curious posture. They approached him quietly so as not to send him into a fright, leaving Fred to gently squeeze Arthur's shoulders and announce their presence in a soft voice. Arthur woke slowly with a crick in his neck and a dead arm. He had been in a deep sleep and struggled at first to come around as Fred explained what had happened with some excitement and showed him his discovery. His tone eventually turning to one of despair as he recounted his lack of success in locating Lavender's hair.

"I don't know what we are going to do, Mr Tilly. We might be stuck here forever," Fred concluded despondently.

Arthur placed a hand on Fred's shoulder. "Ee, lad. Tha's nowt to fret about. Look 'ere."

He put his hand into his pocket and pulled out the lock of Lavender's hair. Fred's jaw dropped in disbelief, reaching out to touch the hair, checking the soft red strands were real.

"I took them for safe keeping while you were sleeping down by the river," Arthur explained.

"You had it all along, all the time I was looking?" Fred exclaimed in exasperation, and then after a moment's pause to think continued, "Can we go home then now? I'm starving and tired."

It had been a long time since he had lasted this long without food, and the thought of his father's pies were causing some tuneful gurgling noises in his stomach, which in turn played on his mind so much, he could barely focus on anything else. Arthur looked out into the moonlight, taking in the simple beauty of the ancient moonlit landscape. He pondered the couple in front of him, who were sat on the wall recovering from their walk.

They had been listening in surprise to the revelation that the whole expedition had developed under a pretence that was entirely unfounded. However, neither of them could shirk the feeling that it had all happened as it was meant to happen, though they had very different reasons for feeling this. For Olicana, something inside her had changed, the world seemed different, her senses broader sharper and deeper than she had known before, as if now she knew beyond the ordinary way of things. It was fate itself to have gone and discover such an incredible object, buried shallowly in what had hitherto been such an inaccessible place. For Captain Fortune, it was all destined to happen to bring him close to Olicana and allow him to prove his care of her. In this respect, carrying her down from Goddodin moor had revealed to Olicana a man of kindness and devotion, to whom she now felt a connection of a depth she had not previously experienced with any other man.

"Come on, Mr Tilly, let's go home now," said Fred, tugging on Arthur's arm and breaking him from his thoughts.

"Aye, lad, we'd best be mekin' tracks or else they'll be sending out a search party for us. It's been nice to make your acquaintance Captain, but we must be on our way," Arthur explained to Fortune, and then he turned to Olicana.

He looked at her and saw in her eyes the very same light he saw in Lavender's eyes, a unique striking spirit that was unmistakable to anyone who knew it.

"What do you see?" Olicana asked.

"I see the past, and the future in your eyes, I see my own grandchild deep within you."

Arthur's words struck Olicana profoundly in her heart.

"Wait. Before you go, can I touch the lock of hair you carry?" she asked, sensing an urge to hold it.

Arthur held out Lavender's hair, just as he had done for Fred. She touched it lovingly, feeling a bond so strong it was as if it were her own hair.

"I have to ask you to leave some of it behind, the future depends on it," she continued, then whispered something into his ear.

Something happened to Arthur in that moment, and it was now impossible to say no to her. He undid the string that held it together and removing a small width of hair, passed it to Olicana and retied the hair.

Arthur and Fred turned to leave, heading back towards the site of Pear Tree Cottage and the Venetius Stone, but they had got no more than a hundred yards when Fred placed his hands in his trouser pockets, then stopped. In his eagerness to leave, he had forgotten the gold case that sat in his pocket.

What should I do with it? he thought, pulling it out.

He wiped it with his sleeve, examining closely the familiar intricate design. The dent he had made in it with his foot was not there. It was remarkably pristine. He opened it up in a sudden burst of excitement that something maybe inside, but it was empty. Taking it didn't seem right. Besides, it was still at Pear Tree Cottage hiding underneath the piano, wasn't it?

"Shall I leave the case with Olicana?" he asked.

Arthur smiled at him but had a curious look in his eyes.

"Aye lad, you do that. I need to go on ahead if you'll be alright on your own. But listen, straight back to the cottage and home to your family, you hear?"

Fred turned around, retracing his steps towards Olicana and the captain while Arthur continued ahead.

"What are you doing?" they both asked as Fred arrived back.

He reached out and thrust the case into Olicana's hands.

"Here, I think you should have this," he offered.

She took the case and smiled softly with her eyes.

"Your work here is done now young Fred. It's time for you to go."

Chapter Thirty

The End of the Beginning

In the moments after Fred first entered the great fireplace, Lavender, grandma and Aunt Margaret stood agog, staring in disbelief at the fireback. There had been a blast of wind that accompanied his action, extinguishing the flames in the instant of his disappearance and sending Delius heading straight under the piano stool to hide. In that split second, it was almost as if a lifetime had passed before them. Was it really happening? Would he be safe? Would he find Arthur? Grandma was frozen in shock, scissors still in hand. Lavender's long hair had blown back by the blast and Aunt Margaret's jowls were wobbling as if she had been leaning out of the window of grandad's speeding lorry. But then no sooner had the smoke dispersed in the room, than there was another whoosh of air and the fire lit again as if nothing had ever happened. An eerie silence followed, punctuated eventually only by the growing crackle of wood in the flames.

They became aware of a subtle break in the quiet by the distant sound of a solo cornet, that grew steadily like the accompaniment to a grand development. The Wades Mill brass band were practicing "Nimrod" from the slow movement of Elgar's variations across the road in the working men's club, sending the stirring sound of brass through the foggy air towards them. Delius peered out from his hiding place, his ears turning and bending as he listened to the music. He moved cautiously at first, then nonchalantly slinked around the furniture and stopped to sit at the front door, staring at the handle. Lavender was watching with curiosity at his demeanour.

"Look at Delius. I've seen him acting weird like this before. He knows something we don't," Lavender pointed out.

"Aye, lass, 'appen he does and what's more, if you let him out of the door, I reckon he'll show you what he knows," Aunt Margaret answered.

Lavender twisted the doorknob and pulled the door towards her, letting Delius silently cross the threshold and disappear, out into the front garden and the slowly building volume of the music. She followed tentatively, her breathing shallow and rapid added to the thickness of the fog which had now become entirely ethereal.

"Wait for us!" grandma called out urgently, while Aunt Margaret grabbed her walking cane, as if arming herself ready for battle.

They caught up with her outside in the pea-soup thickness of the air.

"I can't see a thing," said grandma as they stood together somewhere between the open door behind them and the front gate.

Aunt Margaret instinctively turned her head to the left towards the pear tree. She felt it but couldn't see it, something was disturbing the fog.

"Look!" she said, guiding Lavender and Annie to the direction she had turned to.

A swirling pool of fog swept the ground, coming from the corner of the cottage, followed by a muffled sound, dragging along the path that meandered around the corner and into the garden. The sound stopped in what must have been the vicinity of the edge of the cottage. All three of them gasped in disbelief, the fog marginally dispersed revealing the familiar outline of Fred staggering towards them.

As he approached Lavender his knees buckled under him, and he collapsed on the ground. They all bent down at once in concern and to tend to him.

"Are you alright, Fred?" Lavender said, looking into his dazed eyes.

He peered at her, struggling to focus before his eyes became heavy and closed.

"Did you find Grandad?" she continued, agitating his shoulders to prevent him falling asleep.

"Come on let's get the lad inside," grandma advised, and between the three of them they lifted him up and guided him towards the front door.

When he got back to his feet the music from the building opposite grew in the air and seemed to clear the fog as it did so.

"Ee listen to that. Stirs my soul it does," said grandma, as the shivers encircled her body.

Without warning, they all became conscious of a bright light in the clearing air behind them. Slowly, warily, they turned to face it.

Standing in front of them was Arthur and held in his arms his daughter Mary. The music peaked in volume and then ebbed away for the final bars before returning the now clear air to silence. Mary called out to them softly, in a voice that had become only a beautiful memory.

"Lavender? Mother? Is that really you?" Lavender and Annie tentatively stepped forward.

"Mum?"

"Mary? No, it's not possible," each exclaimed in harmony, as they came face to face with her, then holding her together, in an embrace so tight that their sobs of joy heaved in unison.

They were so caught in the moment that each one of them was oblivious to anything else, until Fred spoke up.

"Wow, what has just happened?" he said, as he observed the spectacle and became reacquainted with home.

The three generations of women released their grip of one another to include a particularly excited Fred Keighley and Arthur, who was still dazed from his experience.

"I'm famished, I don't suppose you have anything to eat, do you?" said Fred.

His statement sent the rest of them into a burst of laughter, all except Aunt Margaret, who looked on in quiet satisfaction.

"I'll put the kettle on, I think we should all go in before we catch our death," Margaret said, leading the way back inside.

For all but Mary, it was a lively conversation as they talked in front of the roaring fireplace. Flames were licking the chimney back and Delius rested contentedly in his normal position, with his bottom precariously close to the heat. Aunt

Margaret came in from the kitchen with a loaded tray of tea and a few doorstep sandwiches for Fred.

"Now then, what wonders have you to tell us, Mary?" she enquired excitedly.

Mary appeared shell-shocked. She sighed and looked lovingly at Lavender, then spoke quietly, "Enough for a lifetime I would think, Aunt Margaret. Suffice it to say; I'm home thank the Lord and thank your blessed father too Lavender. He saved me, but I fear he sacrificed himself so that I could return. If it were not for him ..."

Mary's words petered away as she spoke, her head falling into her hands to shield the weeping tears. Lavender threw her arms around her mum's.

"Don't cry, Mum. We will bring him home, I know we will," Lavender assured her.

A log on the fire shifted its weight and spit quite suddenly and loudly, shooting an ember onto the hearth and turning Aunt Margaret's eyes towards it. They glazed over in one of her ominous stares.

"Aye, lass, you will bring him home, make no mistake, I see it clearly in the flames. But heed this, it'll not be an easy task."

The End

Lavender Bathwater will return....

Lightning Source UK Ltd.
Milton Keynes UK
UKHW032011260622
405003UK00006B/62